## Iain Thayne

Iain is a
lyricist ;
first for
many y
enjoyed
story ac
book has enabled him to expand his
storytelling skills and put a much wider perspective to his work.

CW00863241

Iain lives in Dorset with his wife and travels extensively. Being a self-confessed Grecophile he has visited many of the Greek islands with Kalymnos being his "Favourite Place". Having immersed himself into the local lifestyle, including learning to speak, read and write a little Greek he has applied a unique insight when writing this engaging story.

In this book Iain manages to mix the tragedy, triumph and madness of life in Kalymnos with a heartfelt story of family life, friendship and bittersweet love.

## Note from the Author

For authenticity I have used a number of Greek words and phrases. All the Greek names, places and words are in italics and spelt using English. I have included translations where necessary but as the book proceeds I slowly drop these as I am sure the reader will pick up on the simple translations. Finally, for those that want an extra bit of help or to satisfy themselves as to the meaning or pronunciation there is a glossary at the back of the book.

Regards
Iain

# the DINNER OF LOVE

WOULD THE DINNER OF LOVE
DELIVER ON ITS FOREBODING?

IAIN THAYNE

FOR JANE

# PROLOGUE

## THE MEDITERRANEAN SEA
## SOMEWHERE OFF THE COAST OF EGYPT
## SPRING 1886

The captain of the small, traditional, *Kalymnian* sponge hunting boat had plotted a course to an area he knew was rich in its potential for harvesting sponges. He knew his craft well and was guided by his vast experience of captaining a sponge boat with many years at sea. Having reached his chosen destination, he called out to the crew to ready themselves for work.

They had left the port of *Pothia* after the Easter festivities and the entire community's usual weeklong extended farewell. This culminated in "The Dinner of Love", where friends, families and lovers participated in a final meal before their menfolk departed for the five-month trawl for their ocean bed bounty. This year's fleet of some 300 boats eagerly anticipated the coming season. Each boat had around 6-15 divers, together with all the usual paraphernalia required to carry out their hunt. However, this year would be different, for on board was the *skafandro,* translated from

Greek as "the diving suit". Instead of using the traditional but archaic methods used for years of diving naked and holding their breath, they would use this simple new and revolutionary method. Not only did this mean they could stay on the seabed longer, but crucially they could go deeper - not thirty, forty or fifty meters, but some 60 metres where a fabulous bounty awaited.

Captain *Yainni* instructed *Stavros* to don the suit. Today was his day and the rest of the crew were to ready themselves for the first dive of the day. The suit included a bronze collar to which the heavy bronze helmet was attached. Once on the steel reinforced rubber hose was connected to the valve on the front of the helmet, by the viewing glass which would supply the diver with compressed air. The air was supplied via a hand operated pump installed on the boat. It would be the crews' job to maintain the fresh supply of air once *Stavros* entered the deep.

Just before *Stavros* entered the water another crew member tied a fine string to his wrist. This would be his only communication tool with the boat. Whatever *Stavros* felt in terms of emotion or nerves his demeanour didn't change. He was *Kalymnian*, strong and robust, this was their way. The crew watched as he climbed over gunnels and dropped into the water. As he slowly disappeared the pumping began, and the string line uncoiled, wriggling its way after him.

Captain *Yainni* glanced at his watch; *Stavros* had been on the seabed for over an hour. The measurements on the air hose indicated he was at a depth of 50m. This was new territory, maybe it was time for him to ascend. He gave the signal and the crew member controlling the communication string gave three sharp tugs. This was the signal for *Stavros* to return. The rest of the crew recoiled the hose and the string, watching eagerly to see what this new system would behold. As he reached the surface they could not believe their eyes. Such a bounty of sponges, like they had never seen before. They all shouted in exultation; they could hear

*Stavros'* muffled shrieks of delight as they pulled him on board. Once they removed his helmet he regaled them with the sights he had seen. The captain's hunch was right, sponges carpeting the seabed for as far as he could see. *Stavros* announced it was time for a cigarette and then after a break he would dive again. As he pulled on his cigarette and exhaled a strange smell drifted across the boat, but this was ignored.

Two hours later *Stavros* donned the helmet again and followed the same routine. This time he was down on the seabed for an hour and a half. Before descending into the deep he had told the captain he was brave and strong, and he would reward his favour with a haul so big that they would be able to drink *Raki* all winter. When the signal was given *Stavros* made his way to the surface and sure enough the size of the bounty was clear to see. As before he rested and pulled on another cigarette. Again, the strange smell drifted across the boat as he exhaled, once more it was dismissed. However, what happened next could not be ignored. *Stavros* started to tremble and cried out in agony. The crew called out to captain *Yainni*. What was this? With all his experience, surely he would know? But this was something even he had not witnessed before. *Stavros* complained of a terrible pain in his limbs and chest. This went on for hours with *Stavros* adding that one of his legs wouldn't move. There was fear in his eyes. The crew sensed this but did not understand this phenomenon. What could they do? As they watched on in horror *Stavros* started to lose consciousness, and then he was gone.

Over the next twenty-four years there were a staggering 10,000 horrific deaths and 20,000 cases of paralysis among the sponge hunters of the Aegean. Most victims were *Kalymnians*!

# CHAPTER ONE

## THE DEPARTURE

The sudden piercing shrills of the alarm clock filled the room, slowly increasing in volume and staccato in nature. It did exactly what it is was designed to do. Brought to my senses, albeit blurred by the fuzz of an alcohol infused day and night, my arm floundered in the air like an uncontrollable puppet trying to find the spot to neutralise the noise. I hit the button.

'What time is it?' asked Jane.

I responded grumpily, 'I told you last night, I set the alarm clock for 2.45am!'

'It seems a bit light for 2.45am.' was her terse response as she eased herself out of bed.

Whilst Jane went into her routine of readying herself for the journey ahead, I wearily dragged myself out of bed. The effects of yesterdays "Client Entertaining" had taken its toll and I now wished I had stuck to my promise.

'Yes, I know the flight is at 6.30am and yes I'll be sensible.' Jane had given me one of her looks that required no explanation.

'These are very important clients, and you know people have an expectation when they're out with me. I'll keep things under control and be home around 6am'ish, right as rain.' I arrived home that evening at 11pm, enough said.

As I dragged myself out of bed I glanced out of our rooflight and noticed to the strange hue of light for 2.45am. I stared out into the night sky, but it was not night sky. The dawning of the day was making its stealthy approach, light growing from behind the mask of darkness. I checked the clock, 4am! I checked again 4am!!

'Jane, fuck me! It is 4am. I must have cocked up when setting the alarm.'

'You are joking.' another look from Jane that required no explanation! 'I'm not joking, I can't believe it, what a cock up.' I very quickly moved from my blurred fuzz to the reality of the situation.

My mind quickly turned to our flight, leaving at 6.30am, last check-in is 5.30am.

A quick bit of head mathematics followed, not easy after copious glasses of red and not enough sleep. Highcliffe to Gatwick... around 100 miles... say on average 60 miles an hour... holy shit, about an hour and fifty-five minutes. Right, get our shit together... leave in 15 mins.

My mind wandered; Jane ready in 15 minutes no chance.

Back to the math, leave at 4.15am... 100 mph, arrive at 5.15am. My brain ached at the simple tasks being asked of it. 'Jane, we need to leave in 15 minutes and we're probably still not going to make it.'

In truth Jane was unflappable 'I'll be ready in ten,' and she was. Jane had that innate ability to look good in whatever she wore. Even though she had little time for her full make up routine when ready she was her usual vision of loveliness. No matter where she was or what she was doing her trademark look was never missing. With lip liner and lipstick beautifully applied, her voluptuous full lips adorned with a luscious red tone, she always stood out against a crowd and even at this ungodly hour they were in place. Over the years she had taken great pleasure in planting a smacker on friends, family and any unsuspecting acquaintance and leaving her indelible mark. Once we were ready there was no time for the pleasantries of goodbyes to the our sons, no time for the promised cup of coffee before we left. No final checks for cash, passports, etc. A real case of grab everything and go. Our Audi aptly nicknamed the silver bullet roared off into the barely risen sun.

As we raced through the countryside, heading towards the motorway all around was still. The soft calm of the morning mist hanging gently across the New Forest belied the panic inside the car. I had it all planned out now. Get across the forest in 10 minutes, onto the motorway, foot to the floor and do the remainder of the trip in 45-50 minutes. Drop the car at the airport valet parking and we might just make it. Positive as ever, and whilst knowing the plan required a minor miracle, I relayed it to Jane.

'So, Jane, we can make this, but we need a bit of help.' As was often the case on our jaunts abroad I generally organised things. I would argue this was one of my greatest skills! Jane knew better.

'We have everyone's tickets for the flights so the others can't check-in without us. We need to call Milos and let him know we have a problem.'

This year's trip to the Greek island of *Kalymnos* was going to be a little different. Having visited the island for many consecutive years, with our great friends Milos and Mary we had generally followed a standard routine. However, this year we were also travelling with Milos' old school friend Chris, and his wife of forty-five years Jen. I expected things to be a little unconventional!

Milos, actual name Miles was a veteran of the Greek islands and whilst not classing himself as a "*Grecophile*", simply loved their way of life. Made of hippie stock he was the archetypal early day Greek "*tuoristes*" and delighted in regaling all he met with tales of island visits, sleeping on the beach, eating on the beach and with his penchant for no nonsense vernacular, shitting on the beach. The years of baking himself in the sun and his natural olive skin gave him the sort of colour that most people get either by dipping themselves in mahogany wood stain, or actually being of Greek extraction. A striking feature of Milos was that he was 6' 3" and on *Kalymnos*, against most of the menfolk, this made him virtually a giant. Alongside this he weighed not much more than a wet paper bag, this somehow extenuating his height and giving him a unique look. On one of our earlier trips and returning to Gatwick we were waiting at the baggage turntable. I noticed some people staring inquisitively in our direction, gesticulating and deep in discussion. Eventually one of them meandered over, excused himself and ventured the following 'I hope you don't mind, but me and my friends couldn't help noticing you and we reckon you are Ben Kingsley! You know, the actor in Gandhi, and can we have your autograph?'

Milos stared back stoically and responded, measured as ever 'If you've seen the film Gandhi you might have noticed that he's about 5' 4". I am 6' 3" which puts me literally out of the picture!' As he sheepishly retired to his friends Milos offered up his view on the guy, 'Twat'.

This episode resulted in the nickname 'Stretch Gandhi' becoming one of the many monikers he had acquired over the years. However, in Greece he was always Milos, very simply because the term for anyone over 6' in Kalymnos was *Silos* (tall), and on one *retsina* fuelled night I changed this to Milos and the name stuck.

He also possessed some other key traits which helped him identify as Greek. The first a *"Moustaki"* that any Greek man would wear with pride. Anyone having any semblance of the understanding of the Greek mentality would know that the moustache is in a sense a part of Greek history. The second, an obligatory chain-smoking habit that when on form, amounted to 60 *Assos* (the local Greek cigarettes) a day and thirdly, the ability to drink *retsina* non-stop. It should be noted that he only drank the "Cheap Shit", the local *retsina,* and took great pleasure in using this vernacular when ordering his next bottle. Having spent many years visiting the islands of the *Ionian*, the *Saronics* and the *Cyclades*, around 25 years ago, purely by accident he happened upon the island of *Kalymnos* and more importantly the village of *Emporios*. Our holiday destination and home for the next two weeks.

'Milos, listen it's me, we have a problem.' I tried to make myself sound serious. Over the many years I had gained a well-earned reputation for pulling a fast one, with Milos often being the victim.

'I'm in the car, we've only just set off, got a tad lashed last night and overslept. We're going to struggle to make it, I need you… ' Milos interrupted in his own inimitable style.

'Fuck off Youth, see you shortly.' and the call ended there. My "Youth" moniker, even though I was now 57 was simply because I was thirteen years younger than Milos.

I knew exactly what was going on here. Milos had decided that I was pulling one of my stunts and he was simply not having it. However, there was another reason why he was taking this stance, and that was Mary, Milos' second wife.

Mary had a nervous disposition and in certain situations could not be relied on to hold her nerve. Whilst I loved her dearly our relationship took a long time to reach this stage. Primarily because early in our formative years, in her view I was nothing but a bad influence on Milos. Frankly, I couldn't argue with this, although in my defence leading Milos astray was not a difficult task. I had shared a house with Milos many years ago, when between marriages he lived with one of his old flames Liz. The house, called Pollards, was in the middle of nowhere and deservedly gained legendary status as a party house. Milos had cast his net out across the rugby and cricket clubs he played for and captured several easy to influence youngsters, eager to test their drinking and partying attributes and happy to know there was a place they could crash and burn. By a twist of fate, at the age of nineteen I had decided on a whim that living at home was not for me. One evening arriving home from work I announced to my mum, somewhat bizarrely after she had dished up a burnt pasty for dinner, that it was time for me to make my own way and that I was leaving home. Having gathered up my stuff and deposited it in the back of my Datsun 120Y car I said my goodbyes and left, immediately realising that I had nowhere to go! Subsequently I spent the next week living in the car.

Answering an ad for a rented room in a shared house, I arranged a viewing for the coming Saturday. I turned up at Pollards at the agreed time to be greeted by Milos, naked and suffering from a massive hangover. Furthermore, for some unknown reason there was a van driving round the garden being chased by a dog. Once invited inside the house I noticed a couple entwined, fast asleep on the sofa. Milos told me to ignore them and asked me to wait in the kitchen. Once dressed he showed me the bedroom and asked a few questions about me and what I did for a living. Having told him that I was training to be a Quantity Surveyor, it turned out Milos was a qualified Quantity Surveyor working for a rival building company. Having something in common did the trick and I was offered the room. However, later I found out that Milos had taken a reference on me from a guy he knew at my firm. Considering the shenanigans, witnessed at the house I thought this was a tad rich when clearly it should have been the other way round. What followed was a tenancy of complete and utter lunacy to match that very first meet.

Some ten years later Milos' relationship with his latest flame had run out of gas. Being a creature of habit when it came to having a lady by his side he quickly moved on. As I later found out, he had already been "dabbling" with his then secretary, Mary, and very shortly thereafter Pollards was committed to history with Milos simply advising me, 'I'm shacking up with Mary.' They made an interesting couple with some traits that were firmly at odds with each other. Firstly, their marked difference in height, with Milos at six foot three and Mary at five foot nothing. Having been invited to meet her for the first time down at the rugby club I noticed Milos striding across the pitch towards me, holding the hands of what I thought was a child, which in fact turned out to be Mary! Secondly their drinking habits, which were so diametrically opposed. Milos getting blethered, especially at weekends was 'deriguer', whereas Mary, whilst certainly not tee-total generally steered clear of alcohol. I had never witnessed her tipsy, let alone drunk. Thirdly, whilst Milos always had something to say and would never shy away from controversy, Mary was generally demure and preferred to take the role of the quiet bystander and listener. However, one trait she did have that I never saw Milos display was the very rarely seen ability to lose it, and some, if a person pushed her too far. I hasten to add that I had been on the end of one of her tongue lashings when getting Milos into trouble on a "Company" boy's night out in Cornwall. We got stuck into a very long and heavy session which resulted in him getting thrown out of a bar for falling asleep! Deciding we were enjoying ourselves far too much to look after him we dumped him in a taxi and sent him back to the house where we and the girls were all staying. When we eventually arrived back, and deeming it was my fault for his troubles, I got a full blast of what I imagined a Tasmanian devil's rampage to look and sound like. However, in the morning she apologised and much to my amusement had now decided Milos was to blame and placed him firmly in the doghouse.

When travelling or doing anything associated with either me or an unknown element, Mary's loss of nerve resulted in one simple outcome. The need to crap! Not once, not twice but often several times, hence her nickname "Perky Poos" (her married name before meeting Milos being Perkins). This was a reaction I had witnessed many times and for a diminutive blond she could pack it away in the toilet stakes. Milos knew any sign of an impending issue would send her scuttling away, tightly clenching her buttocks, to, using his vernacular, "The Shitter"...

I could imagine the conversation. 'Who was that Miles?' Mary politely enquired. She never referred to him as Milos. Now here was the blag. Mary had not heard the conversation but obviously knew the phone had rung. The next line would be crucial and still thinking to himself that it was a Youth wind up or was it? He responded positively.

'Just the Youth saying he's running ten mins late.' The first mistake, saying it was me and the second going for ten minutes.

Twenty minutes after our agreed rendezvous time Mary went scuttling off to the Ladies!

'Right Jane, Milos obviously thinks this is a wind up and I'm not going to fanny around making more calls. I need to focus on the driving. I'll take the actionless action approach and let the passing of time tell him the truth.'

Thirty minutes after Mary went scuttling off again!

We were now racing down the M23. One godsend of travelling at this early hour was the lack of traffic. It was not lost on me, and probably Jane too, that one, we were speeding, and two, I was likely to be a tad over the limit. Too late for all that now.

'Ok Jane, I reckon we'll be at Gatwick in fifteen minutes, get ready to peg it.'

Forty minutes after Mary made her third trip to the Ladies!

It was now time to call. 'Milos, it's'… before I could finish Milos interrupted, 'You twat, where the fuck are you?'

'I'm ten min'… again he interrupted 'I've got Perky Poos running back and forward to the shitter and Chris and Jen aren't impressed either.'

Irrespective of all this I knew Milos' main concern. Our lateness would possibly mean no red wine at Weatherspoons ahead of the flight. This would be playing with his routine.

'Listen,' hoping he would this time. 'Tell the check-in we'll be there in 10 mins, get all your bags weighed in and ready and we might just make it.' I got his usual curt response 'Twat.'

As we rounded the departures corner and across to the check-in it was 5.25am. 'What's the problem?' I politely enquired. His look said it all.

Fortunately, both Jen and Chris possessed laid-back natures, a knock-on effect of being of 60's stock and appeared relatively unfazed. Jen's response was of her mould and eloquently delivered. 'Well Iain, he's absolutely correct, you are a twat,' followed by one of her knowing smiles. She leaned forward and gave me a little hug and kiss and I knew we were good to go. We were rushed through check-in and security and by 5.45am we were in Weatherspoons.

'Milos, what do you want?' I enquired.'

'A very large red.' No surprise there.

'And for Perks?' I mischievously enquired.

'She is in the shitter you twat'. After quickly downing a few large glasses of average Shiraz we made our uneventful way to the gate, boarded the plane and before we knew it we were in the air…

……

I had spoken to Jen earlier in the year about coming out to *Kalymnos*. We first met when I moved into Pollards around 40 years ago. On my second night Milos invited me to stay in for dinner and to meet his old school friend Chris and his partner Jenny, known as Jen, who were coming down from London. Whilst I went out for the afternoon and attempted to kick a piece of leather or an opponent round the football field, Milos and Liz prepared a curry, smoked some hash and waited for the lunacy to commence. I arrived back at Pollards around 6pm armed with a bottle of some cheap plonk. Around 7pm Chris and Jen made their entrance.

Milos made the introductions 'This is our new housemate Iain, meet Chris and Jen.'

We exchanged pleasantries and whilst I offered them a drink I noticed Milos reach into his jacket and pull out his tobacco tin. I watched as he filled a cigarette paper with tobacco and then burn a piece of something that looked to me like an oxo cube. This was to be my introduction to smoking dope. As he drew on the joint I noticed a very strange mannerism. It seemed to me he was trying to inhale the whole world and that every ounce of smoke needed to reach the very depth of his soul. His eyes widened, with his whole frame enlarging and then suddenly he exhaled, sending the smoke in all directions by pursing his lips. Milos generously passed the pipe round, Chris took the next hit, Jen declined, and it eventually reached me. In for a penny, I put the joint to my lips, took a deep toot and waited, for what, I wasn't sure.

Being a young man in the 60's Chris had developed an inimitable style, with a sartorial elegance all his own. Like many of his generation, he refused point blank to follow any trend, other than what all the others of the sixties did! Having said that he carried his look well. He had very strong features, resembling those of Milos but somehow different. Maybe more Turkish than Greek. Perhaps it was this that drew them together at school along with their unusual surnames, Snazell and Szumski, not quite your quintessential English. Neither had showed much interest in school life, with a perceived lack of commitment to their studies. This resulted in them being branded as "wasters" with the school wanting rid of them as soon as the system allowed. The one aspect of school life they did enjoy was the sport with rugby and cricket at the forefront. However, there was one further trait they would eventually find out they shared after leaving school and that was being Jaffa's, seedless for the uninitiated. Both would find this out once they were married and this would very much shape their lives and their marriages. Milos very quickly came to terms of a life without kids of his own and managed to push away any thoughts of being inadequate. His first wife didn't quite share his stoic approach to the problem, and it eventually led to a parting of the ways. However, for Chris it played on his psyche and his role as a man. His way of dealing with this was to have a string of affairs throughout his time with Jen, which seemed to me to be nothing more than him trying to prove his manhood. Chris' undoubted love, and no small modicum of talent for cricket saw him play for several teams in and around London, generally playing at weekends. This hobby also afforded him the opportunity to participate in summer cricket tours. As I and Jen found out in time, this gave him the perfect ruse for his extra-marital activities.

At some stage we sat down for dinner, all sense of time had passed and for some reason I felt totally relaxed in my new surroundings. What followed was the first of many stories associated with Chris' life and this first one was to give me a sense of the path Chris had trod. He told me that he had been totally frustrated with his school's inability to educate his mind and decided to leave school as soon as he could and follow his dream to be an entrepreneur. During the evening I lost count of the "brilliant business ideas" he had, and he certainly spun a good yarn. What became clear to me over the years was that Chris had a good brain, but a somewhat unique and alternative take on the way things should be. What also became clear to me over the course of our friendship was that he really wasn't cut out for the life of an entrepreneur!

Despite his waster tag at school Milos was in fact very intelligent and took in far more than the school realised. On leaving school he had found a way to manoeuvre his approach to fit some semblance of normality and secure his future as a Quantity Surveyor with a real penchant for numbers. Chris clearly didn't share this skill and his failure to grasp numbers made his approach to business somewhat archaic. Furthermore, he possessed what he called an alternative to PAYE, which was SAYE (Spend As You Earn). This meant that he was constantly scrabbling around for funds. Apparently following one early business failure he considered joining the Navy as a diver. I remember him telling me this at one of our little soirees and I told him that frankly, I was only ever interested in one sort of diving! I did not have the balls for the first one and my life at that stage was generally organised around using my balls for other purposes. Little did I know how aligned I was to Chris!

Milos leaving Pollards and shacking up with Mary coincided with me meeting Jane. We had a whirlwind romance which resulted in another of my many impulsive moments. On a whim and deciding that my tenure at Pollards was over, I dropped everything and moved with her to Christchurch in Dorset. We settled into our new life well and found a lovely home in the village of Highcliffe. Living by the sea and close to the New Forest, over the years we had a constant stream of visits from friends. Chris and Jen would generally come and see us once a year and had been down to stay with us for a long weekend earlier in the year. I got a call from Jen later in the year to surprisingly announce they would like to come down again. When discussing the arrangements for this latest visit Jen had simply advised me that the weekend may be difficult!

On the Friday evening, and after a splendid meal accompanied by some very fine wines both Jane and Chris had retired to bed, leaving Jen and myself with a rather nice bottle of white port. I had sensed during the meal that Chris was in a different place, he seemed disengaged, and I could sense Jens' unease. The fragility of her emotions was soon revealed as she tearfully broke down before me. I was shocked. In all my time knowing Jen she had carried this presence and strength of mind, the one part of the relationship that could be relied on. I realised things must be bad. As she began to unravel the problems, I decided the best thing I could offer was my ear. I sat listening intently as she slowly and carefully deconstructed their relationship and explained how things simply didn't fit anymore.

'Chris just doesn't get it. We are in real trouble, and he continues to put up this shield of denial. The financial burden of keeping us afloat is wearing me down, Iain I'm 70 now and I am still working like I was 21.' her head dropped as she sobbed incessantly.

I felt it was now time to speak 'Jen, I can't say I am surprised at any of this. It feels like the realisation of many years of Chris' failure to address the problems his lifestyle has generated has finally surfaced and he is taking the easy option and laying it at your door.'

Jen paused for a moment and then replied. 'Yes, I get that, and I am still willing to help, God knows why, but I just can't seem to get through the shield. It is as if the realisation that he now has to face this, so late in life is too great an ask.'

'So, what does he say when you try to talk to him about this?' I gently enquired.

'Talk, talk?' she questioned. 'He just gives me that stare, you know Iain, you will have seen it before. Whenever we get onto a subject he doesn't like all I simply get is this stare.'

Indeed, I had. 'Ok Jen, so here's the nub of the issue and before we go any further. Is it over for you?'

She looked at me intently, I was guessing no one had asked her this question. I knew I was pushing a boundary, one that required honesty and for her to bare her deepest feelings.

I wanted to explore a little thought I had. 'It seems to me that the whole thing with his perceived inadequacies as a man has a big part to play here. If you then throw in the accident he had at work, and how the resultant injuries have further exacerbated the psyche of how he sees himself as a man, then it all seems to point to a dark and unpleasant place. I guess the fact that the business failures have left him with just the state pension doesn't help either. All these things seem to have impacted on his life, almost like disabilities.

'You know that's so true.' Jen had calmed a little, the sobbing had stopped. 'I think he looks at all of you, you know, "The Company" and especially Milos, in amongst all the madness you all seem to have done incredibly well and he feels isolated from this, and maybe even jealous. Whilst you may have a point, I think it is all a little too late, especially on the money front'.

'Jen I get that, but I am guessing that you're at the stage in life where you aren't planning to spend a fortune?' She laughed, 'A fortune, wouldn't that be a nice problem.'

'Yes, but you get my point. Forget the cash for now, surely it is a mindset thing, a sort of removal of the blackness that surrounds his thinking, the self-pity and denial.' I ventured.

She paused for thought. 'Well, going back to your earlier question if I could get the Chris of old back the one that I know and love, then the answer is no.' she said emphatically.

'Wow, that's a big if and are you clear on what that is?' We sat quietly for a moment. I could see in her expression she was still contemplating the enormity of the question, maybe I needed to draw this out.

'All these years we've known each other, but you've never told me how you met? What was it that drew you together? what are those traits you know and love?

Jen stared out of the window, I could sense her brain reminiscing and searching the backwaters of her mind. She looked at me and smiled.

'I was working at a school in Pimlico. I hadn't long passed my teacher training and was really enjoying the lifestyle London offered. I was sharing a flat with a fellow teacher and she asked if I wanted to go with her to a party one of her friends was having, in Chelsea I recall.' She paused for a sip of port. 'As you can imagine, in those times London really was the centre of the swinging sixties, and everything seemed to revolve around having fun and partying. Anyway, I said I would go, and I couldn't help notice this one particular guy at the party.'

'Chris I presume?'

'Indeed, there was something about his look, almost Mediterranean which I found quite appealing, and his dress sense made him stand out. I think he was wearing a pair of purple suede trousers and a rather fetching mohair jumper. Anyway, once we got talking I could tell he was quite a charmer and as we talked I could sense straight away the sexual chemistry. We ended up in the sack, very much of the times and to say that Chris had an insatiable appetite for sex would be something of an understatement. I have to say I found that very appealing and before I knew it we were shacking up.'

'Ok so that's clearly something you had in common.' I noted cheekily. 'But there must have been more?' I asked.

'Well sure, I liked his views on things, in those early days we talked incessantly about all manner of things. We shared the same choice of music and we both loved to party! He had all these madcap ideas on creating his own business and I guess I found that quite exciting compared to my teaching job. However, the bit that finally bonded us together was when I got offered a new job, out in the suburbs away from central London and this gave us the excuse we were both looking for to leave that scene behind. Chris thought this would be a great moment to solidify our relationship and one mad weekend we got married. Miles was our best man.'

'Blimey, that sounds a bit like a whirlwind moment, very you though. It feels to me like you are yearning for the Chris of old but need to find a way for him to have his eyes opened.

'Well yes, and a little bit of sex would be nice.' Jen replied.

"Maybe I can help?, not so much with the sex but let's leave that for now.' We both laughed and the seed was planted.

We finished off the Port while reminiscing about some of the many Pollardian escapades. I was pleased to see her smiling and laughing. 'What's the time?' Jen glanced at her watch. 'Oh, it's about 3am!'

'Bloody hell, Jen I love you to bits, but it's definitely time for bed.' We got up from the table and she moved across to me. She grabbed my hand and looked intently into my eyes. I leant forward. She whispered softly in my ear.

'Thank you Iain, you know you really are a lovely man.' She kissed me gently on the cheek and left to go to bed.

The conversation with Jen only confirmed my suspicions that all was clearly not well. I already knew that Chris was having a difficult time emotionally and mentally adjusting to the 'retirement' phase of his life. I felt that in many ways he had not come to terms with the realisation that all the things he wanted to achieve in his business life had somehow passed him by. A further big change in his life came about when he endured an industrial accident. It was around 20 years ago, when Chris had decided the future for sport was artificial pitches. With the help of funding from Milos he set himself up as one of the leading providers of "specialist sports pitches". As usual there was a lot of blarney around this but with his Cricket and Rugby contacts he convinced Milos and himself that it couldn't fail!. Unfortunately, on somehow securing his first project and applying his laissez-faire approach he had an altercation with a JCB digger and came second. This resulted in him ending up with a severely damaged left leg, often needing a stick when it "played up", the business failing and when asked by Jen about insurance, simply shrugging his shoulders. Last, but not least it meant Milos' lost his investment. This would have a lasting impact on their friendship.

The remainder of his working life was spent in menial jobs, lacking any semblance of job satisfaction as he meandered his way to retirement. What he didn't lose was his incorrigible nature when it came to womanising. Apparently these never lasted very long but I guessed they must have given him some sense of satisfaction. Maybe the attention helped him deal with his insecurities, acting like some sort of psychological crutch. In amongst all this Jen had found a way to let this trait pass her by, for what reason I never asked.

However, over the years I had become massively fond of Jen and indeed Chris and I wanted to help. Whilst even more diminutive than Mary, Jen carried a larger-than-life personality, maintained a trademark blonde "Twiggy pixie cut" and an ability to take front and centre stage. She had a wonderful willowy figure and had kept herself in fine shape. She would often attribute this to the lack of having to produce babies. This was a subject I rarely broached with her as I very much felt this was between her and Chris. I admired and maybe even envied her mastery of the English language and the way her lines were delivered with such intensity and bravado. It was no surprise to me that in her early years she breezed through her school, university, and teacher training years as she was clearly well educated and well read. People generally listened when she spoke, and her views always seemed to me to be very intelligently formed. When I was "on form" I relied on my brash and unashamed bellicose nature, whereas she could hold court without the need for a change in demeanour. Like Chris, Jen had many stories to tell. It seemed to me that being of the sixties era they both had grasped the freedom that it promised. I also realised that she had acquired that other great trait the sixties promised "Sexual Freedom". Whilst not being shy in coming forward about my sexual prowess, my attitude and approach was born out of the laddish male dominated "dressing room" repartee, whereas with Jen it was just simply telling it as it was.

The following morning over coffee and croissants I decided to invite Chris and Jen out to *Kalymnos*. I had woken in the morning and spent some time reflecting on last night's conversation with Jen. Suddenly a very clear vision of an idea of how I could help entered my mind and along with last night's conversations I outlined my plan to Jane.

'Iain, I know this is a lovely thing to do but what about Miles?' I knew where she was coming from.

Whilst supportive of my plans for inviting Chris and Jen to join us on this year's holiday Jane was right about her concerns as to how this would play out with Milos. This holiday would be different in that the events I had in my mind would play havoc with his routine and approach to our *Kalymnian* holidays. When I phoned him to let him know of that I had invited Chris and Jen to join us in Kalymnos his simple response was to say firstly, that as long as it didn't affect his system that would be fine, and secondly, that when it came to any plans, don't include him!

Milos had invented and fully possessed the ability to practice what he called "*The art of doing nothing*". I suspected that he had picked this up from Alberto, an Italian acquaintance we had become friendly with on account of his regular visits to *Emporios*. I found this out accidentally one year, along with the fact that he was CEO of Agip Oil! One day, whilst trying to explain to him what guided our holiday routine, I was amazed when he said, "Ah, La Dolce Far Niente", which translates to '*The sweetness of doing nothing.*' He went on to explain that Italians may wander off to a favourite little spot after a few hours of working to take a little nap, they may be inspired by a nearby cafe and sit down to have a glass of wine, or they may just go home and make love to their wife. I suspected with Alberto that he would take the last option. However nice this thought was, for Milos, "*The art of doing nothing*" was not about work. It was about life itself and the idea that doing nothing was an event in and of itself. My plans for Chris and Jen were clearly at odds with his philosophy!

......

Having boarded the plane, the flight passed by without any drama other than Chris moaning about how the plane's pressurised cabin was playing havoc with his leg! Milos and I ignored this doing our best to demolish the planes supply of red wine. Some three and a half hours after departure we landed at Kos airport. We disembarked the plane and whilst waiting for the bags Milos rushed outside to have a fag. Having collected our bags, we made for the taxi rank. Passing through the terminal doors, I immediately felt the rush of the *Kos* heat. There is something about the way it lifts the mood, the way the warmth on the skin feeds the emotions and gives a general sense of feeling good. It was also a signal to me that the *Kala Kardia* (good heart), our favourite *taverna* on the port of *Mastihiri* was only a ten-minute ride away. We jumped in the first available taxi and in no time at all we were outside the *taverna*.

'A bottle of the cheap shit *retsina Nikolas*.' Milos's vocal calling card rang out across the taverna. The *Kala Kardia* was a typical seaside taverna. Painted in the traditional white and blue of Greece with all its seating outside and under the cover of a canopy. Its focus during the day was to act as a transient staging post for those making the journey to and from *Kalymnos*. Small wicker chairs and tables, adorned with the obligatory paper tablecloth detailing a map of Kos, neatly held in position by small metal clips which seemed to me to be desperately hanging on to the edge of the table. Having visited many times, we always received a warm greeting from its resident waiter *Nikolas*. I often thought this was mainly to do with the fact that he didn't have to hang outside and try to persuade us to visit his establishment, a thankless task at the best of times, but I eventually realised that the Milos call sign gave him and us a unique notoriety. One thing that constantly irked my Jane was Milos' blank refusal to order anyone else's drinks. This was not unique to the *Kala Kardia* and was a constant theme when in *Kalymnos*. In truth this extended way beyond *Kalymnos* but was never more in focus than during these holidays. For those that know the ways of Greece and the role that women play in Greek society, particularly on the islands it was as if Milos wanted to live up to his "Greek Heritage". Jane took no truck with this and whilst generally being someone who liked to sit back and watch the madness unfold, she would take every opportunity to remind Milos accordingly.

We made our way to a vacant table and as we sat down the f un began.

'Milos, I'm sure Mary would like a drink.' she rasped at him. 'Thanks Pipe Up, she's got a tongue hasn't she?' was his terse reply.

His response and the term "pipe up" had become de rigueur whenever any situation arose where Jane felt the need to stick up for Mary. I knew Milos loved Jane and she likewise loved him, and I rather enjoyed their little spats!

*Nikolas* made his way over to our table. '*Yassou Nikolas, Ti Kanis?*' (Hello Nikolas, how are you*)*, I asked as we shook hands.

'*Ime kala, esi?*' *(*I am good and you?), he politely responded.

'*Kala, poli kala,*' *(*Good, very good*)*, I said pulling out a chair.

Enough with the pleasantries I ordered another glass, to share the *retsina* with Milos and a round of drinks for the others, all in

Greek which clearly impressed Jen. We were offered the menus apart from Milos, and I also declined one. *Nikolas* knew that food was not something Milos bothered with whilst in transit. He also knew not to offer him any water 'It's for washing' was his response whenever asked. This always made me laugh as this very simple joke was clearly lost in translation, but Nikolas always afforded him the pleasantry of a smile. Whilst the others viewed the menu I sat back, raised a glass to Milos, '*Yammas*' (The traditional Greek for cheers), and took my first sip of *retsina*. It was crisp, cold, and frankly resembled the taste of turpentine! The *retsina*, a white wine infused with the resin of *Aleppo* pine trees was undoubtedly an acquired taste. Apart from the first glass of the holiday, it was a taste both Milos, and I enjoyed and whilst most British holidaymakers would advise you against it, we were keen advocates. We also loved the price – "The Cheap Shit" coming in at 3.5 euros for a 75cl bottle! The reason I didn't bother with the menu was I knew what was expected of me regarding getting the ferry across to *Kalymnos*. Number one: Milos could not be arsed to walk up the quay to make enquiries. Number two: As I had learnt a reasonable amount of Greek I was best positioned to enquire and furthermore in his view it would be good practice. And number three: it also meant he could keep more *retsina* to himself. I wandered off.

Getting across to the island had always been a lottery. Greek ferry timetables are a contradiction in terms and certainly on our earlier trips generally potluck was the best option. Things had improved over the years and as well as the slow traditional ferry, the *Apollon* which took around 50 minutes to make the 7-mile crossing, they had also introduced a fast speed hydrofoil service, The *Kalymnos Star* which took just 35 minutes. Frankly, my preference was the *Apollon*. I liked the way it meandered across to *Kalymnos*, the metronomic rhythm and gentle hum as it rode the waves, gently caressing my soul and helping me adjust to the pace of the coming weeks, whereas the *Kalymnos Star* was more brutish as it aggressively ploughed its furrow through the waves.

As I wandered up the concrete quay towards the ticket kiosk the blazing sun enveloped my whole body. The gentle breeze softened its harsh nature and either side of the quay the azure blue seas, which matched that of the sky, gently caressed all it touched. I was truly made up to be here. As I surveyed the quay there were no ferries moored but there was an array of people. From my viewpoint it was hard to make out whether they were travellers or locals. However, there were no cars or lorries which meant the *Apollon* wasn't due. As I neared the kiosk, perfectly positioned at the junction of the L shaped quay I stared out across to *Kalymnos*. In the distant haze the unmistakeable shape and characteristics of the *Kalymnos Star* was bulldozing its way towards the quay. Bollocks!

At the kiosk, a fortyish year-old looking couple were engaged in discussions with the lady selling tickets. I strained to hear the conversation and picked up the unmistakeable tones of English. I also picked up the unmistakeable tone of frustration. They stepped back. Clearly the language barrier was creating some sort of uncertainty. I asked the lady if I could help.

'It's sooo frustrating,' she remonstrated. 'We're trying to find out what time the ferry leaves for *Kalymnos*, the lady is trying to help but her English isn't the best!'

What I wanted to say to her in response was that the issue here is that you are in Greece and it's your Greek that isn't the best. However, I reminded myself how hard it had been for me to learn and that the Greeks tend to play up to those that aren't prepared to make an effort. I stepped in, clearly to their amazement:

'*Seegnomee, Ti ora fuevye to polio yia tin Kalymnos?*' (Excuse me, what time does the ferry leave for *Kalymnos*?) in my best Greek accent.

The lady behind the kiosk gave me a huge smile and politely replied. '2pm.' in her finest English!

'*Epharistho*,' (Thankyou*)* I replied.

'*Parakalo*' (You're welcome*)*.

I asked, again in Greek if the tickets were still eight euros and was delighted to hear they were. The look of shock on the couple's face said it all as I relayed the information and ordered two tickets for them and six for us. Feeling smug I said I would see them on the ferry and meandered my way back to the *taverna*. It was now time to call *Pavlos,* our great friend and host whilst in *Emporios*. '*Ella Pavlos*, (Hi *Pavlos*) it's me, Iain.'

'You are here?' he enquired. '*Nai*,' (Yes) I responded.

'What time the ferry you catch?' Spoken in his unique English diction.

I replied, 'Maybe 2pm, you know the system,' already slipping into what Milos and I called our "Greek English".

'*Daxi, Daxi,* (ok, ok) I get *Giorgios* to meet you, see you later Iain.' I made my way back to the table at the taverna.

'Ok Youth, what's the crack?' Milos enquired.

'The *Kalymnos Star* is on its way and is due to leave at 2pm, it's 1.15pm now so mine's a *retsina*. And before you ask yes I've called *Pavlos* and *Giorgios* will meet us as usual with the taxis.'

The shout went up followed swiftly by delivery of a nice cold bottle of *retsina*. As I sat back and enjoyed the retsina and nibbled on some of the "*meze*" (a selection of hot and cold Greek dishes) adorning the table, Jane gave me a smirking glance. Right on cue Mary bit, 'Miles, I don't think we've got time for another bottle, we've got to get our bags and get across to the ferry and what if it leaves early and what…' 'Mary scuttled off!

'Youth give me a break,' Milos pleaded, followed by a similar smirk. We jumped on the ferry at 1.50pm and shortly thereafter we left port.

# CHAPTER TWO

## THE ISLAND OF "SOFT GOLD"

*Kalymnos* is one of a group of islands in the Southern Aegean Sea, located north of *Kos* in a part of Greece called the *Dodecanese*. This is strange in itself as the word *Dodecanese* literally translates as twelve islands but the group is made up of 15 larger islands and 150 smaller islands. There will be some sort of Greek logic to this but best left unexplained.

Kalymnos is relatively small, rectangular in shape and around 21 miles long and 8 miles wide. The population is always a hard number to call as so many of the inhabitants live a transient life driven by the need to find work, often in far flung places. Let's say 11,000. It is mountainous with a complicated topography and mainly barren in nature apart from two fertile valleys in *Vathi* and *Pothia*. I had told Chris and Jen that if they expected to see the almost tropical nature of *Corfu* then think again. However, I found exceptional beauty in its nature. The harsh grey and gold hues of the craggy mountains, when set against the azure skies and shimmering turquoise seas were quite intoxicating. I simply loved the place and had a lot to thank Milos for in finding this strange oasis. Over the years I found that visitors to the island fell into two categories. They either loved it and became entranced, drawn back year after year by their connection with the local culture and the emotional attachment made with the friends and families of the island, or they didn't get it and moved on. Fortunately for us more and more visitors fell into the second category and the delicate balance of the island needing tourism against us wanting it to remain "our island" seemed safely set. Furthermore, our destination and "Home" on the island, *Emporios,* the last village close to the Northern tip was considered by many as too remote and the taxi ride of 45 minutes a stretch too far.

As we crashed our way through the waves, creating a foaming chasm in our wake, the haze of the *Kalymnos* skyline slowly came into focus. Whilst still not being my favourite way to arrive the sense of belonging grew as we approached. One thing about the *Kalymnos Star* was that it created so much noise, especially when sat on the top deck, that we all sat in silence for the journey, rocking and buffeting against whoever you shared a seat with. In the final magical five minutes, with the engines throttled back, the roaring horse stood down and riding on the softer seas protected in the lea of the land we made the final cruise into the harbour.

'Jen, what do you think?' I watched as she intensely scrutinised the vista and her simple exclamation said it all 'Wonderful Iain.' I took great delight in her response. A very good start I thought.

The approach to the port of *Pothia* emphasised the dramatic panorama created. Built like an amphitheatre the hundreds of pristine *Cycladic* houses tumbled down towards the port, every spare piece of land occupied by these traditional Greek homes, dominating the landscape, and creating a sense that the mountain had been whitewashed. As we got closer the green pines and the odd coloured roof, church or building began to break the whitewash and the first sense of the hustle and bustle of the port arrived. As we slowly pulled into the quay side, I grabbed Chris and Jen's attention and pointed to a large sign:

"Welcome to Kalymnos the Sponge Divers Island".

I leaned forward to speak. 'There is a story here that I want you to witness, and I know that you Chris, in particular will have a great affinity with what is to unfold.' They both stared at me inquisitively.

'Soft gold my friends, soft gold.' I said as we prepared to disembark.

Waiting on the quay were an array of taxis, various models in all sorts of condition but all with one trait to separate them from all the other traffic, a silver livery. They were all haphazardly parked waiting for the ferry to arrive. I had come to realise that if you really wanted to know when the ferries were running, they were your best bet. The usual scrum and shouting ensued as taxi drivers vied for business. This was not something we had to participate in as our very good friend and taxi driver *Giorgios* had positioned himself, almost belligerently to ensure he got the right spot and would not be missed.

'*Silos* my friend, how are you?' *Giorgos* bellowed.

'Do you have the *meze*?' he politely enquired.

This was the normal ritual between *Giorgios* and Milos. Over the years Milos had developed a habit of bringing all manner of smoked, cooked, or ready to boil fish "*meze*", vacuum packed for "the boys" to enjoy at *Pavlos' taverna*. *Giorgios* had happened upon this one year and the ritual stuck. Milos one year forgot the "*meze*" and *Giorgios* threatened to drop him in *Vathi*. 'A very long walk for you my friend.'

I suggested Jane jumped in *Giorgios*' taxi with Milos and Mary and I would take the second one with the others. 'Chris, you jump in the front and enjoy the view and I'll get in the back with

Jen.' This was quite deliberate as I knew that all *Kalymnians* liked the opportunity to engage with the *touristes* and this would give Chris the opportunity to chat and tell one of his stories. This would also give me the opportunity to sidle up close to Jen.

As we pulled out of the harbour and headed towards the town the heat was already tearing at my skin. We never stopped in *Pothia*, it was not what we came to *Kalymnos* for, and our sole aim was to get through it as quickly as possible. On one of our very early visits to *Kalymnos* Jane and I decided to visit *Pothia*, much to Milos' chagrin and insistence that it was 'Too fuckin' hot and too fuckin' noisy'. There was only one bus per day from *Emporios*, that left the village around 10am and returned at 4pm. To call it a bus was a contradiction in terms and hair raising would be an appropriate way to describe the journey. Having sorted a taxi, we were back in the taverna by 1pm to be greeted with, 'I told you, you twat.' The only time I ventured that way on future trips was to help *Pavlos* with the "shopping!"

To understand the chaotic nature and cacophony of *Pothia* is to simply say that of the islands 11,000 population, 6,000 live or rather are crammed into this small town. In the summer this is further exacerbated by the constant arrival of tourists and even worse the day "Tour Boats" from *Kos* and Turkey. Deep down I was disappointed at my failure to grasp the nettle of developing my knowledge of some of the wider aspects of the capital, its culture, and its history. I knew of the town's Italian influence and the neo-classical architecture was clearly visible when driving through the small streets and alleyways, but these had always been fleeting glimpses. I knew that you could visit the Archaeological Museum of *Kalymnos* to learn the history of the island and visit the Nautical Museum that detailed all manner of things related to the great *Kalymnian* maritime activities and most importantly the sponge hunting. However, the sponge hunting was one aspect of the *Kalymnian* economy and the way of life I knew a plenty!

I also knew from my time spent with *Pavlos* that there was a special place in *Pothia* related to the sponge hunting, "*The Vouvalis Family Museum*". *Nikolaos Vouvalis* founded *N. Vouvalis and Co*, Direct Sponge Importers and Commission Agents in 1882. He would later in life be declared "Great Benefactor to the Nation". However, for most of his life he used his business acumen and influence to become very rich and create a thriving worldwide business selling what I called "soft gold". I knew this year I would finally visit this place.

We were now through *Pothia* and heading North. Slowly but surely the incessant traffic was easing and the cool draft of the breeze through the window was softening the intense heat. Leaving Chris to discuss some sort of madness with the driver, I conversed with Jen, pointing out various milestones along the journey whilst letting her take in the stunning landscape. Out to *Panormos* and through *Kamari*, these villages more residential than holiday destinations and then as the roads became smaller and more compact, we passed through *Myrties* and *Massouri*, accompanied by the incessant whine of small motorbikes weaving their way down these tiny streets and dodging through any traffic. These two villages were deemed the main holiday destinations on the island and whilst small were typical in nature. No more than 50m from the beach, set in the steep hillside of the landscape, focusing on tourism with small hotels, apartments, shops and tavernas crammed into every space. They also had an additional function as the centre of the islands climbing region with many of the main crags and routes nearby. In October there is a climbing festival attended by some 3,000 lunatics, dangling from ropes as they attempt to scarper up some insanely vertical face. The Island has a reputation as one of the best climbing spots in Europe. Fortunately for us it was way too hot for climbing in the height of summer, so we were able to avoid this madness. As we made our way out of *Massouri* I pointed out *Telendos* to Jen. Part of the

archipelago and the smallest of the *Dodecanese* islands it is very
much a part of *Kalymnos* and is peacefulness personified. Made up
simply of one mountain, one village with no road or cars, a day
on *Telendos* was isolation itself.

We were now on my favourite part of the journey. The upper
Northern part of the island is very sparsely populated with just
the villages of *Arginonda* and *Skalia* to traverse before reaching
*Emporios*. Over the years the road network had vastly improved
and even though many of them were cut from the harsh sheer
steeps of the mountainside I never felt uneasy. As we snaked
through the passes the odd motorbike, car or truck gently eased
by. There was no need to speed out here. The island's size meant
the journeys generally were short and to speed would deny you
the opportunity to take in the majesty of the landscape.
Furthermore, this was goat country and at any minute one of
these fascinating little mountain dwellers could decide to cross
the road. Having passed through *Arginonda* the road dropped
down to the *Valley of Skalia*. An exotic name for such a small
obscure village. I thought it was the sort of name best suited for
one of JK Rowling's Harry Potter novels. Being situated on an
inlet open to the strong summer *meltemi* winds that sweep down
from the North we rarely visited *Skalia,* but as we passed through
I knew this meant we were just ten minutes from *Emporios*.

As the taxi climbed up the road out of *Skalia* I pointed out the
lush *Olianda* bushes lining both sides of the road. Ribbons of pink
and white flowers amongst deep olive-green leaves beautifully set
against the mountains on one side and the sea on the other side. Jen's
silence told me all I needed to know about how she was slowly
being intoxicated by what she was seeing. Even Chris had stopped
talking. I wanted to announce that around the next corner the bay
of *Emporios* would come into view but resisted the temptation.

'My friends, *Emporios*, look.' The taxi driver shouted. He had
beaten me to it and there in all its splendour was "home". Jen did

not hold back 'Wow, that looks absolutely wonderful, it's everything and more than I imagined.' Chris responded in kind, 'Looks great honey.' As we made the final drop down towards the village, I thought about my plans for the next two weeks and I was really pleased about how the holiday had started.

The village of *Emporios* sits on the eastern side of the island and the huge bay is protected from the *meltemi* by the imperious vertical mountains that dominate the landscape. Across from the bay is the very small uninhabited island, *Kalabros* adding further protection from the wind and when looking south the splendour of the *Telendos* mountain can be seen in all its glory. The village sits on a small flat piece of land at the bottom of the mountains with a tiny fishing quay. There is one road in and out and everything revolves around the quay and the compact village square. An array of traditional houses lines the main street down to the quay and the beach road is dominated by four or five traditional *tavernas* and a single shop leading to the square. The pebbly beach is no longer than 200 yards and contains a mixture of tables, chairs, and various forms of sunshades to facilitate long lazy lunches. Further along it is simply sand and sea. Like many things in life, size is not everything! In the winter months the population is no more than a couple of handfuls. In the summer months, even during the tourism season the population still does not exceed sixty, with the only addition being the yachties that regularly choose to weigh anchor and moor up for the evening.

Over recent years a few additional homes have been built. These were a little less traditional, to cater for the various European expats, who like us, had become entranced by the place but had gone the whole hog and made *Emporios* their proper home. However, these were mainly situated on the main drag that drops into the village but none of these had managed to take away from the glorious nature of *Emporios* being in our view, "A proper

Greek Village". As we turned the corner, I pointed out *Harrys Paradise Taverna* on our right. More of that place to come. As we reached the quay and turned sharp right the wonder of the village presented itself:

'Your home for the next two weeks'. I announced.

I simply let them take the rest in. As we passed the tavernas and shop we reached the square. Sited on the far corner of the square was *The Artistico taverna,* run by *Giorgios,* and ably assisted by his wife *Ireni,* their sons *Nikolas, Themelis* and *Nikolas'* wife *Eleni,* this was one of our favourite places in the village. A further 100 yards along the tree lined beach road we took a sharp right uphill turn, quickly followed by a sharp left. We passed St *Giorgios* church immediately on our left, blink and you miss it, then a short rise and low and behold the wonderful "*Mbarba Nikolas*", *Pavlos' taverna* and home of all the madness.

The *taverna* sits high up on a rocky outcrop at the end of village with simply the most wonderful views of the bay of *Emporios.* Built in typical style by *Pavlos* some 25 years ago, on land bequeathed to him by his father, he had fulfilled his dream. Having stood on the land as a boy and declaring the spot as the most wonderful place on earth to have a *taverna* his vision had been realised. Frankly, in our view he was not wrong.

To understand the history and the life in *Emporios* is to understand the *Michas* family. To appreciate our affinity with the place is to witness the relationship between Milos and *Pavlos.* They were kindred brothers. *Pavlos* was the youngest of 11 children! *Pavlos* father, *Nikolas,* had passed some 20 years ago but his life's work, family, and influence on the ways of *Emporios* were everywhere. Whilst having never met him I suspected his nature was that of *Pavlos.* An extremely hard-working family man he had committed himself to living off the land by way of "goat herding". An astute man, during the wartime occupation by the Germans, when food was in short supply along with the ability to pay for it, he had a key role in supplying the villagers with sustenance. In terms of payment, he simply swapped his goods for land. This had resulted in him owning great swathes of the northern tip, perfect for grazing and growing the size of his herd along with various plots within the village. Over the years these various plots of land had been bequeathed to members of his flock with family members now dotted around the village in homes they had built for themselves and their families. At the latest count there were some 40 members of the *Michas* clan, brothers, sisters, in-laws, cousins, etc, dominating village life. The family business of "goat herding" remained and apparently there were more than 400 *Michas* goats wandering around the kingdom of the *Michas*, ably worked by *Pavlos'* brothers, *Thoris* and *Nioti*.

As with all *Kalymnian* families some of *Pavlos'* brothers and sisters had left the island seeking work and had never returned. Unfortunately, one brother had passed away. Irrespective of this the family had a strong bond, typical of what *Kalymnians* value most. However, this family bond, if crossed could be doggedly maintained. Next to *Pavlos' taverna* was the *"Asteri Hotel"*. The term hotel was a stretch beyond imagination, but it was where we stayed. Built and owned by *Pavlos'* brother *Pandalis,* it consisted of two tiers of angular white concrete blocks seemingly carved into the hillside. There were twelve rooms, each with a bedroom, a shower/toilet room, and a small balcony. Simply furnished with brilliant white walls, wooden patio doors and windows painted in traditional Greek blue. The obligatory re-enforcement bars sticking out of the top of the concrete columns, with which it was built completed its Greek heritage. What it also provided when sat on the balcony was the stunning view of the bay, one I had never tired of waking up to. Before the installation of the air-conditioning Jane and I often slept out on the balcony. I might add a very nice place to make love! Milos and Mary shared our love of the place, but lovemaking was off the agenda for Milos. Too much *retsina* and not enough Viagra! Milos particularly loved the price for a room, 35 euros a night, with the last night thrown in for free.

In our early years Milos had picked up the simple fact that *Pavlos* did not speak to his brother *Pandalis*. Very strange considering the *Kalymnians* approach to family and that they were on each other's doorstep. I had decided long ago that this was a subject best left alone.

As we parked on the roughly hewn carpark, directly outside the taverna *Pavlos* and the family were waiting. One of the advantages of the taverna being positioned where it was is that you could view the whole village and the main road that drops into it. Any vehicle heading to *Emporios* could be spotted and one of the family had clearly seen the taxi cavalcade arriving at the village. *Pavlos* was the same age as me, typically *Kalymnian* he was not tall but very thick set with short and powerful arms. With a mop of the archetypal black curly hair and dark olive skin he was as Greek as Greeks can be. However, you should never mistake that he was *Kalymnian* first and Greek second. A position all *Kalymnians* held. This may have had something to do with the various occupations *Kalymnos* had suffered over the years, from the Ottomans, the Germans, and lastly the Italians. As a result, they had held strongly to their *Kalymnian* heritage whilst fiercely maintaining their allegiance to Greece. After a stint as a fisherman and merchant seaman *Pavlos* had saved enough cash to realise his dream. With the land handed over his vision for the taverna slowly unfolded. Both Milos and I admired the blood, sweat, and tears he had obviously shed in committing to the task which took four years. It was L shaped, with two dining terraces and the kitchen in the middle. It must have been massively rewarding the first time he stood on the terrace and imagined long lunches, romantic dinners, laughter, music, dancing, and a place to support a family! Having reached the tender age of 35 and realising his dream he had not found time for the finer things in life, like women! Very strange I thought for a Greek man, but he had simply been "away" to much. The family stepped in and before long a marriage was arranged. A taverna without a wife was unthinkable and unworkable. This was still a route often taken in *Kalymnos* for such affairs and whilst completely alien to me it had a place in the way *Kalymnian* society worked. As *Pavlos* would often tell me 'This is the system.' A phrase that would become his trademark.

*Pavlos* married *Aphrodite* (Affroula) after a whirlwind courtship, if that's the right term in the summer of 1999 and forget the honeymoon, it was kitchen time. Over the years the "arrangement" gave them three wonderful children, *Nikolas, Ireni,* and *Maria,* now 22, 16 and 8. *Nikolas* was a chip of the old block, *Ireni* the spit of her grandmother and *Maria,* whilst being the spit of her mother had clearly inherited her father's tough and dogged nature. They were a wonderful family and our relationship with them all had grown to such an extent that we were treated like family and the feelings were reciprocated. The taverna was open from May until October and over the years various members of the *Michas* clan had supported the establishment taking on various roles. Our favourites over the years being *Kalioppi, Pavlos'* cousin, *Efftechia, Affroula's* sister and the lovely *Fucchiana, Pavlos'* sister. From the age of around maybe 12, *Pavlos* son *Nikolas* worked in the taverna, without complaint. However, when *Ireni* reached "working" age she found it all a complete pain, interfering with either the TV or her social media. When called upon, a hissy fit and shouting match followed. This led to me giving her the nickname of "Diva" a name that has stuck with her today and used by all the family. The arguments generally came to an end once *Pavlos* stepped in!

*Pavlos* had inherited the family *Spiti,* (house) in the village. Originally just two rooms, one for general living and an upper level for sleeping. I could not conceive how such a large family lived in the house and even more surprising how *Pavlos'* mum could "conceive" in such an arrangement. Over the years *Pavlos* had converted and extended the house and being in a prime position in the village I looked upon it with envy. This house was only used by the family in the summer and whilst the *taverna* was open. The only exception being *Nikolas* and *Pavlos* who sometimes stayed in the winter and spring simply because of their affinity with the village. The remaining time was spent in their house in *Pothia* and as *Pavlos* often spent months away fishing it enabled *Affroulla* to sort school life and be near her family. In terms of lifestyle Milos and I often wondered who had got it right.

'*Ella Pavlos.*' (Hi Pavlos) I shouted as I jumped out of the taxi. '*Ella* my friends, *Ella*, journey ok?' he enquired. Milos, Mary, and Jane had already been involved in the greeting rituals with all the family and whilst I introduced Chris and Jen, Milos had already disappeared.

"All ok Iain, how is the family?'

'The family is good *Pavlos*. Lovely to see you and to be back at home.'

'*Nikolas*, still no *Moustaki*!' I cheekily exclaimed. *Nikolas* smiled 'Ah maybe another year Iain.' 'Maybe never,' I replied.

'*Affroulla*, beautiful as ever.' I hugged her tightly as she smiled sheepishly. *Affroulla's* English was non-existent. It was one of the reasons I had a decided a few years ago to learn some Greek so at least we could have some semblance of a conversation. However, we knew each other well enough to know that the sentiments were real.

I turned to *Ireni*, 'Diva!! Still playing up?' I asked. 'Yes Iain,' she playfully responded. Like *Nikolas* her English was now very good. All credit to their aunt *Kalioppi*.

*Maria* had already decided this was boring and had stomped off somewhere.

'*Pavlos*, wonderful to be here, how is business?' I asked.

'A little quiet, maybe not so much now you are here! Come come,' was his knowing response.

As we walked across to the main terrace '*Ella Silos*, call me for the *Meze*,' rang out as *Giorgios* departed in his taxi. As we entered the main terrace Milos was already in his favourite spot, *Assos* on the go, a bottle of *retsina*, with three glasses. Milos was clearly home and as per normal *Pavlos* immediately adopted his rightful place next to Milos. Not much would change over the coming two weeks.

I turned to the others, 'Right you lot, what's your poison?' I asked.

Whilst they deliberated, I made my way indoors and behind the bar to sort the drinks. As usual very little had changed. On the far wall the noticeboards with the same photos from bygone years, maybe now a little more faded and turning at the edges. Later I would point out to Chris and Jen various reprobates we had encountered and the stories behind them. I made my way through the swing gate to the bar with three shelves of spirits including *Pavlos'* favourite Johnnie Walker whisky. The main fridges were reassuringly all in the same place with the same contents. On the bar a small fish tank with *Nikolas'* terrapin, which now seemed way too big for the tank. At the far end of the bar sat *Pavlos'* antiquated music system and various other *taverna* paraphernalia. Jane appeared at the bar. 'Mary and I are going to share a beer and lemonade and make a shandy, Jen wants a water and Chris will have a small beer please.' '*Daxi*,' (*ok*) I replied.

For as long as I could remember when it came to drinks *Pavlos* left me to it. This had fascinated many *taverna* visitors over the years, this strange Englishman behind the bar. On the odd occasion when the *taverna* was really busy, *Pavlos* would engage Milos and me as de facto waiters! Milos as a waiter was an experience not to be missed. His usual opening gambit, curt, matter of fact and always in English 'What do you want?' I particularly liked this when the customers were Greek.

I grabbed a tray for the drinks and made my way outside. Jane and Mary had joined Milos and *Pavlos*. As I looked across the terrace there was Chris and Jen, leaning against the railing that protected the edge of the seating area, in silence taking in the spectacular view. I noticed they were holding hands. Another good sign I thought.

It was around 3.30pm and whilst hot it was very pleasant sitting in the shade of the *taverna*. It was too late to bother with a trip to the beach, all of 5 minutes away and besides before we knew it *Nikolas* appeared from the kitchen with some form of *meze*.

As it landed Chris enquired, 'Who ordered the food?'

'Nobody Chris, it just happens. Get used to it,' was Milos' acerbic response.

Milos and Chris had an interesting relationship. I had never delved too deeply into how it worked. Clearly in their younger days they were great mates. However, I knew that Chris' failure to return on the investment Milos made in his "sports pitches" business left a bitter taste and that he was no longer willing, using his term to "bail him out". Whilst Chris had his laissez-faire approach, Milos would go to all sort of lengths to present a similar mindset, but clearly had all things well thought out and planned. For some reason this grated on Chris, I think he resented that fact that underneath the mask Milos had found a way to get his "shit" together and carve out a career and status that had enabled his lifestyle, and ultimately his retirement doing just what he wanted to do.

The term "The Company" was a *Pavlos* idiom. Along with our regular trips to *Emporios* we also spent every new year, for as long as I could remember in a huge, rented house in Cornwall. This originated from a few of the original Pollards 'family' but had grown to around thirty strong, made up of extended family, kids, and friends and to describe it as a week of madness would massively underplay the lunacy that occurred. One year way back we persuaded *Pavlos* and *Affroulla* to stay with us for New Year and to witness this madness. Since then, many of them had joined us in returning the favour and witnessing the same sort of lunacy in

*Kalymnos.* We called it Cornwall in the sun and *Pavlos* simply called us "The Company".

The afternoon session was drawing to a close and we decided it was time to get our stuff together and make the very short transition to our hotel, the *Asteri.* It was a short walk across the *taverna's* veranda, down a set of steep concrete steps and there waiting for us was *Pandalis.* He wore the look of a man troubled by his past misdemeanours and the isolation of his existence. It was as if the loneliness had literally taken the soul out of him. Lines etched his face, caused by the years of chain smoking and his gait seemed to me to represent the burden of being outcast. Despite all this he was always genuinely delighted to see us, and he greeted us excitedly. His English was as limited as *Affroulla's* and whilst I could hold some basic local vernacular with him, I would hardly call it conversation. He handed out the keys, normal rooms for Milos and Mary and Jane and me. I introduced Chris and Jen and explained he was Milos' *filous,* (friend*).*

'Welcome, welcome,' he gestured and pointed towards one of the rooms on the ground floor *'exi.' (six).* I advised Chris and Jen accordingly.

'Jen, just before you go don't forget "pinkles" on Milos' balcony at 8pm'ish.'

'Okay Iain, see you then,' and off they went. I yelled across, 'Let me know if you need anything once you get settled in, we are up there on the right,' I pointed. 'Number 10, just shout.'

I had explained to Jen on the phone ahead of the holiday that one of Milos' routines in *Kalymnos* before dinner was "pinkles" on the balcony. "Pinkles" being a term invented by one of the company members namely Greeno, and it referred to the ritual of having a little livener, cocktail, or some sort of obscure spirit on a night out before what he termed 'The proper drinking commenced'. It was no surprise to me that in the urban dictionary a "pinkle" was the description of anything involving a lack of

common sense, how apposite for Greeno! To facilitate the taking of
said "Pinkles" I had explained that we all bought a bottle of our
favourite tipple at the airport duty free and stored it in Milos'
fridge ready for commencement of the evening's frivolities. Mixers
would be acquired from *Pavlos,* and Milos would sort the ice. I did
also warn her that keeping the spirit in Milos' fridge did come
with a potential problem. He might drink it! She said she would
keep Chris' in their fridge.

'Well, I am not sure Chris would appreciate Milos gleefully
filching his favourite Gin.' How eloquently put I thought.

Jane and I made our way up to number 10. Whilst this meant
climbing two sets of steps I never complained, even when just the
thought of it made me sweat. It was worth the effort for the view
and the solitude it offered. I also liked the fact that with a little
care and planning I could have Jane from behind, whilst staring
out at the beautiful view. We opened the door and the heat hit us.
'Iain get the air-conditioning on,' Jane pleaded. I grabbed the
controller, set it in motion and before long the soft cooling air
transmitted around the room. In five minutes, we had unpacked
the bags, sorted the bathroom toiletries, and made our way out
onto the balcony.

'That's it Jane, we're home. Look at that view, stunning.' I
caressed her hand.

'I love being here with you.' She looked at me lovingly. I took
her inside and we made love there and then, no foreplay. It was
wonderful and then we fell asleep.

Jane gently nudged me 'Iain, it's 7pm. I am going for a shower
and then I need to sort my makeup and what shall I wear?'

Even though we had been here many years the ritual of Jane's
choice of clothing never changed. In fact, it was the same back at
home. Even though she could look fantastic in a bin bag, she had
some anxieties around herself which manifested in her needing
me to give her the confidence in selecting the right attire.

'How about a nice little skirt and top, I'll throw something on the bed.'

I got up and wandered out on to the balcony, naked and feeling completely at one with myself. It was still a lovely temperature with a very soft tickle of a wind. I looked across to the other rooms to see if we had any neighbours staying in the hotel. Across from us but on a lower level in one of the rooms I could see some clothing on the drier and the patio doors were open. No worries, I knew from that trajectory my tackle was safe from view! I gazed over the balcony to the room directly below us and again clothes on the drier, but the patio doors were closed. As I sat to simply take in the moment and wait for the shower, I caught sight of *Pavlos'* brother *Nioti,* dog by his side walking on the road that leads up behind the *taverna* and the hotel. Whilst I had never met *Nioti*, as he never came to the *taverna* I had seen him many times making this walk, day and night and recognised his dogged gait. I guessed he was off to do some sort of shepherding duty and perhaps select some *Katsidi* (goats) for the pot. On Sundays *Affroulla* would prepare *Katsidi* stew, a wonderfully rich and unctuous dish, perfect with *retsina.*

'Iain, the shower's all yours.' I was done and dusted in 20 minutes, I grabbed the Kraken Rum, Jane's Martini, keys, man bag, phone, and music speaker.

'Are you going to fill the others in with your plans over pinkles?' Jane asked.

'No, I will talk to them over dinner.' and in less than a minute we were on Milos' and Marys' balcony. Mary was sat at the table, beautifully turned out and looking relaxed. 'Mary, where's your drink?' I enquired.

Before she could respond, 'Maria, Maria, where's my shirt?' bellowed out from their room. Maria being the colloquialism Milos used for Mary when in Kalymnos. Like me with Jane, Mary had the same ritual for Milos when it came to shirt selection in

*Emporios*. Up she dutifully jumped, this time Jane didn't bother on the pipe up front. I followed Mary into the room with our bottles. There by the fridge, a freshly poured gin and tonic for himself.

'Usual rules then Mary? Useless git, what would you like?'

'Vodka and tonic please,' she politely replied. I sorted Mary's drink, Jane's martini and lemonade, my kraken rum and coke and took them out to the balcony just as Chris and Jen were moseying over.

Jen was wearing a simple plain pale blue dress, but she still managed to look wonderful. 'That's a lovely little number Jen, there are some glasses by the sink and the mixers and ice are in the fridge.' I advised.

Chris was carrying a large bottle of gin. 'Honey, all I need is a glass and some ice,' said Chris as Jen wandered inside. 'Oh, and some tonic,' he added.

'On the Tanqueray are we Chris?' I knowingly enquired. 'Yeh and I won't be leaving it in there for that git either.' Very wise I thought.

'Okay Jane, music selection tonight is yours, what would you like?' I waited but already had it poised. 'Fairground Attraction please.' I hit the button and the tones of "Perfect" softly filled the air, and it was.

As we were now all seated on the terrace, drinks in hand I offered my salutations '*Yammas*' (cheers) my friends, and Chris and Jen welcome to *Emporios*'.

'Well, it's lovely to be here, it's very magical' Jen enthused. 'Room is nice and simple, great view,' Chris added.

'Not bad for 35 Euros,' Milos exclaimed. 'By the way Miles,' Jen also didn't indulge in the Milos badinage 'When do we pay for the rooms?'

'At the same time as we pay for the food and drink, on the last night,' replied Milos.

'Really, well I get the rooms but how does *Pavlos* work out the bill for food and drink?' she enquired.

'It's the system' Milos simply replied. 'The Youth will explain later.'

'I will but now it's time for Dinner. Drink up and let's head up to the *taverna*. We've got lots to talk about!'

# CHAPTER THREE

## THE PLANS

By the time we made it up to the taverna it was around 9'ish. On the main terrace our usual table was waiting for us. Set for six and adorned with the obligatory paper tablecloth, but this time with a map of *Kalymnos* and held in place by white plastic clips. An array of glasses to cover all eventualities at each place although in mine and Milos' case a complete waste of time. The sound of Cretan music filled the air.

'Youth sort the drinks,' Milos barked out. There were some other guests sat in various positions around the taverna, another table of six, maybe yachties, two tables of 4 and a table of two. I made my way to the bar.

'*Kalispera Pavlos*, (good evening) not too bad tonight with the tables.'

'Ah yes, a little busy but no problem,' he said as he made his way out with a plate full of *Kalamari*, (squid). I grabbed a bottle of *retsina* and two glasses, a bottle of fine *Kalymnian* red for Jane, Mary and Jen and a small beer for Chris. I added a large bottle of water for the table and made my way back out. Milos was in his traditional seat, at the head of the table and the others had parked themselves in various positions whilst leaving a slot next to Milos for me.

'Youth, if Vera is going on the expensive red, I am going to have *Pavlos* adjust the bill,' Milos declared. Vera was my pet name for Jane, long story.

'Actually, Miles I thought you might have noticed Mary and Jen are also on the red,' Jane promptly responded. 'Thanks, Pipe Up.' They were off and running!

*Pavlos* appeared 'What you like Iain?' which generally meant everyone, but this was his system. I suggested a nice little meze starter of *tsatsiki, kalamari*, tuna dip and an *horiatiki salata* (Greek Salad).

'*Daxi*, (ok) and for mains?'

'What's on tonight *Pavlos*? I enquired. 'Have *moussaka*, chicken or pork *souvlaki*, maybe some *dolmades* and fresh fish, what you like?'

'I'll have the *moussaka*, chicken *souvlaki* for Jane, Maria?'

'Oh, the *dolmades* for me please' she said excitedly.

'Chris?' 'The *Souvlaki*, but pork.' He replied.

'And Jen?' 'What's the fish?' she politely enquired.

'Bloody expensive!' Milos quipped.

'You come to the kitchen; I show,' *Pavlos* responded.

'Milos, what you have?' I asked, slipping into my English Greek.

'*Pavlos*, any lamb chops?' Milos enquired. '*Nai*,' *(yes)* Pavlos simply replied. 'In that case I'll have the lamb,' Milos confirmed.

Very Greek I thought! Jen followed *Pavlos* to the kitchen to select her fish.

The food, as ever was magnificent and was devoured with real purpose along with plenty of the cheap shit. Mary hated any waste and would make sure most plates returned to the kitchen empty. Alongside this anything that was left would be served up as

*meze* the following morning. Milos and I had been scanning the
tables to see if we knew any of our fellow diners. The table of six
were definitely yachties, German we thought after hearing a
snippet of their conversation. This was eventually confirmed by
*Pavlos*. One of the tables of four were Greek, *Athenians* holidaying
in *Kalymnos* and apparently *Pavlos* taverna was one of their
favourite haunts and the other table of four turned out to be the
Eriksson's. A Swedish family we had met many times who had a
house in *Emporios*. Lastly, in the corner sat a couple of guys, maybe
mid-twenties, and in Jen's words both "gloriously handsome
young boys."

'*Pavlos*, you know these people?' I enquired.

'Not before but now yes, staying at *Pandalis*. Arrived earlier this
week, Swiss Italian I believe.' I looked at Milos, probably with the
same thought!

As was custom a big plate of melon followed the mains for all
to share. Chris gave it his customary stare and without the needs
for words I passed it his way first. Over the years I had noticed
this intensity when he was eating. I once asked Jen about this, and
she said it all stemmed from his childhood. Chris was one of six
kids and when it came to food he gave no quarter on who should
get the lions share. As we all tucked in it was now time to reveal
the plans.

'Ok you lot, I would like a little moment to outline some of
the things I have planned for the holiday.'

'Let's hope they go better than your plan for the airport,' Milos
quipped.

'Very funny Lofty,' another little Milos moniker easy to work
out. 'Anyway Milos, before you get too excited you won't be
surprised that most of these plans don't include you.' Milos lit
another *Assos* 'The art of doing nothing Youth,' he proudly
declared.

'Yes, I am well aware, and you can sit in your little corner and while away the hours with *Pavlos* doing what you do best, *Assos*, *retsina* and talking rubbish!'

'I resemble that description,' again proudly declared.

'I could see the disappointed look on Mary's face. 'However, Mary I expect you to join us,' she smiled gleefully. Milos played his hard done by card.

'That's it Maria, you go off and leave me on my own, I'll be al…' Jane jumped in and reacted true to fashion 'Now who's being a twat Miles?' I noticed his smirk.

'Right Milos, as this isn't for you, make yourself useful and get behind the bar.' Off he swanned stopping off on his way for a chat with the Eriksson's, poor them I thought.

'Ok, Chris and Jen I have spoken to you many times about our holidays in *Kalymnos* and some of the madness that goes on. I really wanted you to come out here and indulge in some of the madness and the sights and senses that this magical place has to offer. Now one of the things you must understand about planning anything out here is that it may not happen. *Pavlos* has this saying, whenever I've asked him about our plans in the past and when they were happening he would respond 'Maybe today, maybe tomorrow, maybe never. This is the system.'

However, he also could change tack at any minute. One year our great friends the Davies family came out and Solomon (nee Simon) kept asking about when the "special fishing" I had told him about was happening. I had asked *Pavlos* several times and got the stock answer. Then one lunchtime *Pavlos* called out 'Solomon, now you fish.' Solomon looked at me and asked what was happening, declaring that he was ready for a proper lunchtime session. *Pavlos* called over big *Nikolas*, one of "The Boys" and *Nioti's* son, said something I could not decipher, and big *Nikolas* pointed at Solomon and gestured follow me. Frankly, you did not argue with big *Nikolas* who, in my imagination was the closest thing I have seen to Hercules. Calling him barrel chested would be a disservice to the term and I often thought to myself that crossing the *Michas* must mean you've either lost your marbles or never had any. Off they went, with *Pavlos'* son *Nikolas* in tow, returning some 5 hours later resulting in Solomon going missing that evening. Apparently, the fishing ended with a visit to a mate of big *Nikolas* who had a penchant for the local hooch "*Raki*", best described simply as poison! Solomon was a little tender the next day!

"Youth, here's the *retsina*.' Milos filled his glass, plonked the bottle down on the table and wandered off to sit with "the boys". Most evenings, once *Pavlos* had finished with "the service" he would position himself at his and Milos' favourite little corner table, where often various members of the *Michas* clan, affectionally nicknamed "the boys" would smoke, drink, and talk rubbish. Milos' favourite pastime, even though most of it was in Greek he somehow seemed to get the gist.

I continued, 'Having said that, the one thing I definitely know that is happening is the wedding.'

'Whose wedding?' Mary said frowning.

'I had a call from *Pavlos* before we came out. There is a wedding party here this Saturday night. A *Kalymnian* man who married a Danish lady and the family now live Denmark. Apparently, they love *Pavlos'* place and have always wanted their daughter to have her wedding celebration here. *Pavlos* reckons we will recognise the mother and father as they have been here a number of times when we've been here. Anyway, if anyone is going to recognise them it will be Mary.'

Mary was brilliant at remembering all the people we had met over the years together with an uncanny knack of knowing all the *Michas* family names and family lines. Jane found this impossible, particularly as the *Kalymnians* had this habit of naming all their kids after mums, dads, and grandparents. I had lost count of the number called *Nikolases!*

'Sorry Ian? But why would they want us at their wedding,' Jen enquired.

'Three reasons apparently. Firstly, they didn't want us to have to go elsewhere on their account as they know the affinity we have with this place. Secondly, and rather amusingly that they think we will add a little sparkle to the festivities.'

'Well Iain, your reputation seems to know no boundaries!' exclaimed Jen.

'Have you told Milos?' Mary asked. I shook my head. 'No, the miserable git should have stayed at the table. I'll fill him in over the morning *meze*.'

'The third reason is rather special and is one of the things I really want Chris and Jen to witness, The Dance of the *Mihanikos*,' (*Engineer*) I announced. 'The what?' Chris asked. They both looked at me inquisitively.

'So, Chris and Jen, you remember the sign I pointed out as we arrived?'

'Well of course Iain "Welcome to *Kalymnos* the Sponge Divers Island." not much got past Jen.

'Indeed, and Chris, I leant over and told you there was a story here I wanted you to witness.' Chris leant back; I sensed his mind ruminating. 'Soft gold,' he exclaimed 'Yeh something about soft gold.'

'Nice one Chris, good to know you were listening. I've spent many hours whilst here talking to *Pavlos* and various members of the family about the sponge diving history of this island. I've learnt about the riches and lavish lifestyle brought about by harvesting this "soft gold". The archaic diving methods they adopted to enable hunting of the sponges and the appalling tragedy of the terrible toll it has taken on many families of *Kalymnos*. I want you to visit *Pothia*, to see the house and museum of the most important early sponge trader, *Nikolaos Vouvalis*. I want you to witness "The Dance of the *Mihanikos*" (engineer) which depicts the crippling effects of decompression sickness caused by the sponge diving, I want you to meet *Pavlos'* friend *Thassos*, a victim of this cruel affliction and lastly I want us to have our very own "Dinner of Love" a very special *Kalymnian* tradition which preceded the sponge fleets annual departure.'

The table had fallen silent. Before I had a chance to continue Milos appeared.

'Fuck me Youth it's like a library. I thought you were leading the charge round here? *Pavlos* wants some reggae!'. He wandered off 'And by the way, it's your round!'

'*Ella Nikolas.*'(Come*)* I shouted. '*Nai* (yes) Iain, what you like?'

'Two *retsina's*, one for here and one for Milos and another bottle of red, oh and beers for "the boys", *Epharisto.*'(thanks)

'*Parakalo,*' (you're welcome) he politely replied and headed off to the bar.

'Now there are some other plans, but let's leave them for tomorrow. As you heard from Milos I have a little job to do!'

*Pavlos* was clearly ready for some reggae! As well as his love for the traditional Cretan Music, during his time as a merchant seaman he had picked up a penchant for reggae, and in particular Bob Marley. I made my way behind the bar, dug out a CD, given to him by me on a previous trip. Fired up the system and 'One Love' belted out.

'Right you lot, let's have a little dance,' I proclaimed. Over the next two hours we danced, sang, drank, and thoroughly entertained ourselves along with the Eriksson's, the Yachties with even the two "gloriously handsome" Swiss Italians gracing the dancefloor. Milos and "the boys" looked on bemused, not quite your traditional *Kalymnian* or Greek fare but that was "*Mbarba Nikolas*". I didn't remember going to bed.

As the sun rose majestically from behind the mountains and the soft breeze gently swayed the pale cotton curtains across the patio door, I awoke to the sounds of the tinkle of the goats' bells as they made their way across the hill directly behind us. As well as acting as a warning of predators, of which there were few or none anymore on *Kalymnos,* the bells also served to calm the herd and allow for their quick location. For me, the soothing tones were a reminder that I was not back in England awaiting the shrill tones of the alarm clock.

'What time is it Jane?' I asked. I noticed her soft pert little bottom as she leaned over to check her watch. 'It's 8am,' she replied. 'Another half an hour before shower time,' she declared.

'Ok, come over here and have a little cuddle.'

When in Emporios, waking up next to Jane with the sun rising and already warming the morning air, the goat bells tinkling and the pungent smell of the wild oregano drifting on the breeze, I didn't have the need for anything else.

'Love you Jane.' 'Love you too Iain' and we dozed off in each other's arms. I came to with the sound of the shower running 'Do you want to jump straight in after me?' she asked. 'Yeh, give me a shout when you are done.'

I made my way out onto the balcony, naked as usual to get an early feel of the morning sun on my body. Gazing out across the bay the water was still and calm. In the distance a small *Kaiki*, (A traditional Greek fishing boat) was making its way out towards *Kalabros*, the gentle chug of the engine still not loud enough to disturb the peace and tranquillity. Across and down towards the quay the fish farm workers were loading their supplies ready for a day in the baking sun. Not paradise for all I thought. In amongst the moored yachts a few couples were having an early swim off the back of their boat. What a nice way to start the day.

The near silence was suddenly broken by the screeching sound of someone sliding their metal clothes drier across their balcony. Searching the lower-level rooms, I straight away recognised the occupant on the balcony. It was one of the Swiss Italians, he clearly hadn't noticed me and was hanging out what looked like some indescribably small trunks, naked as me! Blimey, wait until I tell Jen he is not just a pretty face!

I quickly made my way back into the room. 'Jane,' I called out.

'I'm nearly done,' she responded thinking I wanted to get under the shower. I went into the shower room.

'I've just seen one of our neighbours,' I explained.

'What, out on their balcony?' she asked.

'Yes, it was one of the Swiss Italians, they are staying in the room across from us on the lower level. One of them was out hanging up some trunks, naked as a jaybird'.

'Really,' she exclaimed.

'Yes, really and if you play your cards right you are in for a treat!' I declared.

'Oh God, you weren't naked as well?' she enquired.

'Yes Jane, but you know the system with the balcony' I cheekily replied. 'Wait until I tell Milos he has some competition for his Budgy Smugglers.' I jumped under the shower.

Milos was one of the few guys I knew that had the front to wear the skimpiest swimming trunks known to man. For years he had worn these ill-fitting speedos that were frankly obscene and a bane of Marys holiday life. Fortunately, our bit of beach in *Emporios*, directly below the taverna was generally very quiet but the sight of anyone coming to frequent the beach sent her into apoplexy. As ever with Milos I decided to assist her in sorting this problem. About 12 years ago Jane and I decided to buy him some Budgy Smugglers for his birthday, which was in June and therefore perfect for our holiday plans. We decided to get the most garish neon pink pair and, on the plane, out in front of the passengers I gave him his present and demanded he opened it. He dutifully did so, almost pissed himself laughing and held them up for all the passengers to see, rightfully earning plenty of cheers from his fellow passengers.

This was nothing compared to the reaction from *Pavlos* when he saw them on Milos. I thought he was going to pass out from the convulsions of laughter. This became a yearly tradition, with us selecting various colours and patterns. However, one year the future requirement became a little trickier, particularly around the choice of colour! More of this later...

Having selected Jane's bikini choice and having gathered up all our paraphernalia for the day ahead we set off to the taverna for breakfast. It was around 9.30am and already a very nice temperature. *Pandalis'* garden and terrace had some beautiful bougainvillea and olive trees and the sound of the bees darting around the lush soft petals and the unmistakable cicada's rasping away but rarely seen, contributed beautifully to the backdrop as we made our way down the steps and under the archway.

'*Kalimera Pandalis*,' (Good morning Pandalis).

'*Kalimera, Kalimera*' he simply responded.

You would always find *Pandalis* under the arch in the morning, sat at a small table, heavily engaged in an *Assos,* and drinking either beer or *retsina*, yes beer or *retsina* or rarely coffee to get his day underway. As we passed through the arch there was no sign from number six, of Chris and Jen but as we turned left, to head up to the terrace we could see Milos and Mary sat in their usual spot in the *taverna*.

Pleasantries offered, we sat at the table. I gave Milos a knowing smile, as he lit a fag *Pavlos* appeared.

'*Kalimera (*good morning*)* Iain, same for you and Jane?'. His way of saying the usual. '*Nai*,'(yes) I responded.

After a short while two coffee's, two fresh orange juices and two slices of cake landed. The cake? Who knows, one year it had been served up, maybe given to *Pavlos* by *Michalis Bouros*, the cakemaker as leftovers and as ever the businessman, he served it up for breakfast. Fortunately, it was very nice, so no-one complained. Milos never ate in the morning which meant Mary, much to her delight got an extra portion. I often thought yep, that is the only portion you will be getting on holiday. As Milos shakily sipped his *metrios* coffee Chris and Jen arrived.

'Morning all', was Jen's salutation. 'A nod was Chris' offering as they planted themselves at the table.

'Did you sleep well?' I enquired.

'I slept wonderfully,' Jen responded. 'Chris had a bit of a problem with his leg. He thinks it was probably something to do with the flight.' Milos mumbled some profanity.

*Pavlos* appeared again 'Iain, what they like?' I looked at Jen and Chris.

'Well coffee and Juice would be great,' said Jen. I could see Chris eyeing the cake.

'That comes anyway Chris.' I said to put him at rest. In no time at all *Pavlos* returned.

'So Youth, Mary gave me the lowdown this morning regarding the wedding,' he took another shaky sip and continued 'Sounds like a good crack, Mary has been racking her brain and thinks she can remember the couple. The bit about living in Denmark did it.'

'Well done Perks, I knew we could rely on you,' I said reassuringly. 'Apparently they are coming up to the *taverna* Friday to sort the plans so let's see'.

'She also said you have some other plans?' Milos asked enquiringly.

'I do indeed but before that I have some news, we have some neighbours,' I declared.

'And?' said Milos.

'Jen, you'll be pleased to know that your handsome Swiss Italian boys are staying across from us.'

She interrupted 'They are not my boys, far too young for me but very nice on the eyes though'. Chris grimaced and shovelled in some more cake.

'One of them was on the balcony naked and I didn't need my glasses!'

Milos interrupted 'So Youth, do you reckon we were right?'

'Right about what?' Jane enquired.

'Well, last night when "the boys" got up to dance Milos asked me whether I thought they were gay?'

'And?' said Jane.

'I told him I wouldn't bet against it.'

Now, what none of the others knew was that Milos and I had already made our mind up, and in one of our usual *retsina* fuelled moments decided to have a £50 bet on who was the giver and who was the taker!

'Milos suddenly got up from the table. 'The bus,' declared Mary. 'Youth?' '*Nai.*' (Yes) I responded.

This was another of Milos' little routines, used to commence the day's imbibing. This was designed to signal his first beer of the morning, timed around when the bus left *Emporios*, usually around 10am! *Pavlos* and I had discussed on many occasions trying to organise the bus not to come. We needn't have bothered as with all things around Greek timetables they did not need our help. On the odd occasion when it failed to show up Milos' frustration was a great source of amusement for *Pavlos* and me. Milos returned with a couple of *Mythos* beers, cracked them open, poured a little of each into two glasses, took his seat and lit an *Assos*.

'So Youth, the other plans?' Milos enquired.

'Well, I call them plans but you know the system. I was hoping that we may have a "special fishing" experience, I am also going to ask *Pavlos* if Chris can meet his mate *Thassos*…'

Milos knew *Thassos* and interrupted 'That's if he's still alive!'.

'Fair point.' Ever the optimist I thought.

I continued, 'We are going to *Pothia*, to visit the house of *Nikolaos Vouvalis*…'

Milos interrupted again 'Fuck me Youth, didn't you learn your lesson about visiting *Pothia* years ago, and who the fuck is *Nikolaos Vou…* what did you call him?'

'*Vouvalis* you wally, and yes I know about visiting *Pothia,* but I really want Chris to see this place. Besides, we will be going early.'

Milos interrupted for a third time 'Yeh, and you'll be back by lunchtime again. Maria, you're not going to *Pothia*,' Milos declared. Jane did not bother.

Mary jumped in for herself. 'Well it depends on what this *Vouvalis* thing is all about, I might like to…'

Again, for a fourth time Milos interrupted. 'Yeh you didn't tell me who the fuck this guy is.'

'Milos, can you just pipe down for a minute,' I instructed.

'Don't you start Youth, it's bad enough with Jane,' Milos barked as Jane laughed.

'Look I'll talk to you about him later. Let's get back to the plans. On the Monday, just before we leave *Emporios* I have arranged a special night for us all at *Harrys*, a "Dinner of Love".'

'Oh yes Iain, you mentioned that last night, sounds very intriguing. What do you think that's all about honey?' Jen asked Chris.

'You what?' Chris was clearly too engaged with demolishing his cake.

Jane stood up and interrupted 'Enough of this. Mary, I am going down to the beach now, are you coming? Jen?'

'I need to go to the toilet first,' Mary responded.

'Quel Surprise,' Milos quipped.

'Are you coming Chris?' Jen asked.

'Yeh I guess so, what are you guys doing?' Chris enquired.

'*Meze* first and then maybe the beach,' Milos responded.

This would be the normal daily pattern for most of the two weeks. Generally, when it came to beach time Milos rarely made it for the morning session. He would prefer to sit with Pavlos, drink *retsina*, talk rubbish and wait for whatever "*meze*" appeared. Depending on my mood I would take either option. Once Chris got into the rhythm of things, he did his own thing. At around 1pm the girls and whoever had made it down to the beach would appear back up at the *taverna* ready for a long lunch, avoiding the hottest part of the day. The table was always prepared and ready, in the same spot, just how we liked it. This pattern only changed when either we decided to have lunch in the village or if some madness occurred.

With most of the plans now in place it was time for the fun to begin!

# CHAPTER FOUR

## KALYMNIAN VIGNETTE NO. 1:
## "CHICKEN FARMING KALYMNIAN STYLE"

Having arrived on the Tuesday, after a couple of days we were well into the natural rhythm of the holiday, following the simple routines that we cherished when staying in *Emporios*. We arrived for breakfast on Thursday morning around 9.40am with Milos and Mary already at the table. The Milos system required a 9.30am arrival for breakfast. Chris and Jen turned up just as the bus left. Having dealt with the morning pleasantries *Pavlos* dutifully delivered the mornings *proino,* (breakfast) with the only variation being Jen and Chris trying the Greek yoghurt with fruit and *Kalymnian* honey, as recommended by me the night before.

'Wow, this honey is pretty special,' Chris commented.

He was clearly enjoying this special breakfast treat as he did not raise his head as he spoke, wearing his eating stare he was totally focused on devouring this simple but delicious fayre. As Milos and I were enjoying our first beer of the day, him on the *mythos* and me on the *brassinno,* Greek parlance for small tins of Heineken simply on the basis that they were green, *Pavlos* suddenly appeared. He pulled up a chair in between us, pulled out his pack of *Assos,* neatly stored in his shirt breast pocket, fumbled around in his other pocket for his lighter, slowly losing patience as clearly it wasn't in his pocket before Milos leant forward, ignited his lighter and got the job done. *Pavlos* took a long drag, leaned forward to rest his elbow on the table and both Milos and I knew something was coming.

'Iain, maybe today we have some business to do,' *Pavlos* declared.

'Is this one of your plans Youth?' Milos asked.

'How the fuck do I know, he hasn't said what the business is yet,'

'How erudite you twat', Milos promptly responded.

*Pavlos* took another drag 'Miles,' *Pavlos* also didn't use the Milos moniker. 'You know *Yianni,* yes?'

'What *Solonaki?'* Milos replied.

'Yes, Yes *Yainni Solonaki.'* We both knew *Solonaki.*

'He has work this summer. Looking after a chicken farm. He called me yesterday, he needs some supplies. I said I will come' *Pavlos* explained.

Milos looked at *Pavlos* 'Solanaki working, I thought he had retired?'

'Ah yes, but big problem with the money,' *Pavlos* said chuckling. 'You, Iain and Chris to come, maybe leave in an hour,' he declared as he got up and headed to the kitchen.

Now with *Pavlos'* plans there were a couple of things to remember. Firstly, he did not ask you he simply told you and secondly, Milos was required to go. Whilst this clearly was at odds with his "art of doing nothing" routine, for *Pavlos* Milos was happy to bend the rules.

At this point Mary got up and headed to the ladies!!

Chris, who had been listening intently, asked the obvious, 'Who is this *Yainni* bloke?'

'You don't want to know' Milos retorted.

'I'll be the judge of that' Chris said, rather agitated. Milos continued.

'Ok, so this bloke *Yainni*, I have known him for 25 years and the Youth maybe 20 years. I met him the first time I came out to *Emporios*. He was working behind the bar for *Pavlos* when the *taverna* opened. He is an old mate of *Pavlos* and was prepared to work for not a lot of cash as long as he got free food and beer thrown in. He is also the one who introduced me to the local *raki*!'

He took a pull on his *Assos* and continued 'He is originally from *Crete* and "Cretin" would be a very fitting description of the bloke. Lovely fella, but I wouldn't trust him as far as I could throw him.'

Mary returned sheepishly from the ladies.

'Milos, remind me, was it Darwin, Australia where he worked?' I asked.

'Yes, just like a lot of the *Kalymnians* he had a lengthy spell out there, believe it or not as a plumber. *Pavlos* reckons his plumbing was a tad dodgy.'

'He must have done the showers in the *Asteri* then,' quipped Jane.

'Very funny Jane and in fact true,' Milos responded. 'I think he was out there about 15 years; he had a bit of a reputation as a womaniser and...'

'*Yainni* a womaniser, I don't think so,' Jane interrupted.

'Don't be so surprised Jane, apparently he had a bit of a problem with a couple of women he was seeing at the same time! Anyway, one of the guys he was working with was heading back to *Kalymnos* and he took the option of doing a runner, came back with the guy and here he stayed.'

'So, is he a bit of a Cretan Adonis?' Jen enquired.

At this point Milos nearly fell of his chair. Then, having composed himself, 'I would describe him as charismatically ugly!'

This was a reasonable description in my mind. However, like most Greek men *Yainni* had this belief that he was god's gift to women, and I had certainly witnessed him turning on the charm, all delivered with a nice Aussie twang when speaking English. His "*moustaki*" worn with pride, together with a nice fisherman's cap, finished off the look and like Milos he loved to tell a story. He had married a *Kalymnian* lady but that had ended in divorce. Having produced a couple of kids that were now grown up he spent most of his time working for them and sleeping in the shed at the end of his ex-wife's house. The house was in a very pleasant bay called *Ambelli*, which was a little open to the meltemi wind but ok and "the boys" had commandeered the beach to open a bar called "*To Piratees*" (pronounced The Pi-ra-tees). His two sons *Stavros* and *Manolis* were a chip of the old block when it came to the ladies and their beach bar, whilst a little ramshackle and decked out in all manner of shabby chic rubbish, it was very popular with the climbers. With some of the meanest dub reggae around pumping out across the bar, the two lads dressed like Jack Sparrow were a sight to see. *Manolis* played the part incredibly well and whilst *Stavros* had now married and produced a couple of kids *Manolis* was very much single. I once asked *Yainni* if *Manolis* would like to settle down?

'He likes the Italian ladies too much' *Yainni* had told me. Indeed, he did and watching him turn on the charm was just like seeing *Yainni* in "*Mbarba Nikolas*" all those years ago.

......

We had one of our strangest *Emporios* incidents at "The *Piratees*" a few years back. *Pavlos* had a received a call from *Yainni* saying *Manolis* had run out of *retsina* and could he let them have a few crates to see them through until the next delivery. No problem said *Pavlos*, and he would bring some over by boat. Having announced to *Affroula* that he was going to deliver some "shopping" to the *Piratees* he gathered up Milos, Mary, Jane and myself and we headed down to the beach. I helped load up a few crates of *retsina* and noticed a bag with what looked like a couple of large bottles of water.

We headed out of the bay in *Pavlos* rubber boat and made the very pleasant journey across to the *Piratees* beach which is situated to the left of *Kalabros*. Along the way *Pavlos* pointed out the new house he was getting built for our Italian friend Alberto. Sat up on the hillside with dramatic views of the bay, a swimming pool, and its own personal beach it was certainly going to be a wonderful place. The journey was only five minutes and as we cruised up to the beach *Yainni* and *Manoli*s were waiting to greet us.

'*Yassou Pavlos*, (Hello Pavlos) you have the *retsina*' *Manoli*s enquired. '*Nai, Nai,*' *Pavlos* responded

'And you have the "shopping",' *Yainni* added. '*Nai,*' again Pavlos responded.

'What shopping is he on about Youth.' Milos enquired.

'Not sure, but I did see a couple of bottles of water in a shopping bag,' I responded.

Milos stared at me quizzically, I could see his mind whirring 'Ah maybe the *raki*, big catastrophe.'

He was not wrong on both counts. Indeed, the two water bottles were local *raki* and the ruse of the delivery of the *retsina* was nothing more than an excuse for *Yainni* to get *Pavlos* away from the *taverna* and over to the *Pirates* to get stuck into a session on the *raki*, "shopping" indeed!

The next two hours involved lots of talking rubbish, shouting, *meze*, dub reggae, some fantastic Italian eye candy, *Manoli* acting up and *Pavlos, Yainni* and Milos getting stuck into the *raki*. I stuck with the *retsina*, wise move. By the time the session was well underway *Yainni* had roped in a few German couples who he had invited to try the islands best *raki*, not so wise. Drinking the *raki* should come with an Island health warning and for Milos it had its usual effect, of inducing sleep.

Milos had a simple system when it came to offloading the ballast tanks, ie: taking a leak. He would simply head to the water, roll about like a walrus, and relieve himself. We were all sat at the table enjoying the afternoon sun, continuing to drink and talk rubbish when Milos, having crashed out in one of the hammocks suddenly appeared from behind us. Clearly still under the influence of the *raki* he stumbled his way past us to the to the water's edge, no more than two meters away to unload. At this point Mary shrieked loudly at him to remove his sandals and shorts before getting in. Tottering about he managed to remove his sandals and then attempted the tricky balancing act of removing his shorts. As they dropped to his ankle he bent over, rather ungainly to attempt to slip them past his feet, unfortunately revealing in his dayglo green budgy smugglers a large red and brown stain in the posterior area for all and sundry to see. Mary shrieked even louder for him to get in the water as soon as possible but all this did was draw attention to the horseplay unfolding before our very eyes. *Pavlos, Yainni* and I were in stitches, Jane simply covered her eyes and the Germans sat staring incredulously, muttering something that I didn't know or want to know what it meant until he finally managed to unleash the shorts and throw himself into the water. The sorry episode concluded with Jane announcing that the colour of all future smugglers would need to reflect the status of his "Chalfonts"…

......

Meanwhile back at the *taverna*, having finished our breakfast we were sat at the table patiently waiting for *Pavlos* to give us the nod that it was time to leave. Much to our surprise he appeared from the kitchen with a tray full of *meze*, including a bowl of mussels brought out by Milos, a basket of bread, plates, forks, glasses, and a bottle of *retsina*.

'Is the business cancelled *Pavlos*?' I enquired.

'No but maybe no food where we go and some *retsina* required for the trip,' he said mischievously.

Mary headed to the ladies as *Pavlos* laughed.

'Well Jane, we may as well help "the boys" with this lovely little spread, especially the Moules before we head to the beach,' Jen announced.

'Ok Iain, have the *meze*, a little *retsina* and then leave.'

'Do we need anything *Pavlos*?' I enquired.

'No, no problem, have everything you need.'

'In that case, Milos pour me a *retsina*,' he obliged accordingly.

'Well Milos, this will be a first. I have been to the fish farms before, but a chicken farm? I don't recall *Pavlos* mentioning them before.'

'Me neither Youth, lovely mussels though,' and we all tucked into the *meze*.

*Pavlos* appeared 30 minutes later in which time two bottles of retsina had been dispatched. I was rather looking forward to our little trip.

'Shall we head to the truck *Pavlos*?' I enquired.

'*Oki, Oki*, (no, no) to the beach down. We get the rubber boat,' *Pavlos* explained.

I looked at Milos, the normal response followed. 'Catastrophe!'.

This was his response whenever a *Pavlos* plan started to unravel. 'Miles why are you going on the boat, and you've had loads of *retsina*,' Mary admonished him.

'No problem Maria' he announced as she headed off again.

We gathered up our stuff, which in my case simply consisted of my beach towel and my man bag. We waited for Mary and then all headed to the beach. The girls were going to follow their normal routine and spend the rest of the morning on the beach at what we called "Our own little bit of *Emporios*". *Pavlos* arrived at the beach in his truck with the outboard and we readied the rubber boat for the trip. We loaded up about six carrier bags of what I presumed were supplies and at this point I probably should have asked the obvious 'Why the boat?' but had learnt over the years to trust *Pavlos*. When it came to Milos' view on anything associated with *Pavlos*, he would respond 'I trust him with my life!'

Just before we left, I seized my moment 'Jane, if I don't make it back, all the cash is yours.'

'You Twat!' Milos declared and off we went giggling.

As we set out across the bay l looked lovingly back at the village. There is something very special about travelling around an island on a boat. You get a very different perspective of the land and its place in the vista, seeing the size of the village slowly shrink and the sheer magnitude of the hills and mountains that dominate the skyline. We headed out towards *Kalabros* with just a little breeze. I could see some wind rippling the water out towards the channel between *Kalabros* and *Emporios*.

'Much wind out there *Pavlos*?' I enquired. 'Maybe a little round the corner, but no problem.'

'Which way are we heading, towards *Skalia*?' I asked.

'*Oki*, (no) out past the fish farm, towards *Leros*' he responded.

This surprised me as I was not aware of any roads that led out to the northern tip. All supplies that went out to the fish farm went by boat. Chris was sat next to *Pavlos* at the back of the dingy in deep discussion, probably some tale about a business he was once involved in selling boats. Milos and I were at the front of the dinghy and enjoying the trip. As we moved into the channel *Pavlos,* as ever was right, just a little wind. Very nice I thought as the fish farm came into view. Seven or eight huge great circular nets, like giant fishbowls, interconnected with platforms and maybe five or six guys toiling away in the sun. Not for me I thought. As we gently motored on past the fish farm the sea spray from the boat gently cooled my skin. Way in the distance Milos pointed out the island of *Leros*, jutting out of the sea like some ancient beast from Greek mythology. We were now in the main channel. The sea had lost its turquoise hue and was now intensely dark but still shimmering from the sun dancing on the waves. I could see the very tip of the island now and over to our right what looked like a couple of sheltered bays, one more visible than the other. *Pavlos* steered towards the bays.

As we made our way past the first bay, I noticed how barren the area was. No sign of buildings, of people, of human existence, not even any goats, just the rocky outcrops, small bushes, and trees and what looked like a small landing area. How tranquil I thought. As we made our way to the second bay and rounded a small peninsular of rock the same vista appeared, however I could make out some strange structure floating in the sea. I turned to *Pavlos,* and he was already laughing!

'Milos, what the fuck is that?' I asked. 'Well, I think I know what it is but not sure I want to believe it,' he responded.

'*Ella* Iain, *Kotopola Farma kalymnian stul,' (Chicken Farming Kalymnian Style) Pavlos* announced still laughing.

'Milos, are you telling me this is *Yainni's* chicken farm? At sea?'

'He's mad enough that's for sure,' Milos retorted.

As we drew closer to the structure, I could now see it in all its glory. A floating pontoon constructed, or should I say a thrown together mix of large blue bin type containers, all roped together with a platform made up of wooden pallets lined with some form of plywood. It looked like it measured around ten-by-ten metres with a small timber shed at one end and something that resembled a timber chicken coup at the other end. Much to my amazement there was a load of the scraggiest looking chickens I had ever seen, jerking, and bobbing about as they appeared to be pecking at the deck. I was lost for words.

'*Ella Yainni, Ella,' Pavlos* shouted.

Suddenly the door to the shed opened and there before us was *Yainni,* looking like a dishevelled Robinson Crusoe type figure.

He had his same fisherman's cap on, full unkempt beard, short sleeve shirt and shorts, his knee was bandaged and no shoes. In fact, he looked more like a vagrant. I noticed he hobbled over to the edge of the platform as *Pavlos* shouted, first something in Greek to *Yainni* and then secondly to me to throw him the rope.

As he tied us off *Yainni* greeted us 'Miles, Iain, my friends, welcome to my farm,' he declared in his broad Australian English accent.

'*Yainni*, you're taking the piss calling this a farm,' Milos declared.

'Ah my friend you better believe it, I'm gonna make a lot of money selling these chickens.'

'The only thing you are going to make is a lot of chickens seasick!' Milos cheekily retorted.

Calling these poor little excuses "chickens" would be questionable under the Trades Description Act but fortunately this did not apply in *Emporios*. *Yainni* extended his arm and pulled us up onto the deck. The first thing I noticed was the precarious nature of the structure and calling it a platform was a contradiction in terms.

'*Yainni*, this is Chris, Milos' old school friend.' He offered Chris his hand.

'G'day mate,' said Chris, perfect for *Yainni's* vernacular.

'Ah *Pavlos*, you have the supplies?' *Yainni* asked.

'Nai' *Pavlos* responded.

'Miles, you have a cigarette. I am desperate, ran out a few days ago. Milos pulled out his *Assos* and handed one to *Yainni* who lit it immediately.

'*Yainni*, what you do your knee?' *Pavlos* enquired whilst holding in a laugh, he had clearly noticed the bandage and the hobble.

'Bloody bastards the other night. A fast ferry from *Leros* created a big wake and I didn't see it coming. As it hit the platform it knocked me over into the chicken coup,' by now Milos and I were laughing.

'Must have knocked me out and I came to, covered in chicken shit.' Now even Chris was laughing.

'Could hardly walk as I must have caught my knee as well, had to make a bandage out of my other shirt,' he explained.

'Ah *Yainni* my friend, this is not a good system,' *Pavlos* announced 'Maybe stick to the plumbing!' Milos and I were still laughing.

'Too old for the plumbing now, anyway *Pavlos* I'm gonna make a lot of money with these chickens,' *Pavlos.*' look said it all.

'Come and have a look at my shack,' *Yainni* instructed.

We gingerly made our way across the platform to the shed. It looked around six feet by four feet, no windows that I could see and a single access door.

'*Yainni,* why does the door have a lock?' Milos politely enquired. *Yainni* looked at him inquisitively.

'Well Miles you never know if anyone is going to break-in.' he stated obviously.

'Break-in, fuck me you don't even have a roof!' said Milos mockingly. All I could hear was *Pavlos* laughing and muttering 'I don't believe, I don't believe.'

Inside the shed was a makeshift bed, some bags of what I presumed were chicken pellets, a very small generator, a few belongings, and a rather pungent odour.

We had all noticed the hole in the corner 'Well my friends everyone has to go.' *Yainni* exclaimed.

That was the cue for further fits of laughing. *Yainni* grabbed a small plastic bag and held it out for all to see.

'Look at this my friends, all I have left to eat,' inside were a handful of olives and what looked like a solid piece of ropy cheese. '*Pavlos,* the supplies,' barked *Yainni.*

*Pavlos* made his way over to the boat with *Yainni* in tow. He jumped into the boat and passed up the carrier bags as *Yainni* carefully inspected each one. At around bag four he stopped, reached inside, and pulled out a large plastic bottle. '*Raki*' he declared, opened the bottle, and took a big swig. His smile said it all.

After loading the rest of the supplies into his little shack and passing round the *raki,* which of course I declined, *Pavlos* announced it was time to leave. I can't say I was disappointed, and my worry was that before we knew it *Yainni* would get into one of his stories, the *raki* would take a hammering and we would all be left stranded on the platform.

However, there was one last sting in the tail. *Yainni* announced that he had to get a delivery of some of the chickens to his contact and had arranged for them to be picked up at *Pavlos' taverna.* A couple of cages appeared from behind the shed and he proceeded to shove around 20 of the forsaken birds into each cage. Getting off this excuse for a chicken farm and being eaten seemed to me a small mercy for the chickens.

We loaded them into the boat and bade our farewells to *Yainni.*

'Come back and see me next week my friends,' *Yainni* shouted.

'Maybe never,' *Pavlos* muttered and chuckled as we set off for *Emporios.* Milos and I assumed our same positions at the front of the boat, mainly so that we could remain upwind of the birds and were pleased when we rounded the bay and *Emporios* came into view. As we got closer to the beach the ladies spotted us and made their way to the landing point. I grabbed the rope, jumped into the sea for the final few yards and pulled the boat onto the beach.

'Oh my god, what's that smell and what's in the cages?' Jane enquired.

'It's the Chickens and the Chickens,' I declared.

'Don't worry they are not for *Pavlos' taverna.*'

'Well, they don't look like they're fit for any *taverna,*' Jen wisely declared.

'Milos, *retsina* time I believe. Ladies let's lunch'. We never did ask what happened to the chickens.

# CHAPTER FIVE

## THE LONG NECKS

It was Friday lunchtime, and we were sat at our usual table enjoying a very nice *meze*. Along with the usual Greek salad we were working our way through some very nice *horta*, (a Greek equivalent of spinach) some cheese *saganaki* (fried cheese), *tstasiki* and a rather large plate of *sapsari* (small fish). The *retsina* was flowing and Chris and the ladies were having small beers. The temperature was a very nice 34 degrees with a soft, pleasant little *meltemi* blowing now and again through the *taverna*. Milos and Mary were already brown as berries and Chris, Jen and Jane were not far behind. I was still in my red to brown phase, and all was well in the world. There were several other tables occupied, but no one we knew, which kept *Pavlos* and *Nikolas* busy through most of the lunchtime. We had a little moment of madness when the diva refused point blank to do the washing up. A lot of hollering and screaming was followed by the diva launching herself into the small accommodation unit next to the *taverna*, slamming the door and shouting what I guess was the Greek equivalent to an English teenager's petulant "It's so unfair". It never ceased to amaze me how nobody in the *taverna* reacted to this extremely loud dissension and carried on as if nothing was happening. Eventually when the pace of service had waned *Pavlos* pulled up a chair, plonked himself down, helped himself to a glass of *retsina* and lit an *Assos*.

'Ah pah pah Miles, what you do?' asked *Pavlos* frustratingly.

Milos knew *Pavlos* well 'I think the Youth's nickname for *Ireni* is spot on, maybe send her to work with *Yainni!*' We all chuckled.

*Pavlos* suddenly looked out across the village, something had clearly caught his eye as he took a long drag on his cigarette. 'Maybe the people Iain?' 'What people?' I enquired. 'Look, look, two taxis,' he replied.

Sure enough, as we scanned the hillside two taxis rounded the bend at the top of the village and started the descent down the hill. Not much got past *Pavlos*. He leaned forward, stubbed out his half-finished cigarette and shouted something to *Nikolas*.

'*Pavlos*, what people?' I enquired again as he stood up. He shrugged his shoulders.

'Maybe the wedding people,' and headed off to the kitchen. I knew *Pavlos* well and this didn't mean maybe.

'What's happening?' Chris enquired from the far end of the table. 'The wedding people, heading this way apparently' I said.

'Oooh, how exciting' said Jane. 'I wonder if the bride is with them?' Jane loved a wedding. We all turned to watch the taxis make their way through the village and then disappear momentarily behind *St Giorgios* church then re-appear to make the final ascent to the *taverna*. As they climbed up the small incline to the car park, *Pavlos* made his way across the patio to greet them.

As the dust settled from the taxis parking, we watched as the occupants from the first taxi got out. Two men and two women, mostly Greek by their looks and they made their way across to the gate. We watched as *Pavlos* welcomed them, greeting them with a kiss which indicated he knew them well.

'Mary, do you recognise them?' I asked.

She peered intently, searching the memory banks. 'One of the couples look familiar, any idea Miles?'

'Yeh, the guy maybe but the lady, not sure' Milos responded.

I was racking my brain and like Milos I thought I recognised one of the guys. While all this was going on, we had failed miserably to keep tabs on the second taxi. What a mistake! Suddenly into view came three of the most fantastic looking ladies I had ever set my eyes on.

'Milos, Milos, have a bloody look at them,' I exclaimed.

'Jesus Youth, Maria, you're fired.' Milos declared.

'Oh Miles!' Mary reacted accordingly.

'Don't worry Mary, they are definitely out of his league, and mine as well.' I added.

They were introduced to *Pavlos* by what we had now decided was the father and one of them was clearly the bride. As it happened we quickly determined which one was the bride as she bore all the hallmarks of a Greek beauty, rich olive skin, luscious folds of raven curls and a face befitting Aphrodite, the Greek goddess of love, beauty and most importantly sex. Just like *Aphrodite* she was sculpted as a most desirable deity. She was also very tall, unlike a *Kalymnian* lady and elegance personified. The other two, whilst equally beautiful, tall, and elegant were stark in contrast as they were blond, porcelain like and clearly not *Kalymnian*.

'Those two are clearly Danish,' Milos declared. He had been listening after all. They were all exquisitely dressed, in long summer maxi dresses and seemed to float as they made their way across the *taverna*. 'Look at their long necks,' Milos added.

'Iain, put your jaw back in place!' Jane had clearly seen I was a touch enchanted by these visions of beauty.

*Pavlos* came to our table ready to introduce the father when suddenly Maria blurted out '*Vasilis*, you're *Vasilis*,'

'Bloody hell Perks, where did that come from,' Milos asked.

'*Yassas* (hello) my friends, very nice to see you and you remember me yes?' *Vasilas* said smiling broadly.

'I do now, great to see you and *Pavlos* tells us you are here for your daughter's wedding,' Milos said.

'Yes, yes, it is going to be a great day. I have to discuss the plans with *Pavlos* inside but will talk to you later,'

'Ok *Vasilis*, talk later' Milos responded as *Vasilis* and his entourage headed into the *taverna*.

'*Ella Nikolas, Ella, Ella*' I called out.

'*Ella* Iain, what do you want?' *Nikolas* asked.

'Did you see those ladies *Nikolas*, very beautiful yes?'

'Yes, yes, Iain maybe I dance with them on Saturday night.' *Nikolas* exclaimed.

'Not if I get to them first.' I responded.

'Ah maybe you are a little old Iain,' he responded chuckling as he headed off to the kitchen.

'He's done you there Youth,' Milos added as the others laughed.

We continued our lunch discussing the merits of maxi dresses in this sort of heat and wondering what sort of outfits they would turn up in for the wedding celebration. Jane and Mary were deep in discussion on what they were going to wear but knowing that we were being invited I had already sorted Jane. I knew Chris and Jen would take the attire element in their stride and as for Milos and I it would be the usual approach, shorts and shirt, with Milos probably wearing his flamboyant Carlos Santana shirt, another present we had bought him some years ago and me in my favourite pink floral number!

Just as the girls were thinking of retiring to the beach and asking if we were joining them *Pavlos* called out from inside the *taverna*.

'*Ella* Iain, *Ella*,' (here Iain, here) Blimey looks like my lucks in,'

I said as I headed into the *taverna*.

'*Ella Pavlos*, what you want?'

'*Vasilis* wants to introduce you to his family and has something to ask,' *Pavlos* said.

'Iain, you know my wife *Sofia*, this is our daughter *Eleni*, and these are her friends Freja and Isabella, they are the bridesmaids. I believe *Pavlos* has told you we would like you to join us at the wedding celebration tomorrow evening,' explained *Vasilis*.

'Hi, and yes I do. Lovely to see you again *Vasilis*, *Sofia* must be a few years since we last saw you. I didn't know you had such a beautiful daughter,' ever the charmer. 'Nice to meet you *Eleni*, who's the lucky guy?' she giggled shyly.

'And Freja and Isabella, I'm presuming you're Danish? 'Yes, yes,' they said obviously understanding my English prose. 'You'll make lovely bridesmaids!'

'*Vasilis*, it is very kind of you and your family to invite us and we are very much looking forward to joining the celebrations. *Pavlos* had told me you will be having a special dance "The Mihanikos". We are looking forward to seeing this as well' I said.

'Ah yes, you know this dance? my family have a strong connection with this dance.'

'Yes, I know this dance and its history, it will be very special and my friend Chris.' I pointed him out. 'He was injured at work, damaging his leg. Sometimes he walks with a stick. I have brought him here so he can learn about this story.'

*Pavlos* Interrupted 'Iain, *Vasilis* has something to ask.'

'Not so much me but my daughter,' *Vasilis* responded.

*Eleni* spoke '*Pavlos* tells me of your reputation,' 'which one?' I said jokingly.

'He said you often play music in the *taverna* and entertain people. After the traditional Greek music, we would like to dance to some more modern music, would you do this for us?' She asked.

'*Eleni*, that would be a pleasure and an honour. I will speak to

*Freja* and *Isabella* when you arrive on Saturday, and they can tell me what music you like.'

*Eleni* grabbed my hand 'Thank you, thank you, I forgot to mention my husband to be is called Lucas. It will make our evening special.'

At that point *Vasilis* and *Sofia* also thanked me and said they had lots to sort with *Pavlos,* so I bade farewell and left them to finalise things. 'See you all Saturday and I hope the ceremony goes well.'

I headed back to the table whilst also giving a knowing nod and grin to *Nikolas.* 'What was that all about Youth,' Milos enquired.

'Ok, so *Vasilis* wanted to personally invite us to the evening bash, but also turns out that as well as the *Mihanikos,* the daughter wants some music to dance to and thanks to *Pavlos* and my reputation I am now the official DJ!'

'Right up your street Iain,' remarked Jen.

'Indeed, looks like *Pavlos* has got a lot of sorting out to do so why don't we head down to the beach,' I suggested.

We gathered up our stuff and spent the rest of the afternoon lazing beside the sea reading, chatting, the odd swim and in Milos' case sleeping with the occasional offload of the ballast tanks.

Once the sun's path had moved away from the beach we headed back to the rooms to ready ourselves for the evening's entertainment. *Pavlos* called down to me from the balcony 'Up Iain, up.'

'What do you think he wants?' asked Jane.

'Pass, but It's ok, I was going to pop up anyway to get some mixers. I'll see you in the room and I'll see you lot later for pinkles.'

I made my way up the steps to the *taverna* and *Pavlos* was sitting in his usual spot, *Assos* on the go and a small glass of *raki*.

I went to the bar, grabbed a glass, a bottle of *retsina* and joined *Pavlos*.

'*Daxi Pavlos?*' (Ok). '*Nai.*' (yes) he responded.

'These people, you know the wedding people.' '*Nai*' I said.

*Pavlos* took a sip of *raki* and continued 'Have very strong history with the sponge diving.'

'I know this *Pavlos*, you have told me before.'

'Yes, but you know my friend *Thassos?*' *Pavlos* asked.

'*Nai*, the one who is going to talk to Chris yes?' I responded.

'I never told before, but they are family, you know, cousins. This family many problems over the years with the diving. This is why they have the *Mihanikos* at the wedding, to remember.'

'I understand *Pavlos.*'

'Ok, tomorrow at the wedding you will learn more but also tonight, we have lot of work to do, many people tomorrow evening, maybe you go to the village tonight, is ok?' *Pavlos* asked.

'No problem *Pavlos*, we go to the *Artistico* to see *Giorgos* and *Ireni.*' Pavlos laughed.

We talked some more whilst working my way through the *retsina* and then I headed up to the room. The two boys were on their balcony and as I passed I said hello. Which one I thought mischievously? As I went in Jane was lying on the bed.

'Blimey I thought you would have showered by now.'

She gave me one of her looks 'I was waiting for you!' We went into the shower room and enjoyed a lovely moment under the soft spray of the cool water! A very nice start to the evening!

Once ready we headed down to Milos' balcony for pinkles. Our little frolic in the shower had made us slightly late and Chris and Jen were already there. I had already told Jane about tonight's plans. After fixing the drinks and getting Milos' album selection for the music "Alive She Cried – by The Doors" loaded and the sound of "Gloria" resounding in the early evening quiet I could sense Milos remonstrating and then the inevitable question.

'Youth, what did *Pavlos* want?' Milos enquired.

'He wanted to let us know that he had lots of work to do, or should I say more like *Affroula* has lots of work to do in the kitchen. To prepare for the wedding celebration tomorrow and would we mind heading down to the village tonight.'

'So, what's the plan Youth?' Milos enquired impatiently.

'We are going to the *Artistico*,' I declared. 'Oh lovely,' Mary responded.

'You'll love the food Jen,' Jane added.

'Yeh but be warned, *Giorgios* the owner may get his guitar out, catastrophe!' Milos exclaimed.

As we enjoyed our pinkles and The Doors I told them that *Pavlos* had given me some more information on the wedding. It turned out the daughter *Eleni* is one of Denmark's top models as were her friends the bridesmaids. She was marrying one of Denmark's top ice hockey players, a bit of a lad by all accounts and they were Denmark's glamour couple, a sort of Danish Posh and Becks. Apparently, another reason for coming to *Emporios* and to *Pavlos'* taverna was that in their view no paparazzi would ever find it!

Having made sure Chris was listening, lastly I told them about *Thassos*. That *Pavlos* had told me he had family connections with the wedding people and that they had a very big history in sponge diving. *Pavlos* had said there was more to learn.

'Right you lot, drink up. It's time for the madness of the *Artistico*,' I declared.

The *Artistico* was named to reflect the owner *Giorgos'* penchant for the arts but especially music. It was positioned in a brilliant spot with the main seating area no more than four metres from the beach. The lighting and the ambience created a very nice vibe, only ever ruined, in Milos' opinion by *Giorgos'* guitar playing. *Giorgos* believed he shared an uncanny likeness to Carlos Santana, which in my view was a fair shout. However, his guitar playing did not hit the same dizzy heights, but I really enjoyed the crack when he played and had spent many evenings singing along with him and any other unsuspecting guests. There had been a bizarre incident many years ago when some mad Scotsman, called Billy was holidaying on a yacht and suddenly declared his desire to play along with *Giorgios* and disappeared to get his instrument. About half an hour later the unmistakable whine of the bagpipes cut through the air and from behind the tree-lined beach Billy appeared, in full tartan regalia playing "Scotland the Brave". He was summarily greeted by Milos. 'I fuckin' hate the bagpipes, so stuff them where the sun doesn't shine mate.' Fortunately, Billy decided, quite rightly to ignore Milos and carried on resulting in Milos 'Fuckin off' back to *Pavlos' taverna*, missing what turned out to be a great night. Billy asked me later what was wrong with the "big man". A day on the *retsina*, some *raki* and around 50 *Assos* was my reply.

# CHAPTER SIX

## THE ARTISTICO

The walk to the *Artistico* took 5 minutes. I had a quick chat with Jen on the way down and told her I wanted a bit of time with her tonight. Fine she said but you'll need to make it happen. As we approached, the *taverna* was in full swing.

'Will we get a table?' Chris asked.

'No problem, all sorted,' I responded.

Knowing *Pavlos* as I did, he would have phoned *Giorgos* to let him know we were coming down. Anyway, as far as *Pavlos* was concerned we were family and the *Michas* name went before us. Sure enough, as we arrived I could see a table set for six, we didn't ask just simply made our way to the table. *Giorgos* appeared from the kitchen and spotted us.

'Ah Milos, Iain, Jane, Maria, friends, welcome, welcome back, you found your table!' Unlike most *Kalymnian* men *Giorgos* spoke softly, with a very gentle lilt, almost feminine which matched his stature.

'*Giorgos*, a bottle of the cheap shit.' was Milos' welcoming demand. *Giorgos* expected no less, and as he proceeded to greet us all individually I introduced Chris and Jen.

'*Ella Ireni, Ella*' he softly shouted, beckoning his wife. This was greeted with a high pitch shriek and her shouting something which I roughly translated as 'I'm fucking busy in the kitchen George.'

*Giorgios'* wife *Ireni* was an indomitable lady not to be messed with. *Kalymnians* had long wrangled and debated the simple question of who was in charge, the men, or the women and whether they had a matriarchy or patriarchy. This was at odds with most of Greece but that was *Kalymnos*. In my view there was only one winner at the *Artistico*! *Giorgios* had disappeared into the kitchen followed by some more shouting, ignored by all the patrons and suddenly *Ireni* appeared.

'Iain *mou*, Iain *mou*,' (*My Iain*). *Ireni* exclaimed. She was wearing her obligatory apron and a huge smile as she grabbed me and gave me a big hug, I think she had a soft spot for me and whilst she liked Milos I always sensed a little disdain. She probably worked out that the relationship between Milos and Mary was at odds with how she thought things should be.

'*Ireni mou*, wonderful to see you. You're looking lovely as ever!'

'Ah give me a break' she responded. *Kalymnian* by birth *Ireni* had spent some years in America and her English carried an American twang.

'Lovely to see you Jane, Ah Miles you have honoured us with an appearance,' she said somewhat sarcastically. 'How do you put up with him Maria?'

Milos responded in kind. '*Ireni*, I see the service is the same, where's the cheap shit?'

She ignored him so we introduced Chris and Jen and she said she would see us later after the service.

*Eleni* appeared from behind the bar, *Pavlos* was her uncle and she had married *Giorgos'* son *Nikolas*, the usual *Emporios* complications. We had known *Eleni* since she was a youngster as her mother *Fucchaina* worked in *Pavlos* kitchen for many years. *Fucchaina* and Jane had a very special closeness, which considering neither spoke the others language was remarkable, but it showed language did not need to be a barrier. Whenever they met up the sheer joy and love for each other was evidenced with tears. *Eleni's* father had died from tetanus when she was a child. I always felt she wore this tragedy in her demeanour. However, she was a lovely lady and most importantly she had arrived with the *retsina* and the menus.

'*Eleni*, nice to see you, a bit faster next time with the service,' was Milos' greeting.

'You could always get it yourself!' she responded sardonically.

'How are the children?' Jane asked.

'OK, hard work, you know.' She took the rest of the drinks orders and said she would come back and take our food orders shortly.

The *taverna* was almost full. It was very popular with the yachties with some large tables of guests. This would mean guitar time later. We all pondered the menu but instead of *Eleni* to take our orders we got *Nikolas*.

'Hello my friends, very good to see you. I heard you were in the village.' *Nikolas'* English was very good. 'I knew we would see you soon, especially as Iain is here.'

When Milos holidayed in *Kalymnos* with just Mary it was rare for him to venture beyond *Pavlos'*. This was one of the reasons Mary liked it when we were there.

'How is business *Nikolas?*' I enquired.

'Good, good lots of boats but not so many in the village.'

'And how is your brother *Themilis?*' I asked.

'*Themilis* is away doing his national service, in the paratroopers jumping out of helicopters.'

'Yes, that sounds right up his street' I exclaimed. He took our orders and headed off towards the kitchen.

In Greece they still had mandatory military service. Bizarrely this could be taken between the ages of nineteen to forty-five. I was not surprised *Themilis* had taken the Army option as this only required nine months service whereas the Navy and Airforce was a twelve-month stint. Furthermore, he was a bit of an oddball character and jumping out of helicopters would be the sort of madness he would enjoy. When Milos first happened upon *Emporios* he travelled with two other great friends of ours, Habs and his good lady Space. They had been taking a very long lunch in the *Artistico* and for some strange reason *Themelis,* then aged three decided it would be a great idea to club Habs round the head with a piece of 3 x 2, which still today remains a complete mystery as to why he took such action. Whenever I reminded him of this, he simply said Habs must have done something to annoy him! I often wondered how this approach to annoyance would manifest itself later in life should someone else "annoy" him, but *Giorgos* had assured me he had now grown up. No chance was my view but perhaps the Army would do the trick.

Half an hour later our food appeared. Mary had persuaded Chris and Jen to have the seafood spaghetti and when it landed Chris' eyes lit up. Jane and I decided to go for the chicken *souvlaki* and a Greek salad whilst Milos and Mary shared an "*Aristico* Special Pizza". Not very Greek but it wasn't called special for nothing. We were the last at the *taverna* to eat and *Giorgios* was already walking the tables announcing the imminent arrival of guitar time. I had got chatting to the people on the next table, Belgians sailing on what they said was a very sleek sixty-foot yacht. It was their first visit to *Kalymnos* and the *Artistico*. They had asked me if I had visited before, and I explained our relationship with the place. A very nice lady in their group asked whether I had heard *Giorgios* play and what to expect? I said she was in for a treat. She also unwisely told me she could play. I called *Giorgos* over.

'*Giorgos*, this lady plays the guitar.'

He gave her one of his big smiles 'You will play with me?' he enquired.

Her look at me said it all but the group had now caught wind of what was going on and she was dispatched to get her guitar from the yacht.

'Chris, Jen, how was the spaghetti,?' I enquired.

Chris gestured at his clean plate 'Superb!'

'That was really fantastic, can we thank the chef?' Jen asked

'Yes but you'll have to do it later.' I replied as *Giorgos* was now at the table, guitar in one hand and a stack of song sheets in the other.

'Iain, you hand these out for me' *Giorgios* asked.

'*Daxi* (ok). I made my way round the tables doing what I do best.

The Belgian lady had arrived back at her seat and was busy tuning her guitar, looking a tad nervous. As I sat back down *Giorgios* made his move and the taverna fell silent.

'*Yassou* everybody and welcome. I hope you have enjoyed our service and now I will play a song for you, I will hope you will know this song. My friend Iain, he has passed the words for this song. I know Iain well and he will sing but you will join in, yes. This song I believe, written by an English man, Whittaker.'

'Roger.' I shouted.

'He should be Rogered,' Milos quipped.

*Giorgos* continued 'It is called "The Streets of Luundon," delivered in his inimitable style. As he was about to commence, he turned to the lady with her guitar.

'I play this song in the key of H!' he announced.

Milos and I nearly fell of our chairs with laughter. The lady looked at me incredulously. 'Did he say the key of H?'

*Giorgios* struck up the first chords, playing in his very own time which I found impossible to describe, not resembling 4/4 or 3/4 or any 4 just what he thought was the right meter. The lady struck up and I could instantly tell she could play.

'Have you seen the old man in the closed down market, kicking up the papers with his worn-out shoes...'

And then the chorus

'So how can you tell me you're lonely...'

And our favourite bit 'Let me take you by the hands and lead you through the streets of Luundon... I'll show you something that will make you change your mind.'

At the close of the song everyone gave a resounding cheer, with loud applause, and unfortunately from one guy the call for more. Milos wanted to shoot the guy. His next rendition was a version of the Beatles Let it Be and he should have!

Before he could strike up his next song, I suggested a tune from our lady guitar player. She obliged with a traditional Belgian song, accompanied with singing by her fellow guests. She followed this with a very nice version of Simon and Garfunkel's Mrs Robinson, with *Giorgos* providing a backbeat using his homemade *cajon*, a plywood beatbox once again tapping to his very own meter. After some more songs *Giorgos* declared a break for drinks and announced that he would be back for more. Milos decided that this was his opportunity to split and suggested we get the bill. This was my chance.

'Ok, get the bill but I am going to stay and have a few more *retsinas* and a few more songs, besides *Ireni* wanted me to have a drink with her and she is still in the kitchen. Anyway, what's the time? I asked.

Jane jumped in 'Well it's 10.30pm and you know me, I am ready for my bed.' A further chance.

'Me and Maria are definitely offski,' Milos declared without consulting Mary.

'What about you Chris?' Jen asked. 'I am ready for my bed,' said Chris.

'Well, I'd rather like to spend a little time with *Ireni*. She sounds an interesting lady.'

I made my move 'I am definitely staying. Jen, if you want to stay no problem.'

I looked at Jane 'What do you want do?' I already knew how she would respond. When Jane wanted to go to her bed she went.

'I am happy to walk back with Miles and Mary, you stay, and I'll see you later.' Everything now depended on Chris.

'I want to give my leg a little rest and I'm definitely ready for bed.' Chris looked at Jen. This was the moment.

'Well honey, you head on and I'll get Iain to look after me,' Jen stated. 'Is that ok with you Iain?' Bingo!

Milos called out to *Eleni* for the "*Logiarasmo*" (the bill) and as she bought it to the table *Ireni* appeared.

'What's a matter with you, why are you going so early,' *Ireni* demanded to know.

'The *retsina*, to expensive here *Ireni*,' said Milos, deliberately to wind her up. I jumped in before she could react.

'*Ireni mou*, I'm staying and so is Jen, she wants to have a drink with you.'

After settling the bill and bidding *Kalanichta*, (goodnight) to all and sunder the others disappeared up the street, with Milos tottering and hanging on to Mary as the day and night of imbibing had clearly taken its toll. *Ireni* invited Jen and me to join them at the family table opposite the kitchen. The Belgians were still at their table along with a few others, probably waiting for the next instalment of guitar heaven!

The evening heat was still very appealing, and the gentle breeze just kissed the skin. It was now very dark, and the stars were evident, along with a beautiful glistening moon with its shard of light shimmering on the still water. A very nice night for a stroll along the beach. Later I thought.

*Giorgos* was already sitting at the table as *Ireni*, Jen and I joined him.

'Iain how did your friends like the food' *Giorgos* enquired.

'Marvellous, I've been waiting to thank you. The seafood spaghetti was to die for,' Jen responded.

'I know this' said *Giorgos* proudly. 'My wife is the best, you know this Iain.'

'*Nai Giorgos*,' I said.

*Ireni* jumped in 'Ah that Miles, he drives me crazy sometimes. What is it with him and *Pavlos*, and the *retsina*, it's the same?'

'Don't worry about it *Ireni*, he and *Pavlos*, they are like brothers. You know he loves you, but this is his system, Milos likes to play up to his reputation,' I explained.

'Yes, and one day I will live up to mine,' she retorted.

'What are you having to drink, on me,' I asked. 'I will join you on the *retsina*,' said *Ireni*. I could see *Giorgos* was already on the *raki*.

*Ireni* headed off behind the bar and re-appeared with another bottle of *retsina* and a glass. She filled her glass and topped up ours. '*Yammas*,' she declared as we touched glasses and then she stood up, thanking all the other guests and proclaimed a loud '*Yammas*' across the taverna.

I took a long sip of *retsina* '*Giorgos*, a few years back, I don't remember how many, but you were playing, and I was singing.'

'Ah, to many years with you Iain,' *Giorgos* interrupted.

'Yes, Yes I know *Giorgos*, but listen, this particular year *Ireni* sang,' I could see him ruminating.

'I think I remember this Iain,' *Ireni* suddenly declared. 'Maybe 4-5 years ago,' she suggested.

'Good, good, there was a bunch of people eating here, off a very nice gin palace moored in the bay. I got talking to them, mostly English people but a Turkish boat' I added.

'Ah yes, this I now remember,' said *Giorgos*.

'I was telling them about the sponge diving and it's place in *Kalymnian* history. This was after you and I had performed. One of the guys asked me a question on how the tragedies of the diving had affected the women of the island. I told him that the best way to hear this answer was through a song.'

*Ireni* Interrupted 'Now I definitely remember.'

'Great, so I would really love Jen to hear this song and of course the other guests. Will you sing it for me *Ireni mou?*'

She paused for thought 'Yes, yes *Ireni* you will sing?' This was *Giorgos'* way of asking.

*Ireni* deliberated some more, took a sip of her *retsina* 'For you Iain I will sing, but you will tell the people why I sing.'

'*Daxi*, thank you *Ireni mou.*' I stood up.

'Ok everybody, can I have a moment of your time please?' The *taverna* slowly fell silent as the guests turned towards me.

'Sorry to disturb the peace and tranquillity of the evening. I hope you all speak English. As you know *Giorgos* said he would be back to play. Well, we have a very special moment for you. *Ireni* is going to accompany *Giorgos* and sing for you,' I could immediately sense the anticipation building.

I continued 'I will explain the song, one which I had the privilege of hearing a few years back. I am sure you will all know that *Kalymnos* is the sponge diver's island. Yes?' Most of the guests responded, either shouting yes or nodding. *Nikolas* and *Eleni* came out from the kitchen, obviously hearing me speak.

'*Kala, Kala*, (good, good), So, you will know that these sponges, soft gold as I call them created great wealth for the Islands merchants and that the hunting of the sponges was at the heart of *Kalymnian* life for many years,' the nodding continued.

'This song tells of the dark side of this trade, the heartbreak, the terrible toll of death and disability it brought to the sponge divers and their families and ultimately it's about the loss of love.' You could hear a pin drop.

'Ireni will sing a *Kalymnian* woman's Lament, "The Taste of the Brine". *Giorgos, Ireni*, the floor is yours.'

I grabbed two chairs, positioned them in the same spot where

*Ireni* had sung this for me before. I grabbed Jen's hand and led her to a chair in the prime spot in front of them. I also asked the lady guitar player to join Jen. I went back to the family table, behind *Giorgos* and *Ireni* but right in the line of Jen's vision.

*Giorgos* explained that as this was a traditional song *Ireni* would sing it in Greek, but no translation was needed, just listen and maybe after if you want to know more, see Iain! Cheers *Giorgos*.

The taverna remained still as *Giorgos* began playing, softly but intently as if this music was the heart of his soul. The acoustic hum washed across the taverna, capturing all who were listening. I noticed *Nikolas* and *Eleni* holding hands. *Ireni* had closed her eyes and was gently swaying in her chair, letting the music take over her inner being, I could see the emotion already in her face. Jen was already entranced.

With her eyes closed she began, first a sweet hum rolling and tumbling to *Giorgios* soft rhythms. Her fingers tightened on her knees as she leant forward, and she began:

Ever since our lives began
Aman, aman!
We have known the taste of brine
Aman, aman!
Mingled with our blood, the sea
Aman, aman!
Floods our veins with poetry
Aman, aman!
Floods our eyes with bitter streams
Aman, aman!
Floods our lungs and drowns our dreams
Aman, aman!
Oh Sea, oh bitter sea
Aman, aman!
Oh, bitter is the life

Aman, aman!
When they found you in the sea
Aman…!

As she finished there was a moment of silence, everybody captivated by this haunting song, *Ireni's* emotion and *Giorgos* playing, they were one, they had love.

'*Bravo, Bravo,*' *Nikolas* shouted breaking the silence, accompanied by everyone in the *taverna* whooping and clapping. I was only interested in on thing, my gaze focussed on Jen. She caught my eye and the tears told me all I needed to know.

As the guests went to *Ireni* and *Giorgos* to thank them I went over to Jen and pulled her close. I looked intently into her eyes. I sensed her need to be held, to share this emotion.

'That was magical, but you knew that would do this to me, didn't you,' she whispered softly in my ear.

'Yes, I am not sorry, it's all part of my plan' she grabbed my gaze again. 'Is that why you wanted some time with me tonight?' She asked.

'Yes, and I want to explain, but let's have a little drink and then we will have stroll.' She kissed me gently on the cheek 'You really are a special man Iain.'

'I know,' I said cheekily.

We went back to the family table and spent the next hour reminiscing and drinking with me being accosted by some of the guests, firstly to thank me for making the evening so special and secondly to explain the lyrics. This is what I do I thought.

It was now time for our stroll, we bid *kalanichta* (goodnight) to the family and told them we would see them for lunch in the next few days. The only table of guests still in the taverna were the Belgians and we thanked the lady for her beautiful playing and wished them a safe onward journey. The night was now perfectly still, the odd flotsam and jetsam of noise drifting up from the other *tavernas'*. The air was still warm and as we walked the small part of the road adjacent to the beach the glimpses of the sea through the trees drew us in.

'Let's have a little stroll on the beach, there is a lovely little secluded spot at the far end,' I suggested.

'That would be lovely Iain.'

I grabbed her hand and led her down the steps to the beach. We stood still and took in the picture before us. No words were necessary. The peace of the night sea set against the imposing shadowy mountains. The odd night light from the yachts dancing on the water like some firefly and the very gentle lap of the sea. We slowly wandered up the beach, no more than 50 yards.

'Let's sit here,' I suggested. A sandy little alcove set into the rocks, hiding the village with only the yachts in view. As we sat down Jen nestled in close.

'How are you enjoying life in *Emporios*?'

'Oh it's wonderful Iain, it just keeps getting better and tonight, you had it all worked out didn't you?'

'Not quite, but once I knew we were heading down to the *Artistico* a little plan came to mind.' I explained.

'Well, I am not going to complain, but I wasn't ready for the song. She sang with such emotion and even though I didn't know the words the sadness was so evident I couldn't hold my tears,'

'I know,' I pulled her in closer.

'And when you explained the translation to that guest it all made sense and I know why you put me right in front of her. I knew you were staring at me, but I couldn't look at you, I didn't want you to see my tears even though I knew you could.'

We heard a little commotion down the beach, it was the Belgians making their way out to their yacht. I changed tack a little.

'So how has Chris been?'

'He has really loved it so far, it has taken him away from all the darkness that surrounds him back at home, we've talked a lot but still not about the things I need to talk about. I guess the worry is that the reality of life at home remains.'

'Yes, and for you both.'

I engaged her eyes. 'Jen, I first met you, what was it, some 40 years ago. I feel I now know you intimately, well not intimately but you know what I mean,' she looked coyly at me.

'But Chris, other than the odd story about his businesses he has never opened up about himself, his anxieties, his demons. You get a sense of them through his demeanour, but he doesn't seem to have the bonds of friendship I have with the likes of Milos and the company.'

She held my gaze 'But that's one of the problems. He doesn't have any friends really. You all have each other and "The Company" but we aren't part of that. Even his friendship with Miles has waned over the years. Have you ever known him call you? Any visits to see you is always because you or I have organised it.

I interrupted 'And how does he feel about that?'

'There are some things Chris just dismisses, as if he is scared to confront them. He simply chooses to ignore them!' Another change of tack.

'I've had this holiday in mind ever since we had that talk earlier in the year, round my dinner table, you remember?'

'God, how could I forget.'

'Listen, what I got from that night was that Chris was in a lot of trouble, not just because of what his problems were doing to him but in my mind, and more importantly what it was doing to you. The one person who has provided so much solace when he has needed it. The care and affection you give, seemingly unconditionally for so long, the rock of the relationship, fuck me, now even the provider, but more than anything else your love! And I know he is so lucky to have been gifted that!'

Jen sat silently, hanging on my words.

'That song tonight, it is just a small part of what this holiday is all about. I am trying to get Chris to see something, to have an epiphany. I know I cannot do it through words, but you can help, keep talking to him. There is more to explain but I need to let things unfold a little more and if all goes to plan "The Dinner of Love" will be the defining moment. There will be more moments like this.'

'Well Iain, after tonight I can hardly wait. As I said earlier you really are a special man.' She cupped my face in her hands, held me there for what seemed and age, then pulled me forward and kissed me, sweetly and gently.

After around fifteen minutes I suggested we take a stroll back to the *Asteri* and before we knew it, we were saying goodnight and heading to our rooms. A wonderful night and all going to plan. I didn't remember my head hitting the pillow.

The day of the wedding party had arrived. We decided to give *Pavlos* an easy day not having to look after us and following our usual breakfast routine we headed down to the beach, even Milos making a rare morning excursion. Later we would head down to the village for lunch, or rather cocktails to see another *Eleni* and her husband *Costas* at "*To Kyma*" (The Wave), one of the roadside *tavernas* but with the main seating area on the beach.

Whilst we were all sat having breakfast at the *taverna*, Milos had asked me how the evening finished up at the *Artistico*. I told him and the others that we had a few drinks, talked some rubbish but the highlight of the evening was when *Ireni* sang, a beautiful but sad lament of love lost to the bitter sea. Chris said he would have loved to hear that. Be patient I thought, your time is coming. Jen added that the song made her cry. She didn't elucidate other than to say she hoped we would all hear her sing.

After a very pleasant morning on the beach Milos declared it was lunchtime and that we should head down to *To Kyma* (The Wave). As the others set off on the short stroll down to the village

I left via the beach as I had decided to do my usual swim there. Having done this many times there was in my view no better way to arrive for lunch, besides which I could do my Daniel Craig impression. On arriving at the water's edge, with the others already seated I launched myself out of the sea, dripping with sea water I puffed out my chest and mimicked the scene from Casino Royale as I made my way out of the water. Slight problem, I did not have the chiselled body, or the blond locks but I did have the tight trunks!

*Eleni* was already waiting for me, laughing with the others as I traipsed my way up to their table.

'Ah Iain, lovely to see you but maybe you should walk?'

'Very funny *Eleni*, I thought you liked my James Bond impression?' I said as Jane threw me a towel.

'Yes, but I think maybe you are more, how you say Miles "Steptoe"! The others shrieked with laughter.

'You twat Milos, you set her up, anyway Ghandi, you can hardly talk!'

'Iain, I have *Costas* making you a Mojito yes?' *Eleni* enquired.

'*Nai Eleni*, you know me too well, *epharisto*' I said as she made her way up the beach and across to the *taverna*.

'You do have a bit of Steptoe about you,' Jane said giggling.

'Very funny, now let's get on it,' I responded.

We spent the rest of the day drinking cocktails, eating *meze*, and talking rubbish. We got chatting to an English couple and the husband had a few to many margherita's resulting in him declaring he was "pisshed". This meant we were able to enrol him in "The Accidental Sean Connery Club". This special club was inaugurated many years ago, when Mary's daughter Jodie and her mate Guns came out to *Kalymnos* with us. Jodie had a penchant for getting lashed, probably something to do with having Milos as a stepdad! This would often result in her finding it a little difficult not to slur her words. One day over a rather long lunch this occurred, and her speech drifted into full slurring which to me sounded like a perfect Sean Connery accent. I pronounced I was forming a new club and she was now a founding member of "The Accidental Sean Connery Club". From that point onwards anybody reaching this standard of inebriation and meeting the simple membership criteria was automatically entered into the club. I had lost count of the number of members!

# CHAPTER SEVEN

## THE WEDDING PARTY AND
## "THE DANCE OF THE MIHANIKOS"

'How do I look?' Jane asked. 'Wonderful, you'll upstage the bride,' I replied.

'Don't be stupid! Shall I wear these sandals?'

'Yes Jane, I thought we had already agreed your clobber for the night?'

'I know but just want to be sure I look right,' she replied, seeking re-assurance.

'Right as rain, now let's get going. It's pinkles time.'

Jane looked stunning in her simple white cotton dress. As we headed down to Milos' room, we greeted *Pandalis*, sat in his usual evening spot close to the hotel's perimeter fence, beer on the table and *Assos* on the go surveying the bay. It seemed such a lonely way to experience such a wonderful view.

Mary was sat outside the room in a very pretty blue and white striped dress.

'What do you think Jane,' Mary asked as she stood up and did a little twirl.

'That looks lovely Mary.'

'Thank you Jane. Bloody hell, you always look great,' she responded.

'Maria, shirt.' Milos demanded from within the room. 'Please would be nice,' Jane added.

'Ah, you're here then Pipe Up, Maria Maria, shirt!'

'Yes, yes I'm coming, I thought you were wearing your Carlos shirt,' Maria replied.

Maria disappeared into the room. 'Milos, drinks,' I demanded.

'Please would be nice,' Milos responded sarcastically.

'Get fucked!' was my simple retort.

A few minutes later Milos emerged, with Carlos, drinks, and Mary in tow. 'Nice shirt Youth' he declared.

'Touché my son, I am looking forward to tonight. I suspect we may get a tad lashed,' I ventured.

'I'm looking forward to seeing those birds, all done up to the nines. Fuck me they had long necks,' Milos exclaimed.

'Jesus, if that's the main thing you noticed Mary has no chance,' I added jokingly.

'Well, I'm looking forward to seeing the groom,' Mary said somewhat surprisingly.

'Fuck me Maria, he's hardly going to look at an old granny like you,' said Milos with his usual aplomb.

'touché,' Mary responded, much to Jane's delight.

'*Kalispera, Kalispera,*' (good evening, good evening), Jen announced her and Chris' arrival.

'Oh Jen, you look nice,' Jane said.

'I would,' I added smiling mischievously.

'Wouldn't I be so lucky Iain!' Jen replied mockingly.

Yes, I thought! Jen had a very chic flowery number on.

'Not bad for a septuagenarian,' Milos announced.

'Thank you Miles. I love you to!' said Jen.

'Evening Chris, nice garb fella.' Chris was displaying his usual unique sartorial style, a crumpled off-white cotton suit with a yellow t-shirt emblazoned with a red star!

'Drinks?' I enquired.

'Usual please,' Chris replied. 'Jen, your turn for the music tonight, what would you like?'

I had my finger poised 'Well a little bit of Van Morrison would be nice.'

I hit the button and as Van the Man's Moondance struck out from my Bose system, I went off into Milos' room to sort their poison. Shortly after, I returned with their drinks and in Chris' case a glass with a can of tonic and some ice.

After some idle chit chat I decided it was time to grab everyone's attention 'Ok, so as well as gawping at the lovely eye candy tonight, and that counts for all of us according to Mary.'

'Eye candy for us ladies, have I missed something?' Jen interrupted.

'Yes, Mary has the hots for the groom,' Milos replied. 'I never said that' Mary responded.

'Mary happened to mention that she was looking forward to seeing the groom.' I explained.

'Yeh, she thinks he might like a bit of GILF!' Milos said laughing.

'Milos shut it you twat and listen for a minute. So back to where I started, as well as gawping at the ladies we have something far more important to witness, the dance of the Mihanikos.' I focussed on Chris and Jen.

'You remember I mentioned this dance when I told you about the plans. We have seen this before but for you two this will be a first. It's a very special and emotional dance, one steeped in the history of the island. This dance depicts the crippling effects of decompression sickness caused by sponge diving.' Everyone was listening intently.

I continued 'It has a special place in the history of the family of the father of the bride and with his cousin *Thassos,* who Chris will be meeting next week. You remember me mentioning this as well?'

'Yes, Yes,' Jen said, and Chris nodded.

'Chris and Jen, one last thing, when the dance is announced I want you to take a couple of special seats that I have sorted with *Pavlos.* I will point them out and give you the nod when you need to take them, all *daxi?'* (ok) I asked.

Both nodded. 'Great, in that case drink up and let's get this party on the road.'

We finished up our drinks, I placed the glasses by the sink in the room and once Milos had grabbed his *Assos* we all took the short trot up to the *taverna.* As we approached the terrace area the sound of traditional *Cretan* music slowly came into the ether. The *taverna* was alive with the sound of chatter and people clearly enjoying themselves. The two terraces were festooned with lighting and flowers and the tables were all beautifully decorated with special tablecloths and matching posies of flowers. *Pavlos* and the family had obviously been busy all day. We were delighted to see that our normal table was empty, and *Nikolas* caught sight of us as we made our way through the bar and out on to the terrace.

He called out '*Ella* Iain, your usual table is reserved for you.'
'*Epharisto* (thankyou) *Nikolas,* very kind,' I said.

'Iain, tonight we are very busy with the service, you will look after the company yes?' *Nikolas* asked.

'No problem *Nikolas,* this is the system!'

As we took our seats *Vasilas* had obviously spotted us and came over.

'Welcome my friends, welcome. We are so pleased you are joining us. We will have a great night yes?'

'Very much so but I'm not sure about the dodgy DJ later,' Milos said grinning in my direction. 'How was the day?'

'Very beautiful, my daughter shone like the sun and the

ceremony was very emotional. It was very special for me to see my daughter married here in *Kalymnos*. We have a big history here, not all as wonderful, but this is the life' *Vasilas* said.

'We know a little of your history and the *Mihanikos*, we very much look forward to seeing that and having a great night, we're delighted to share this evening with you,' Milos responded.

'We will talk later, I have lots to do, you know as the father.'

'No problem *Vasilas*, go and do your duties and we'll watch the night unfold,' I said as he left us.

I headed into the bar to be greeted by *Efftechia, Affroula's* sister.

'*Efftechia*, what a lovely surprise,' I suddenly remembered she had about as much English as her sister.

*Signomee, ti eperochi ekpliki,* (sorry, what a lovely surprise),' In my best Greek. She grabbed me and gave me a big hug and a kiss on both cheeks. I knew she was pleased to see me. I met her when she was working in the kitchen with *Affroulla* on our first ever trip. A couple of years younger than *Affroulla* she was just as shy. Now here we were, some 20 years later and the passing of time had seen her confidence grow, she was a beautiful young lady then and that had not changed. Like many women on the island, she spent a lot of time without her husband, who worked in Darwin. Her life revolved around her children, even though they were now young ladies. It felt such a shame that they were not sharing their time together, but this was the way in *Kalymnos*. It made me realise how lucky Jane and I were.

I called out to Jane '*Ella* Jane, *ella*' as she made her way into the bar I said, 'Look Jane.'

She spotted *Efftechia*, shrieked and a rushed over to give her a hug. As they embraced I spotted Jane's tears, nothing unusual here! *Kalioppi* suddenly appeared from the kitchen on hearing the commotion in the bar.

'Oh Iain, *Pavlos* told me you were attending the wedding, it's so nice to see you'. *Kalliopi, Poppi* for short, was another cousin of

*Pavlos*. Her father *Giorgos* was married to one of *Pavlos* sisters and they lived in the village. She had spent a large part of her life in Australia, returning to *Emporios* when her father decided it was time to settle back in *Kalymnos*. She spoke with a strong Aussie twang and was convinced that because of this and the time spent away she would never be accepted as a true *Kalymnian*. This seemed to weigh on her mind along with the unfortunate early death of her two twin brothers. As far as I knew she had remained single her entire life and doted on *Pavlos* son *Nikolas*. Clearly she loved *Ireni* and *Maria*, but *Nikolas* held a special place in her heart. Maybe to replace the loss of her brothers. Fiercely Greek Orthodox she spent a lot of time running errands for the church together with her job, managing her own English language school. Her other passion was her hatred of the Turks. We ribbed her often on this, but she would never let it go. As far as she was concerned, they were barbarians of the highest degree and would always be her enemy. As a little side-line she kept around eight sunbeds on the beach which we sort of hired when we stayed, with her and Milos often arguing over the price. We saw less of her these days as her parents were now very old and she had taken on the task of looking after them. I had a lot to thank her father for as it was he who had regaled me with stories of the sponge diving. A diver himself he also carried a few "problems" associated with his diving exploits.

'I see he's got you back in the kitchen, blimey it's years since you used to grace this bar.' I said.

'Ah well, it's nice to reminisce sometimes but I'm only for tonight,' she replied and turned to Jane.

'Hi Jane' They embraced and more tears! I left them and made my way into the kitchen which was a hive of activity with *Pavlos* and *Affroulla* looking very hot and bothered.

'Ah *Pavlos*, the big service tonight, big problem eh?'

'*Nai* Iain, no service for you,' he responded laughing. Then I saw *Fucchaina*.

'*Fucchaina*' I shouted '*S'agapo!*' (My love*)*, I grabbed her, and we hugged each other tightly.' I asked *Pavlos* if I could take her for a minute.

'Yes, yes, no problem, I know the system with Jane.'

'Jane look.' I shouted. The tears were there before they embraced. Jane held *Fucchaina's* face and stared intensely into her eyes. Wanting to express her deep love without the need for words. They had a special bond. Jane had cried when *Pavlos* told us many years ago how she had lost her husband to tetanus. Since those days she had dressed in the traditional black mourning dress together with a headscarf which she never took off, even when working in the sweltering heat of the kitchen or taking a cooling dip in the sea. Jane simply wished she could take away her pain, but I knew that Jane's love, and friendship was enough.

I made my way behind the bar and sorted our drinks, eventually taking them out to the table.

'Fuck me Youth, it's like a desert out here. Your service is rubbish!' Milos growled.

'I got waylaid,' I said.

'You'll get laid out if you take that long next time,' he responded.

'I was talking to *Effiechia, Poppi* and *Fucchaina*. Much more interesting than serving you!'

'What, are they inside?' Mary interrupted excitedly.

'Well, they are hardly anywhere else,' said Milos sarcastically.

'Yes Mary, ignore the twat. Take Jen in to meet them,' I suggested.

Mary jumped up, grabbed Jen, and headed into the bar. All sorts of shouting and shrieking followed.

As I sat down and poured a *retsina* for Milos and myself he grabbed my arm. 'Youth, have a look at them'.

'Have a look at what?' I enquired.

'Fuck me, are you blind? Over there,' he pointed. 'The long necks, you know the bridesmaids. What a pair of stunners, and their mates too! A real bevy of swans!'

He wasn't wrong. As I gazed across the tables I couldn't help but notice the number of beautiful people thronging the terrace. All exquisitely dressed and looking suitably sophisticated and cool. I searched the area looking for *Eleni* the bride. I don't know how I missed her. Talk about stunning! She was wearing the most beautiful cream A-line V-neck dress, adorned with sequins and lived up to the billing I had given her of *Aphrodite*. Her hair was gently tousled and held back by a simple rhinestone headband.

'I would,' was my simple remark.

'You should be so lucky, anyway the competitions a tad high quality. Did you spot Adonis?' Milos asked.

I hadn't, even though he was stood next to her. Sure enough, he also lived up to Milos' billing. The archetypal Dane with a shock of blond hair, tall, muscular, and even to me as a fella, extremely good looking. Jane, Mary, and Jen were making their way back to the table.

'There you go ladies, your eye candy is on display,' I declared.

'I would,' was Jen's simple remark followed by a glare from Chris.

'You'll have to fight Mary off first,' Milos added deadpan as ever.

At this point *Nikolas* arrived with a tray load of food, a special *meze* that all the guests were being served. I could see Chris eyeing up the fayre and suggested we all tuck in. Along with all the usual dishes the star of the show was *Affroulla's* lamb, slow cooked, infused with oregano and served with sliced potatoes. Needless to say, there wasn't going to be any left for the morning *meze*!

All the guests were seated and doing what Greeks do best, eating, drinking, shouting, and laughing. Even the Danes seemed to understand the crack and the cacophony, together with the *Cretan* music created a wonderful atmosphere. I kept our drinks flowing and at some stage *Pavlos* appeared with a few bottles of champagne from *Vasilas* which was greeted enthusiastically by Jen, 'Is it Dom Pom?'

'Probably more like Pomagne knowing *Pavlos*,' Milos quipped.

'Well, whatever it is, I presume we have to save it for the speeches?' Jane asked.

'No, they don't do speeches. Eat and then dance is the system here.' Milos replied.

On that basis we weighed into the champagne readying ourselves for the following entertainment. I decided it was now a good opportunity to pass on my best wishes to the bride and groom and to speak to *Freja* and *Isabella* about the music for my DJ spot. I made my way across to the main table.

'*Eleni, Lucas*, on behalf of my friends and myself can I wish you both a wonderful life together. We are so pleased to be sharing this special evening with you.'

'Ah yes,' she turned to *Lucas*. 'This is Iain. My father told you about him and his friends. They have met many times before when visiting *Kalymnos*,' *Eleni* said.

'Nice to meet you Iain, *Eleni* tells me you are going to be our DJ for later. That is very good of you,' *Lucas* remarked.

'Well I wouldn't quite call it DJ'ing but I'll do my best. Anyway, I need to speak to *Freja* and *Isabella* about this, so I'll leave you in peace. Have a great night and see you on the dance floor. By the way I am very much looking forward to the Dance of the *Mihanikos*.'

'Me to, I have not seen this before.' *Lucas* said.

Lucky bastard I thought as I made my way across to *Freja* and *Isabella's* table.

'Hi ladies, can I firstly say how wonderful you look. I hope you are having a lovely day and it looks like tonight is going to be great fun. Did you have time to sort the music you'd like?'

'Thank you and yes it's been great, this is such a lovely island. Following our little chat on Friday *Freja* and I compiled a list. Is that ok?' *Isabella* asked.

'We wondered how you would find the music?' *Freja* added.

'The wonders of the internet ladies,' I replied. 'I am relying on you two to lead the dancing so don't let me down,' I added.

'Well only if you join us,' Freja said.

I contained myself 'That would be my pleasure ladies.'

What I really wanted to say was "Well a double header with you two wouldn't go amiss".

I made my way back to our table as the company were getting stuck into the wedding cake.

'Good job you came back now. Chris was eyeing up your cake,' Jen said as she watched Chris speedily devouring his piece.

'He's welcome to it, I am purely *retsina* all the way now,' I replied as my plate was quickly dispatched to Chris.

'How were the long necks youth?' Milos enquired.

'I wouldn't climb over them for you,' I said as I filled my glass with retsina.

'I have their list of music and they want me to have a little dance with them.'

'Now there's a very nice little double header Youth.' He knew me too well.

As the festivities continued, we noticed the band setting up. Having been to a few island weddings before, we knew the importance of having a live band, particularly for the dancing and none more so than the Dance of the *Mihanikos*. As usual there were three members, one on a violin, one on a "*Lauto*", a small banjo like guitar, and one on a "*Tsambouna*", similar to a bagpipe, but made from goatskin. The thing I found funny about this was Milos really liked listening to this music but when I reminded him of his hatred of the bag pipes, he would steadfastly refute it was anything like the bagpipes. This was the contradiction of Milos' approach to life. Whenever we went to an event on *Kalymnos* where one of these bands were playing, they were all given the moniker of "The *Bazouki* Brothers", another contradiction of terms as none of them were playing the "*Bazouki*" but this was the system.

......

We had attended our first wedding around 10 years ago, another *Michas* relation which finished reasonably early for a *Kalymnian* wedding. The *Bazouki* Brothers band playing at the wedding decided it would be a good crack to come back to *Pavlos taverna* for a drink and to play a few songs. As usual I ended up last to bed, leaving them still drinking and playing at around 3am! When I eventually turned up for breakfast, a tad hungover and a little bereft of energy, Milos greeted me with a simple "Big Problem Youth". The said *Bazouki* Brothers were still sat on the other terrace and whilst not playing were still drinking! *Pavlos* said he had left them around 5am, with a bottle of his favourite Johnnie Walker Black Label Whiskey and here they were still drinking. I asked *Pavlos* when he thought they might finish, and he told us that they had put an order in for lunch! We decided it would be best to avoid this and spend the morning on the beach. Whilst down there a fair amount of shouting and commotion drifted down from the *taverna*. When we decided to head back up for lunch, we could not believe what we saw. Of the three, one was comatose on the table and the other two were attempting to eat without much success. Whilst I knew the term "Roaring Drunk" I had never actually seen it but in my view what we witnessed for the next two hours was as close a definition I could imagine. *Pavlos* told us they had polished off another bottle of Scotch and were demanding more, but he had run out! Around 3pm having thoroughly entertained us, themselves and having managed to wake up their mate they decided they should leave. We watched in pure incredulity as the one doing the most shouting, obviously thinking he was compos mentis, bundled his fellow band members into their car, threw a load of money at *Pavlos* and drove off. I remember saying to *Pavlos* about drink driving, etc and wasn't surprised at his response "This is the system Iain". I ventured to Milos that we would have probably been dead before reaching the car let alone drive…

......

Fortunately, we had already decided that this was a different *Bazouki* band and after a very short sound check they got underway. We loved the *Cretan* music, it had a unique style and tone, seeming to harness a sound that you would easily recognise as ancient Greek. There were influences of Byzantine music, both in the lamenting singing and in the use of the drone notes with the instrumentation giving an eerie, mysterious element. Whenever people asked me about it, I simply said you just need to hear and experience it.

During the first song some of the guests and their tables were re-positioned, clearly to create a space for dancing. After the first song the *Lauto* player announced the next song and I recognised the word *horos*, meaning dance. A loud resounding cheer followed and as they struck the first notes. *Thoris, Pavlos'* brother appeared and took to the floor. I had watched *Thoris* dance for many years. In his younger days he was considered one of the best on the island. This together with his swarthy looks, irascible charm, and ability to convey the emotion of the dance through his movements was really something to see. He had spent many years dancing at *tavernas* for the *touristes* and I had no doubt that this, together with a few "liaisons" with some of the lady *touristes* had cost him his marriage. Even though he was now in his late 60's he could still turn it on.

Whilst many of the dances required simple steps, Pavlos had always told me that it was the need for balance and timing that set apart the great dancers. As *Thoris* smoothly transitioned across the floor the clapping, whistling, and shouting started, this seemed to inspire his dips and ankle taps and the flamboyancy of his style. I knew what was coming next and he started to invite guests to join him. Slowly guests made their way onto the floor, coupled arms at the shoulders and followed his lead. Before long there was a train maybe 15-20 long in joyous harmony. We decided for this first dance we should let the guests take centre stage. For the next half hour or so *Thoris* led several dances, one in particular where the bride *Eleni* and her beau joined in, together with the bridesmaids, Jane, Mary, and Jen. Milos and I took great pleasure in watching the girls attempt and cock up of what in our view were simple steps. I took even greater pleasure watching *Freja* and *Isabella*, once again elegantly dressed in maxis but this time a little more revealing at the hips.

The band leader announced a short break and at the same time I noticed *Pavlos* talking to a fellow Greek, but not someone I recognised. However, he was dressed in the traditional dance costume associated with the *Mihanikos*, simple black trousers, white shirt and a *Kalymnian* fisherman's cap. I decided the break would be a good opportunity to check the music system to ensure it could be connected to my i-pad. I wandered over to the band leader who was now stood by the sound desk chatting with one of the guests. I excused and introduced myself and was about to explain the purpose of coming over when he said that *Pavlos* had already spoken to him about the music for later and had pointed me out. He said his name was *Yainni* and he showed me the auxiliary lead that could be used to feed the i-pad directly into the desk. I explained that I was going to use tracks from my playlist together with songs selected by the bridesmaids which would be accessed via YouTube. He showed me the fader for the auxiliary feed and said that this would simply fade the music in and out as required. He also showed me the feed for the microphone, and I asked him what time they were finishing, he simply replied 'When the party finishes.' Somethings never change!

He then told me they were going to resume the dancing in

about 15 minutes, starting with the *Mihanikos* and asked if I knew this dance. I told him that I did but two of my fellow guests were here to witness it for the first time. He said he would be making a small speech to inform the guests about the dance, its place in *Kalymnian* history and also a small bit about why the family wanted this dance at the wedding. *Yainni* then pointed out the guy *Pavlos* had been speaking to when I came over and he told me he would be performing the main role of the disabled diver. Thanking him I said I would see him later when it was time for my slot. He suggested this would be in around 45 minutes, but this may change. I told him I knew the *Kalymnian* system, and he smiled as I walked back to the table.

'All sorted Youth?' Milos enquired.

'Yes, we are good to go, all disco'd up and ready for when I get the nod.'

'What time you on?' Jane asked.

'Maybe around 45 minutes, the next round of dancing is starting shortly and then when it finishes DJ Youth will be in the house,' I explained.

'Might be a good time for bed Maria,' Milos replied chuckling to himself and drawing on yet another *Assos*.

I turned to Chris and Jen 'You see the two seats over by the mixing desk?' They both nodded. 'When I give you the shout you need to plonk yourself there for the *Mihanikos*. It will be the first dance after the break.'

Chris Interrupted me and pronounced forthrightly 'I'm not doing any fuckin dancing, especially with my leg.'

'Now now Chris, keep calm, and listen to what I said, you don't have to do any dancing and that's why I have sorted the seats. This is not a dance where people join in. You just simply need to watch and enjoy.'

'The leader of the band will do a little speech about the history of the dance and why the family have this at the wedding.'

Milos interrupted this time, 'How the fuck are we supposed to understand what he's saying?'

'Because he'll be speaking in English you twat!'

'Sorry, was I supposed to know that?' Milos enquired.

'No, but if you stopped interrupting you would!'

'Right, before they get underway who wants a drink?' I asked.

'Another bottle of the finest red for us ladies, unless of course there's more champagne?' was Jens predictable response.

'I'll see what I can do,' and headed to the bar. I accosted *Pavlos* round the back of the kitchen and he duly obliged with the champagne. I grabbed another couple of bottles of *retsina* and made my way out to the table just as the band leader was placing the mic in the stand and adjusting the height.

This was my nod. 'Chris, Jen, top up your glasses and make your way over to the chairs,' and off they went, with Chris still looking a little perturbed as to what was going to happen next.

*Yainni* tapped the Mic.

' *Yassas, Yassas* (hello, hello), all please gather round or take your seats,' he requested and eventually all the guests duly obliged.

'On behalf of *Vasilas* and *Sofia* we welcome you to the celebrations of the marriage between their daughter *Eleni* and *Lucas*. For those that don't know, the tradition of songs and dancing at *Kalymnian* weddings is very strong and an essential part of island life and history.

I know we have some guests that are not *Kalymnian* or Greek, but we welcome you to join us in the dancing. But before we have the traditional wedding dances, we have a very special *Kalymnian* dance for you to witness. As song and dance is deeply engrained in our society so is the history of sponge diving. For many years it was the main source of our economy and our social life revolved around it. Whilst it created great wealth it came at a terrible cost. Many men, young and old were lost to this trade and even more were left paralysed, afflicted by the bends.'

The *taverna* had fallen silent. He continued.

'*Vasilas* has very strong links with this history and his family were deeply affected. As part of today's celebrations, it is important to remember those times and to give thanks for what we have today by paying our respects to the past. Our first dance will be The Dance of *Mihanikos* where we remember *Vasilis'* family and all *Kalymnian* families burdened by this history.'

I could see Chris and Jen's anticipation in their faces. As *Yainni* and his fellow players prepared themselves, three traditionally dressed male dancers took to the floor. They linked arms at the shoulders and readied themselves in silence. Then the Greek guy I had seen talking to *Pavlos* appeared at the side of the dance area. Hunched over a walking stick he stood very still, eyes transfixed on his fellow dancers. After what seemed an eternity the band struck up, playing at a medium fast tempo, driven by the *Lauto* with the *tsambouna* and violin wailing mercifully.

The dancers began, stepping and circling in perfect rhythm with the music, swirling and kicking with energy and fire, their movement expressing the joy of their dance. After about a minute they stalled their movements, other than gently bending their knees to the rhythm of the *Lauto*. They had positioned themselves directly across from the guy with the stick, their gentle swaying seeming to invite him to join them. As they did this the music dropped in tempo, to a slow drone, sombre and tuneless.

Suddenly the guy with the stick started to quiver, reaching his stick forward to support his weight. Seemingly imploring his legs to move which were shaking violently, he looked at his fellow dancers who watch him with pity and fear. They know his suffering. He makes his first steps towards them, small and unsure, using all his force and strength to will his useless legs to move. The sense of his frustration and helplessness is clear, but he does not submit. Slowly but surely, edging his way to the dancers, he eventually reaches the one closest. He puts out his hand for support and is grateful when his fellow dancer sustains him. The dancers encourage him to move but he is frozen to the spot, shaking in despair.

Once again they begin to step, and the bond is broken. They move away to the same rhythmical steps as the tempo increases. As they circle, he feels their energy and remembers when he could dance. The music slows and once again he is offered a hand which he readily accepts, but still his legs will not respond. The sheer frustration sees him drop his stick and grab his legs, using all his upper body strength and balance as he physically tries to move them, but they will not respond.

The same tragic scene repeats two more times. I can sense the whole *taverna* silently willing him on but on the third time the effort has taken its toll and without his stick he stumbles to the floor. The *taverna* remains silent. The dancers slowly sway within reach as he fights to regain his stance, summoning all the strength he can muster. The violins high pitch wailing seems to match his inner cries for mercy from the pain.

The dancers stall, they sense something.

Suddenly the man is up, no longer burdened, the music accelerates to full tempo and in sheer delight the disabled man is no more. The guests begin to shout, whoop and whistle, imploring him to dance. He throws his stick, dipping, swirling, and kicking. For the final time the dancers offer their hand, and they move again, this time all together in joyous harmony, he is free from the affliction, he is saved. This is the joy of life.

As the music finishes the rapturous applause starts and I am lost in the moment. The same emotions when I first witnessed this dance. I immediately think of *Thassos*, his pain, and his suffering. His story will be told. Oh shit, I have forgotten about Chris and Jen, my gaze is drawn to their seats, I see Jen and she is sobbing. I want to go to her, but this is not my place. Chris is holding her hand, staring intently at her. He whispers something in her ear, and she says something back to him.

'Fuck me Youth, that was intense, get the *retsina.*' and the moment was gone.

As I returned from the bar Chris and Jen were back at their seats and deep in conversation with Jane and Mary. There was nothing I needed to say. Another part of the plan successfully delivered. The band was already playing and the social dancing underway. We spent the next half hour watching the guests, especially the long necks, try their hand at the dancing. Then Milos took to the stage with Mary, displaying his very own unique and flamboyant interpretation of Greek dancing. I simply laughed!

After around forty minutes I notice *Eleni* heading our way, with her gaze directed straight at me.

'*Yassou,* I hope you are all having a lovely time. Iain, it is time for you to live up to your reputation. We are ready to party,' she exclaimed.

'It's been wonderful so far and I am ready to go,' I responded.

'Yeh, and all that's about to change' Milos said sarcastically.

'Well, I'm rather looking forward to seeing Iain in action,' said Jen, having clearly regained her mojo. I nearly replied but thought better of it.

'Ok *Eleni,* I have the list and we'll be underway in five minutes.'

'*Daxi,* I'll see you all on the dance floor,' *Eleni* said as she elegantly sauntered off back to her table.

'Right you lot, I expect the usual carnage and let's show them that these old gits still have it'

'Less of the 'old' Youth!' Milos remonstrated.

I made my way across to the sound system, had a little chat with *Yainni* to check I had everything sorted and gave the mic a couple of taps...

'*Vasilas, Sofia, Eleni* and *Lucas* and all you wonderful guests, can I have your attention please. My apologies but my Greek and

Danish are not worthy of this announcement'.

'Nor is your bloody English!' Milos shouted.

'My apologies again, this time for my friend, he's a twat!' Only our table laughed.

'I am honoured to have been asked by *Eleni* and *Lucas* to play a few, shall we say, modern songs for them and for you to dance to. I know they would be delighted to see you all join in and if there are any songs you don't like, please see *Freja* and *Isabelle* as they chose them!' At least the long necks laughed.

'Let's get this show on the road with a bit of Scandinavian magic.' I hit the button and the first bars of Abba's Dancing Queen rang out. Immediately *Isabella* and *Freja* were up, followed by lots of other guests along with Jane, Mary and Jen and the dancing was underway. At the same time Milos retreated to his normal spot.

For the next hour or so I belted out the tunes with the highlight being Toots and the Maytals "What's My Number" which included getting all the guests involved in banging the tables to the counts in the song's chorus. As well as enjoying watching all the guests it was great to see Jane, Mary and Jen letting their hair down. I was also cognisant that Chris was sat on the table on his own and his demeanour told me all I needed to know. Still work to do I thought.

I suddenly felt a presence behind me. It was *Pavlos*.

'*Ella Pavlos*, a great night. You like the Dj'ing?'

'*Nai* Iain, but after this next song you take a break, no music, we have something to do, you know the system yes?'

I knew exactly what this meant. As the last beats of Michael Jackson's Billie Jean tailed of I announced it was time for a short drinks break. I received a very loud cheer together with applause, with *Freja* coming over and giving me a kiss on the cheek to say thank you, very nice! I noticed *Nikolas* watching and gave him a wry little smile.

Along with the guests we made our way over to our table and
Milos seeing this decided to come over and join us.

'Actually Youth, that was very good. How much did you pay
the long neck to give you a kiss?'

'It's the years at charm school paying off,' I replied.

'I saw *Pavlos* talking to you a minute ago, what did he want?'
Jane asked.

'A little break, for the next tradition.' Before I could explain
Milos interrupted

'*Dinamatives*', (dynamite) his timing was perfect. Suddenly an
almighty explosion rang out, the guests initially gasped then as the
boom resonated around the mountains the cheers and whoops
began. Another blast, this time so close that the initial shock wave
shook the floor with the aftershocks reverberating around us and
the mountains. The cheering and shouting increased as four more
blasts rocked the *taverna*.

'Wow, I didn't expect that. God it felt so close, but I couldn't
see anyone,' Jen said.

'That's only because they don't want you to see them,' Milos
replied. 'I noticed big *Nikolas* leave our table a few minutes ago
following a quick chat. I might have heard the word *dinamatives*. It's
the system for the weddings, old dynamite left over from the war.'

'Bloody hell, that's a bit old, is it safe?' Chris asked.

'No' was Milos' simple and curt response. I felt a tap on my
shoulder. It was *Pavlos*.

'Ok Iain, now more music to play.'

Making my way back to the mixing desk and not bothering
with any intro I smashed straight into a bit of Robin Schulz
"Sugar" which immediately did the trick. I spent the next hour
doing my thing and along with all the guests had a great crack.
Managing to play most of the songs on Freja and Isabella's list,
together with a few of my own. I announced my last track would
be Candi Staton's "Young hearts run free". I wished the bride and

groom a long marriage, thought "Lucky Bastard" he's in for a good night and hit the volume. As the song played out I thanked *Yainni* for the use of his equipment and said the party was now his responsibility and went over to join "the boys". They had all moved over to their usual the corner table with Milos, Mary, Jane, *Pavlos* and the family. Chris and Jen had clearly left! I hoped that was a good sign. The party and *retsina* flowed along with all manner of *meze* dishes long into the night.

I remember my final thoughts as Jane ushered me into the room. *Pavlos* and dynamite "*Catastrophe*"!

# CHAPTER EIGHT

## KALYMNIAN VIGNETTE NO. 2:
## "FISHING KALYMNIAN STYLE"

Sunday had passed in the haze of the recovery mode after
Saturday's party exuberance. It was now Monday, and we were
nearly one week down. It had been a very nice, quiet lazy
morning on the beach with a long lunch talking rubbish. My
main task earlier in the day had been to source, through *Affroulla*
some sort of tincture for Chris to apply to his leg. As well as it
"playing up" he'd managed to get sunburnt, and this was
exacerbating the throbbing. So much so that when they turned up
for breakfast Chris was limping and using his stick. Fortunately, I
succeeded in my task and after a decent application during
lunchtime he said it was feeling better.

After lunch, the girls declared they were heading down to the
beach for the afternoon. Milos decided it was too much hassle to
make the short walk down to the beach and would be staying in
his rightful spot next to *Pavlos* for the afternoon. Chris announced

that he was heading to his room to keep his leg out of the sun and would see us all later. I decided that this provided an opportunity to have a little chat with Jen and told Milos I was going down to the beach to "look after the girls".

We positioned ourselves in our usual spot under the shade of the tamarisk trees that lined the water's edge. These old, gnarly trees have the perfect foliage, not unlike pine leaves that allow enough of the sun's rays to permeate through to the skin whilst removing the harshness that results in overheating and sunburn. The water's edge was literally a metre away and this allowed a little bit of soft cool sea air to waft over you as well. When ready for a nice cooling dip, or in Milos' case an emptying of the ballast tanks, it was hardly an effort to get there. There were three trees and having laid out our sunbeds in pairs under each tree, with a little distance between them all, it was a peaceful little haven for the afternoon. Jane and Jen slipped very quickly into reading mode, Mary decided a nap was in order and I decided it was time for a little bit of Diana Krall through the earphones.

After about an hour I noticed Jen preparing herself for a little dip. A perfect time for a little chat. Jane rarely swam, one she didn't like the touch of any weeds on her body, two, believe it or not she thought the water was too cold and thirdly, if she did swim she didn't like to go out of her depth. I made my way down to meet Jen at the water's edge and we made our way through a little channel in the weeds.

'This water is so inviting, it's wonderful.'
'Yes it is, shall we have a little swim out to the buoys?' I asked.
'Why not,'

*Pavlos* had two buoys for yachts positioned about 30m out from the beach. These enabled yachts to moor up, either for the day or overnight with the simple premise that the user would visit the *taverna* at some stage during the stay. However, today they were both empty. As we got close I told Jen that there were some short ropes connected to the top of the buoys, which the yachties used to assist in the tying off procedure and that we could grab them to suspend us as we dangled in the water.

'Have a look down to the seabed, you can just about see the mooring block, follow the rope,' I said as I laid suspended on the surface.'

'Wow, it's deeper than I thought. The water is very clear,' she declared as she too floated on the surface.

'When I look at this, I think of the early day sponge divers, imagine them down there, no swimsuit, no breathing apparatus, a rock tied around their waste and just a line back to the boat.'

Jen took another look 'I didn't think anyone could hold their breath long enough, let alone get down that deep,'

'You've got lots still to learn about this story.' I changed tack.

'The other night, when the Dance of the *Mihanikos* finished I noticed Chris whispered something in your ear?'

'Yes and no doubt you saw my tears as well,' she said almost apologetically.

'I expected the tears,' I replied as she interrupted me.

'I know, I know all part of the plan! Isn't this all supposed to be about Chris?'

I held her gaze. I could see she was a little perturbed. 'Before I answer that, lets head back to the beach and we can chat whilst drying off on the sunbeds.' I was worried my answer might upset her. There was a place for tears but not dangling off a rope in 30m of water!

We gently stroked our way back to the beach. Jen led as I followed behind her, Jesus even her swimming was elegant. Once through the channel we stumbled up the last couple of yards on to the sand.

'Nice swim?' Jane shouted across.

'Yes' I replied. 'Very refreshing, you going in?'

'You must be joking.' I knew the answer before I asked. I

wandered over to my sunbed, gave Jane a little kiss, grabbed my towel and headed over to Jen's sunbed. I watched her drying herself off, not bad for 70!

I perched myself on the adjoining sunbed 'To answer your question, no.'

She looked at me quizzically and then laid her towel out on the sunbed. As she made herself comfortable, she stared hard at me.

'Well, aren't you going to explain?'

'Look Jen, all of these plans, the ones completed so far, and the ones to come. Of course they are about Chris, but in my mind, they are just as much about you. Any relationship is about two people, how they operate, how they feel, how they support each other, how they understand each other, how they grow together. Look at Milos and Mary, look at Jane and me. We have all been together a long time. When I look at all these things, I believe we are at one with where we are at, we have found a way. So, if I ask you those questions, what would you say?'

She stared hard at me again, she played with her hair and positioned her sunglasses high on her forehead to hold it back, as if buying time to challenge herself, to be open, to be honest.

'You are asking me questions you already know the answer to, I laid myself bare when we sat at your dining table. I haven't spoken to anyone else like that,' her tone was slightly disgruntled.

'That's my point.' I could see my response disappointed her.

'Let me explain, my point is that until both you and Chris deal with these questions together, then things will not only be unresolved, but they will worsen. You remember the big question I asked you, about you and Chris'.

Which one?' she said tersely.

'C'mon Jen, you know, the one that really matters, do I really need to spell it out?'

Momentarily she looked away, I could sense she was uncomfortable. 'You are making me wish I never answered that question, but ok, make your point.'

'As I said, until Chris knows that's a question you are prepared to answer then he will carry on the same. I know you have been doing lots of talking already but do you think he could even contemplate you leaving him? Because for me that is what this is all about. That is what I am trying to get him to see. If you have no fear of losing what you have then what does it mean to you, surely you have to be more precious than that?'

She pulled her sunglasses down from her hair to cover her eyes and laid back on her sunbed. I waited for her response.

'Precious, wouldn't that be nice. Anyway, back to your first question, he simply asked me why I was crying.'

'And?'

'Well, I said I thought that was pretty obvious and that all I could think about whilst watching the dance was *Ireni's* song at the *Artistico*.'

I leant in closer 'And how did he react to that?'

'He said he wished he had heard the song but anyway the dance was mesmerising'.

'Was that it?' I asked.

'We said we would talk some more but everything was so hectic around the wedding.' I sensed this had left her a little disappointed.

'I need you to talk to him about this, I need to understand more about where he is at. Look, tonight at pinkles I am going to set out all the remaining plans. But just so you know we are going fishing tomorrow morning.'

Jen jumped in 'Chris fishing! Are you mad?'

'Yes, but there is method in my madness. I am glad we had this chat as I intend to talk to Chris on the fishing trip and see if I can get him to open up a bit about the dance.'

'Good luck with that one. Anyway, I look forward to hearing all the remaining plans tonight.' I could sense her mood had lightened.

'One last thing though. I need or should I say I want another evening like we had at the *Artistico*.'

'Well, we could eat there again.' She suggested.

'I didn't mean the eating part!' I got up, ready to head back to my sunbed.

'Ahhhhh, ok well again you'll have to sort that out,' she responded as she elegantly rolled over onto her front.

'Before you go be a darling, can you rub a little suntan lotion on my back.'

'It would be my pleasure,' and I duly obliged.

I made my way back to my sunbed next to Jane, who was still avidly reading. Mary was flat out. Jane asked me if everything was alright with Jen, and I told her we had a little chat about her and Chris and the plans. I moved my sunbed out from the shade, put in my earphones for another dose of Diana Krall and enjoyed the last hours of the softened afternoon sun.

It was around 8.30pm and Jane and I made our way down to Milos and Marys room for pinkles. Jane's tan was now lovely and golden, and she looked gorgeous in a floral top, white shorts, and a tan pair of traditional *Kalymnian* sandals. Both Milos and Maria were sat outside knee deep in their drinks.

'What you having Youth? And for you Jane?' Milos politely enquired,

'Blimey Miles, that's very nice, are you ok?' Jane sarcastically replied.

'He's probably been on the job!' I suggested. Milos gave me one of his looks as he stood up. Mary sat quietly with a sheepish grin.

'There's life in the old dog yet' I declared just as Chris and Jen turned up.

'Was that something about dogging?' Chris asked.

'Not quite, I doubt that phenomenon has reached Emporios yet,' was Milos' response followed by 'What do you two want?'

'Usual please, Is he ok?' Jen enquired.

'Not you as well!' Milos shouted as he made his way into the room and shortly thereafter appeared with a kraken and coke for me, a martini and lemonade for Jane, a gin and tonic for Jen and a glass with some ice for Chris.

'*Yammas, Yamma*s' he declared as I asked Chris for his choice of music. After what seemed an age, he requested a bit of Pink Floyd and I obliged. The soft sound of David Gilmour's guitar appropriately filled the still warm air.

I took a long sip of the kraken and revelled in the delight of the surroundings, truly this was *Arcadia* for me, and I didn't need much else.

'Right you lot, listen in for a minute as I want to outline the rest of the holiday plans. We're now just about one week in, and all is going well.'

Milos interrupted 'Shall I have a sleep then?'

'In a word no, you'll be pleased to know that the very first item involves you, and before you jump in with your art of doing nothing you have been selected by *Pavlos*.'

Milos immediately responded 'Ah, *catastrophe* Maria!'

'Wait a minute, wait a minute, and that includes you Maria, you don't know what's involved yet. It just so happens we are going fishing, tomorrow morning!'

'Not a fuckin chance,' Chris exclaimed as Mary made her way to the toilet!

'Mary was it something I said?' asked Chris. Jane raised her eyebrows knowingly at me.

'No Chris, and like Milos you have also been selected, it's a boy's trip. We'll be leaving the *taverna* at 7.30am!'

'Is this definitely a plan Youth?' Milos asked.

'It's a *Pavlos* plan, you know the system.'

'Excuse me but why is Mary so concerned about a bit of fishing?' asked Jen. I kicked Jane under the table, I looked at Milos and he simply grinned.

'Probably because it involves Milos and the sea, a bit like the trip to the chicken farm,' I said. 'Anyway, let me get on with the other plans. Mary, hurry up,' I shouted. As Mary made her way back to her seat, I continued.

'So that's fishing Tuesday, a day off Wednesday with maybe cocktails and lunch at *Eleni's*. On Thursday *Thassos* is coming to the taverna for the afternoon and that's you tied up Chris. On Friday we are going to *Pothia*.' Milos interrupted.

'Maria, you're divorced if you go!'

'Get that in writing Mary,' Jane said as she and Mary giggled to themselves.

'Blimey, it's worse than having kids. So *Pothia* Friday, *Pavlos* has some "shopping" to do and is going to take us down and we'll get a taxi back. We'll visit the house of *Nikolas Vouvalis* and the *Kalymnos* Nautical Museum and yes Jane, before you mention it, you can get some more *Kalymnian* sandals.' She smiled and mouthed thank you.

'Oh, if they are like the ones you have on, I'd like a pair of those, they really are very nice,' said Jen.

'Sorry', Chris interrupted. 'Can we go back a bit, I didn't really catch the *Thassos* bit.'

'Chris I'll talk to you tomorrow about this, on the way to the fishing.'

Chris interrupted again 'What, you mean maggot drowning?'

'Precisely,' I lied. 'Moving on, Saturday is a special day here in *Kalymnos* isn't it Milos?' He looked at me quizzically for a momen...

'Ah yes, the hunting weekend.' Milos declared.

'Fishing, now hunting, is this turning into some sort of safari?' Chris quipped. Quite funny I thought for him.

'I'll explain later but let me finish, Sunday is *katsidi* day, (goat stew day) and maybe too much *retsina,* and on Monday, to close things off it's the "Dinner of Love" at *Harry's Paradise taverna*.'

'That all sounds great and very interesting Iain, but I'd really like another night at the *Artistico* as well.' Jen announced. I caught her gaze for maybe three seconds, and it told me all I needed to know. Sometimes words are simply not needed.

'Well of course Jen and maybe a trip to *Eleni's* for dinner as well. Everyone ok with the plans?'

'Youth, if you pull all that off it will be a minor miracle. Talking of miracles any chance of you getting the drinks in Chris!' Milos said as he held out his glass.

Chris' look said it all as he got up, snatched the glass, and headed into the kitchen as we all had a little giggle. As I said sometimes words are simply not needed.

'Don't forget ours as well honey!' Jen shouted.

After the drinks and some more badinage we headed up to the *taverna* for what turned out to be a relatively quiet night, apart from *Pavlos* confirming tomorrow's fishing trip and Milos taking on Sacha, one of the Swiss Italian boys at Jenga. The Milos double entendre's were in full force throughout.

'You can only use one finger to poke that' and 'These blocks aren't sliding very well, they need a bit of lubrication'. Furthermore, the question and therefore the bet remained unresolved!

I awoke to Jane poking me in the side. 'Wake up Iain, it's 7am. You've got to be at the *taverna* in half an hour.'

'Is it really, I could do with another hour, if you know what I mean.' I said as I pulled her close.

'Later Iain, and I'll hold you to that!'

Having dragged myself out of bed and following a quick shower I threw on my shorts, t-shirt, and trainers and headed out onto the balcony to gather my swimming trunks and towel off the drier. The bay was perfectly still, a nice quiet morning for fishing I thought. Heading back into the room, I grabbed my shades and was ready to go.

'See you later at the *taverna*, I reckon we'll be back in time for a bit of breakfast.'

'Be careful won't you.' Jane said knowingly as I made my way out of the room.

I knocked on Chris' door as arranged and he duly appeared casually attired and in flip flops.

'They won't be any good for today,' and pointed him in the direction of my trainers.

'You also need to bring your trunks and towel as we may have a little swim.'

'Off the boat?' he enquired, I laughed.

'What's so funny?'

'Oh nothing, I was just thinking of our last little boat trip, to see *Yainni*!'

'Yes, things don't get much crazier than that. Anything else I need?'

'Not that I can think of. Is your leg better today?' I enquired.

'Much better thanks.' I was pleased knowing what was ahead.

Chris went back inside for a couple of minutes and re-appeared, adorned in trainers with a bag which no doubt had his gear. We headed up to the *taverna* where Milos was already sat carefully sipping *metrios* coffee and pulling on an *Assos*.

'How are you? I asked.

'Alive and vertical,' Milos responded as he took another shaky sip, holding the cup with both hands.

'I see the usual effects of the *retsina* are in place! What time are we leaving?'

'*Pavlos* is just sorting a few things and said we will get on our way once you two arrive.'

'Do we have time for coffee?' Chris asked.

'Ask *Pavlos*, he's behind you!'

'Morning *Pavlos*, do we have time for coffee?'

'*Nai*, but quickly though, *nes* or *metrios*?'

'*Metrios* for me.' Chris confirmed.

'And for you Iain?'

'*Nes epharisto.*'

*Pavlos* headed behind the bar and sorted the coffees. Soon after *Pavlos* joined us at the table, lit an *Assos* and we sat quietly enjoying the serenity of the morning view. After 10 minites he announced it was time to leave and he said he would meet us at the truck.

I told Milos to get in the front with *Pavlos* and I would jump in the open back with Chris. I knew there would be some beer crates in the back, and we could use our towels as a cushion. As we jumped in the back *Pavlos* appeared and once settled off we went.

'Is it much of a journey?' Chris asked as we reversed out of the car park.

'Maybe 20 minutes.' As we left the car park and down the hill, we turned sharp left to head up the road behind the hotel.

'I thought we would be heading through the village, I didn't see much activity heading this way when we went to the chicken farm,' Chris commented

'*Pavlos* has a special spot for the fishing, very nice and secluded. Sit back and enjoy the ride, much better out here than in there with the chimneys!'

'I see there are no rods in the back, is all the fishing gear on the boat?' How observant I thought!

'Don't worry, *Pavlos* has all that sorted, anyway how's the holiday been so far?' I hoped he would open up.

'Well, I have to say that it's been a little different. I didn't think this would be my type of holiday but it has been good because I can just sit back, watch and enjoy things.'

'That's great. I had a little chat with Jen down on the beach yesterday, she said you seemed a little more relaxed and not so stressed. I think she is really enjoying the peace and tranquillity as well.' I wanted to poke him softly.

It worked. 'Why did she mention stress?' he asked and gave me one of his stares.

'I guess because she thinks you've been a bit stressed lately, have you?' This clearly touched a nerve. I wasn't concerned if he answered or not. I knew he would pick this up with Jen later, which could be difficult for her, but I would get the answer I wanted either way.

'Maybe a little, I had some counselling, it's still on-going but the truth of the matter is the whole retirement thing has given me too much time to reflect. Then there's my bloody leg.' He said as he massaged his thigh.

'I hope the counselling helps. This holiday, it's a bit like counselling and you of course have Jen.' This poke was a little harder and all I got was another stare. A change of tack.

'What did you think of the Dance of the *Mihanikos*? I could see it was a bit emotional for Jen. But what about you? As someone who has suffered an injury trying to earn a living it must have resonated with you?'

For a moment he gazed out across the island. 'It was mesmerising, truly mesmerising. The intensity of the guy trying to regain his ability to dance was almost too painful for me. The way he was grimly holding on to the stick, I could feel his frustration and obviously that did resonate with me.'

'You can see why Jen was reduced to tears then?'

'Well yes, I asked her about that, and she said that it wasn't just the dance, it was the song she heard in the *Artistico*, was it *Ireni* who sang?'

'Yes,' I said.

'She wanted to explain but there was too much going on. I must admit I have been meaning to pick up on this, but you know how it is. We haven't been doing a lot of talking lately.'

Milos suddenly shouted from in the cabin 'Hold on guys, the proper road ends shortly, it's an old track from here and will be a bit bumpy.'

'Ok,' I shouted back. I turned to Chris. 'About another 10 minutes from here.'

'I thought you said it was a 20-minute drive?' he responded.

'Sorry, I should have said, it's one of the reasons I told you to wear your trainers. The track ends shortly and then we are on shank's pony. About a ten-minute trek down to the fishing spot.' Leg willing, I thought.

'One last thing on the *Mihanikos*, when you meet *Thassos* and hear his story, I want you to think about the emotion of the dance, the fragility of the dancer, the pain and torture he is suffering. But listen carefully to what he really lost.' The truck slowed. 'Going back to our earlier conversation, I really want you to talk to Jen about the singing at the *Artistico*. It's very important for the rest of the plans. Will you talk to her tonight, before you meet *Thassos*?' He didn't respond.

The truck came to a halt. I grabbed Chris' shoulder 'Have that chat tonight, please,' and I jumped off the back.

*Pavlos* and Milos exited the cabin, *Pavlos* asked if we had everything and before we knew it we were off. I remembered there was no discernible path down to the bay and that we just simply had to follow him. We were now well off the beaten track, goat country and for *Pavlos* being from herding stock for him, making his way across this terrain was second nature. Not so for us. I shouted ahead.

'*Pavlos, ciga ciga* (slowly slowly). 'No problem, just follow.' He shouted back.

We were heading down hill and the fishing bay came into view. Fortunately, at this early hour the temperature was still nice and cool as trekking our way in the blazing sun would not have been anybody's idea of fun.

'Chris, have a look over there, that's the fishing bay,'

'I can't look up, too busy concentrating on winding my way through these rocks and trying to follow *Pavlos*,'

'You ok Milos?'

'*Nai*, I know where I'm going,'

'Blimey that's a first,' I said.

'Very funny Youth and stop talking. I'm also trying to concentrate.' I could hear his heavy breathing in his speech. No doubt due to the 60 *Assos* a day!

We continued to drop down and I could now feel the fresh breeze coming off the sea. As we reached the final ten metres, I stopped to let Chris and Milos catch up.

'Not a bad spot for a bit of fishing eh Chris?' I watched as he surveyed the scene. The bay was rugged but beautiful and untouched by visitors. Even though it had an element of shelter, being on the Northern side it was still open to the wilds of the *meltemi*. Fortunately, today there was little wind. There was no discernible beach, just rocks at the water's edge and I knew there was very little shelf before it got deep. I didn't feel the need to explain anything about the water to Chris. However, I could tell by his grimace he obviously had a few queries.

'Iain, where is the fishing boat?'

'Did I say anything about a fishing boat?'

'I thought you did, but ok what about the rods.' I sensed a little impatience in his tone.

'Did I say anything about rods?'

'Very funny Iain. This is getting boring, I thought we were going fishing?' he said, even more impatiently.

'Now, now Chris, just playing. *Pavlos* has all the fishing gear, he's probably sorting it now. Let's head down to where he is.'

We made our way down to where *Pavlos* stood on a flat little rocky outcrop. With very little wind this early, the water looked very inviting.

'Iain, maybe the swimming gear, yes,' *Pavlos* suggested. By his side were some netting bags, a set of flippers, a mask, a speargun and a small plastic carrier bag. I suddenly remembered from previous trips that he kept most of the gear stashed in a little hideaway.

Milos was already changed, and I was stripping off. Chris looked at me, obviously very confused but was now following suit. I suggested he came closer to where *Pavlos* was stood.

*Pavlos* was closely scrutinising the horizon. He put his hand into his pocket and pulled out his cigarettes and lit an *Assos*. Following a little more scrutinising he bent down, picked up the shopping bag, reached inside and pulled out a small package of what I knew was dynamite. It was a T shaped lump, wrapped in parcel tape, around four inches long and in the stubby tail of the T a small black fuse was poking out. I looked at Chris and his face said it all. He clearly recognised what it was. He probably also noticed *Pavlos* was smoking!

After another quick scan of the horizon, he reached up to his mouth and grabbed his cigarette. Even though I had done this a few times before I couldn't deny the apprehension, the nervousness along with a touch of excitement. I glanced at Milos who was smiling, and Chris who wasn't…

He held the cigarette to the fuse. I knew you had to be calm and precise when lighting the fuse. I also knew this was German dynamite, left over from the war and a little fragile! I thought of Milos' view on anything to do with *Pavlos*, "I trust him with my life". I wondered if Chris felt the same. It seemed like an age as he waited for the precise moment. Then suddenly it was in the air, heading about fifteen metres out into the bay. As it hit the water I counted in my head, one, two, three, four, boom. The water erupted and almost simultaneously the compression wave hit the rocks.

Chris' reaction was priceless 'For fuck's sake, and I was worried about drowning the maggots!'

"*Pavlos* reached down, grabbed the netting bags and passed them to me.

'Iain, now you fish!' As I prepared to launch myself into the water, I could already see the stunned fish rising to the surface.

Chris, Milos, *Ella*!' I shouted. I threw them a bag each and dived in. The water, although deep and cool was invigorating. I turned to watch Chris and Milos launch themselves into the briny. We all swam out and started to collect the fish.

I tapped Chris on the shoulder 'Look, *Pavlos* is coming in.' he was stripped down to his trunks with the flippers, mask and speargun in hand. 'Yet another sort of fishing!'

He jumped in, donned his flippers and mask, and disappeared beneath the surface.

'Just like the *Kalymnian* sponge divers, but no soft gold round here.' I exclaimed. We continued collecting the fish.

'Not like the old days fishing down the pits then Chris!' Milos shouted.

'You pair of bastards!' was Chris' terse response.

'Any idea where *Pavlos* is?' I asked knowing full well what he was up to. I waited as we all gently treaded water.

He appeared right next to Chris, thrusting the speargun out of the water to reveal a huge Moray Eel, about two feet long, with a huge ugly head and a body full of muscle, writhing and violently thrashing the water as it tried to escape the harpoon. Chris' reaction was priceless and of the mould, just like the first time *Pavlos* pulled this stunt with me, he simply crapped himself.

As *Pavlos* wrestled his way back to the rocks with the eel we followed with our bounty. We carefully picked our way across the rocks at the edge of the water and once out watched as he expertly despatched the eel.

'Ok Iain? *Pavlos* asked.

'*Nai Pavlos*, very good fishing today.'

'*Nai, Nai*, and the nice *meze* for lunch.' He responded smiling broadly.

We gathered up our stuff and made the relatively short walk

back to the truck. As we walked, I thought about how for many years this ritual of catching the day's food, albeit with a slightly different method, would have been at the heart of *Kalymnian* life. The simple notion that the sea could provide all that they needed was an idyllic thought. Of-course the sea was eventually to show the price human life would have to pay to harvest one of its other bounties.

Once we reached the truck, we made the very pleasant little journey back to the *taverna*. As we dropped down the final hill and passed round the back of the *Asteri* the *taverna* came into view. I spotted Jane and the girls sat at our table. I then remembered it was still quite early.

I shouted into the cabin 'Milos, what's the time?'

'Around 9.30, Just in time for a little coffee and then the bus leaves!'

We parked up in front of the *taverna*. We gathered up our belongings, the catch and made our way across the terrace, followed by *Pavlos* with the eel. As the girls came into view, they were all laughing. Obviously, Jane and Mary had briefed Jen on the fishing!

'Oh my god, what is that?' Jen shrieked as *Pavlos* presented his catch.

'Lunch,' I responded.

'Wow, it doesn't get fresher than that. And how was the fishing Chris?' Jen enquired smirking knowingly.

Chris responded, deadpan as ever 'It was a blast! Anyway, fuck the bus I need a beer now.'

# CHAPTER NINE

## THASSOS' STORY

Wednesday passed normally with the usual routine of breakfast, beach, lunch, beach, nap, pinkles and dinner. It was a very warm day and even Milos made it to the beach for both sessions. After a very pleasant dinner we joined 'The Boys' for the usual repartee. It remained very warm into the evening, Jane and I decided it was a lovely night to spend on the balcony. Having moved the clothes drier and the patio furniture we were able to put the mattresses on the tiled floor.

I'd never lost my lust for Jane and still found her massively attractive. The feeling of intimacy and love we shared was something special and these feelings, together with the intoxicating atmosphere of the *Kalymnian* night sky made it truly wonderful. In the height of passion
Jane decided we were probably making too much noise and she said she had heard someone say something, not in English but

something audible. Taking a sneaky look over the balcony I carefully surveyed the apartments and told her I couldn't see or hear anything. I lied! And returned to Jane's arms.

In the morning we moved the mattresses back into the room and re-arranged our balcony. Looking out across the hotel I noticed two people sat on the balcony of the room directly below us. They were in conversation with another couple on the balcony adjacent. Listening carefully, I deduced they were German. We hadn't seen them before. I remembered there were clothes on the drier of the balcony below us when we arrived, but we hadn't seen anyone using the room since. I decided those people must have left and these were new people and maybe they knew the couple across from them. I would ask *Pavlos* as trying to get this type of information out of *Pandalis* was way too frustrating. Just before we left for the *taverna* Jane asked me if I thought they were the voices she heard last night, and if it was how embarrassing. I told her if she did hear something it was probably them. I lied again!

On the way up to the taverna we passed some pleasantries with the new arrivals, gave our normal simple greeting to *Pandalis,* and as Jane joined the company at the table, I made my way inside to the bar.

'*Kalimera (*good morning*) Pavlos*'

'*Kalimera (*good morning*)* Iain, what you like?'

'This morning *Pavlos,* for Jane poached eggs on toast,' I said grinning.

'Ah yes Iain, maybe you cook this.' *Pavlos* witnessed many years ago my attempt to get *Fucchaina* to make this and declared it a "catastrophe."

'No problem *Pavlos*, I will do. Will you sort coffee and Juice for Jane?'

'*Nai,*' he responded as I made my way out to the table.

'I am making poached egg on toast for Jane, any other takers?'

'That sounds nice, but *Pavlos* has already cut me some cake.'

Jen said.

'I'm sure Chris can sort that for you,' I responded.

'I can what?' Chris interrupted.

'Eat my cake honey,' Jen responded mischievously with a very cheeky little smile.

'So, you're in Jen, what about you Mary?'

'No need to ask Youth,' said Milos as Mary mouthed yes please to me.

I made my way back into the bar.

'*Pavlos*, what time today for *Thassos*.' slipping further into my English Greek.

'Maybe 11am and stay for lunch.'

'Great, and you will set up a table, across on the other terrace?'

'Yes, Yes Iain. I have spoken to *Thassos* and everything no problem.'

'*Epharisto Pavlos*, (thanks), now I cook.'

'*Kalimera Affroula, (good morning), simera magirevo*, (today I cook) 'poached *avro* (egg).'

'*Daxi Iain* (ok), *vlepo kai gelo* (I watch and laugh!).'

Affroulla passed me a frying pan, followed by some eggs and bread.'

'*Pou eina to Diva*' (Where is the Diva?), I asked.

'*Koimamai*' (Sleeping). She shrugged her shoulders and we both laughed.

I got busy and rustled up three very nice portions of double poached egg on toast. I duly delivered them to the eagerly expectant ladies who devoured them with gusto. Chris gave me a classic stare stare, as he had obviously decided he'd definitely missed out!

The bus arrived, together with beers for Milos and me. Shortly thereafter *Pavlos* joined us at table, stole an *Assos* from Milos, leant back, and shouted something in Greek, which I roughly translated to the others as '*Ireni*, get out of bed you lazy git!'

After a few beers and some talking rubbish, *Pavlos* called *Nikolas* and gave him the task of preparing a small table and two chairs in the opposite terrace. He duly obliged.

Milos watched inquisitively and turned to *Pavlos* 'What is this?'

'Iain, you speak of this,' *Pavlos* responded.

'It's a table and chairs' I stated.

'Yes, we know that you twat,' Milos replied. 'Do I have to ask the obvious?'

'Ok, you all know the plan today. The table is for *Thassos* and Chris, a sort of storytelling table. He should be here around 11am but you know the system.'

Jen put her hand on Chris' 'Well if that's the case honey I'm going down the beach. Are you girls coming?'

'I'll be heading down,' said Jane.

'Me to,' said Mary. 'Have I got time to go to the loo?' she added.

'Christ, you've been twice already this morning, what are you worrying about?'

Jane didn't disappoint 'Miles, I'm sure Mary doesn't want her bowel movements broadcast to everybody. It might have been something she ate.'

'Thanks Pipe Up, she certainly eats enough!'

'It's not my fault, I just like my food,' Mary responded, almost apologetically.

'Yes Mary, we'll wait for you,' Jane said as her look gave Milos a nonverbal dressing down.

'What are you doing?' Jane asked me. 'I'll be staying up, to say hello to *Thassos*, then maybe the *meze* and talking rubbish with Milos and *Pavlos*'

'Ok honey, we'll see you at lunch.'

Mary returned from the toilet and the girls gathered up their stuff and headed off down to the beach. After around half an hour and a couple of bottles of *retsina Pavlos* announced that *Thassos* was coming and sure enough five minutes later a shiny new Mazda pulled into the car park.

The door opened and *Thassos* pulled himself out of the car, steadied himself on his stick and carefully stumbled his way across the rough terrain of the car park. *Pavlos* had made his way over to the gate, opened it and helped him over the step. He gave him a warm greeting, sat him at the table and headed off to the kitchen. *Thassos* made himself comfortable, removed his cap and hooked his stick over the edge of the table. I could see him looking in our direction. Thassos was 52, an archetypal *Kalymnian* in looks but not so much in stature. Whilst still a very good-looking man his disabilities had caught up with him, he was blind in one eye, often in pain and despite being afflicted by the bends when aged 21, up until five years ago had still been diving! Only in *Kalymnos* I thought.

I made my way over to the table, pulled out the opposite chair and planted myself down.

'*Yassou* (hello) *Thassos*, really nice to see you. How are things?'

He gave me a huge smile and spoke softly '*Yassou* (hello) Iain my friend, I am as well as can be expected. How is your holiday with Miles?'

His voice no longer carried that *Kalymnian* strength, as if it were now carrying the strains of the affliction. The constant pain was worn in the furrows of his brow, and I found holding his gaze unnerving due to the blindness in his left eye. However, *Thassos* would always put me at ease by the sheer joy and warmth he expressed when meeting up. Whilst he may have lost a lot, he had kept that *Kalymnian* openness to friendship and general bonhomie for foreigners. The diving accident, if that was the right term had resulted in him being officially "invalided", which meant he received a pension and by the vagaries of the Greek pension scheme a car! Alongside this he had used his time wisely to become very proficient in the English language and helped out now and again at *Poppi's* English language school.

'We are having a wonderful time as usual. You know we were at *Vasilas'* daughter's wedding last Saturday?'

'Yes, *Pavlos* told me when he called.'

'I thought we would see you there' I said. *Thassos* looked beyond me, out into the bay momentarily to gather his response.

'Some things are hard for me to experience now, like the dance. You know my story Iain.'

'I do, I also know your strength, your bravery and the way you have adapted your life. I admire your willingness to be open on the things you have faced and must continue to face. On that front I want to thank you for agreeing to speak with Milos' friend Chris.'

'Well, I am looking forward to meeting him. I have known Miles for many years, and he is a fascinating character. We have talked many times, about the sponge diving. I have listened to him talk of this friend, about his business exploits and of his accident. I expect he may be the same?'

'Fascinating yes, but maybe not the same *Thassos*, but you can decide. I have told him very little about you other than you were a diver, that you were afflicted with the bends. I want him to hear your story from you, also the sponge diving history. He knows your family are connected to *Vasilas*. I am trying to get him to see something. I think you can help.'

*Thassos* leaned forward inquisitively 'For me to help I need to know what I am supposed to be helping?'

'It's in your story, that is all you need to know. Forgive me if I am vague but this is about an epiphany, an awakening. Your part in this is a cog in the wheel I have been spinning all week. Everything is leading towards our final night here in *Emporios*. I will only tell you this little bit more and that is it revolves around love.'

*Thassos* stared at me intensely, I knew what this word meant to him. I was knocking at a door that had remained shut to him for many years.

'*Thassos*, I am sorry for bringing this to your table, but we are to have our very own "Dinner of Love". I can think of no-one else who is more able to convey what this meant, in the history of the island, of the people, and most importantly you.'

I sensed his anxiety just as *Pavlos* arrived with a glass, some ice, and a small bottle of *ouzo*.

'Thankyou *Pavlos*, will you sort me some lunch for later?'

I interrupted '*Signomee*, (sorry) *Pavlos*. *Thassos*, after speaking to Chris we would be delighted if you would join us for lunch. I know Mary and Jane would love to see you and you can also meet Chris' partner, Jen.'

'That would be very nice.' He replied as *Pavlos* headed off to the kitchen.

'*Pavlos*, I will be back over shortly, some more *retsina* for me and Milos.'

'Ok *Thassos*, if it is alright, I will bring Chris over to meet you. Shall we say lunch in a couple of hours, when the girls come back up from the beach?'

'*Nai* Iain' *Thassos* said as he carefully placed some ice in his glass and poured a slug of *ouzo*. 'But you will join us? I would like that.'

I stood up, to get a quick moment to decide on my answer.

'Ok Thassos, I wasn't planning to but if that is what you would like that's fine. I will just listen as this moment is for Chris. One last thing, I suspect Chris won't do a lot of talking but that isn't a problem. This is a listening exercise for him. I'll bring him over in a minute.'

I made my way back over to our usual spot. Milos was pouring me a *retsina*.

'How is *Thassos*?' Milos asked.

'In his words as good as can be expected. A nice new motor with the pension though!'

'What was that?' Chris asked.

Milos responded '*Thassos*, as part of his pension he gets a new car every 5 years. It's the system.'

'Blimey, someone should have a word with our lot back home.' Chris said clearly feeling short changed.

'I don't think so Chris, in my opinion it is one of the reasons why the Greeks have got themselves in shit street with the austerity measures, too much out and not enough in.' was Milos' simple philosophical response.

'Yes Miles, but the trouble with opinions is they are like arseholes, everyone's got one!' said Chris somewhat aggressively.

I could sense a little friction building and jumped in. 'Indeed, they do Chris, and some people's opinions are like their arseholes, full of shit! Now enough of all that, come over and meet *Thassos*.'

Chris grabbed his bag, cup of half-drunk *metrios* and followed me across to the other terrace to *Thassos'* table.

'*Thassos*, this is Milos' friend Chris.' *Thassos* attempted to get up.

'Hi *Thassos*, no need to get up on my behalf. Very nice to meet you. I hear we have a bit in common?'

'I believe so, take a seat.' Thassos said as Chris sat himself down. 'Iain will stay with us, is this ok?'

'No problem for me.' Chris confirmed. As I sat down *Thassos* began.

'Your friend Milos has spoken of you before. This has been when we have been talking of my history with the diving and my accident. This we have in common yes?'

'Well, I believe the history of my accident is probably very different to yours, but it certainly left me with some problems. The only diving I have ever done was purely for pleasure. Me and Miles did some diving on holiday out in the Maldives. Oh, and I did have a mad moment when I was younger, I thought about joining the Navy, as a diver but the pull of a business life was too strong. I doubt I would have liked the discipline either.'

'You know modern day diving is very safe but still requires a lot of discipline. However, the history of diving on this island is different, very different,' *Thassos* took a sip of his *ouzo* and looked out across the bay.

'This wonderful island, my home, you look across the bay and all looks serene. Our lives are inextricably linked with the sea, but out there, beyond the land it is very different and not so serene. I will tell you this history, it is a story to match that of any other island. It is a story of life and death, a story of incredible riches and terrible loss. To understand my story, you need to understand the history. But before I begin tell me a little about your life now'

'Not much to say really. I had this industrial accident, my leg got crushed. It plays up sometimes and when it is bad I need a walking stick, like yours,' Chris said as he pointed at Thassos' stick. 'The accident really affected my ability to work, and I never really found what I was looking for, I did various fairly boring jobs and now I am retired,'

*Thassos* looked a little puzzled 'There must be more in between, a wife? children?'

'Wife yes, her name is Jen. We've been married over 45 years. She is here with me. You'll meet her later but no children, again for another day.'

'So, you have love in your life?'

Chris leaned back in his chair, scratched the back of his head, buying some time to answer.

'Of sorts,' was all Chris was prepared to venture.

'Ok, I sense something here.' *Thassos* must have remembered my words regarding Chris' lack of openness. 'But maybe this is for you and your lady, not me. But I will talk to you of this at some stage as this plays a big part in my history and that of the sponge diving.'

*Thassos* dropped another couple of lumps of ice into his glass and gently poured in some more *ouzo*.

'Sit back and relax as this will take some time.'

'I'm in no rush *Thassos*, take as long as you want,' Chris said as he leant back into his chair.

'Let me begin. You will have seen the sign in the port in *Pothia*

"Welcome to *Kalymnos*, The Sponge Divers Island". Chris nodded.

'And you will have seen the sellers and their sponges lining the streets. Behind all this is a story, spanning over many decades. It is a story of hunting, a story of human endeavour, of people testing their human spirit. It lies at the heart of *Kalymnian* society and family life as for a man to survive here he must work. On this island he has no choice but to brave the deep. Like many hunters there is danger in the chase, but the danger here is not the bounty you see displayed on the streets. It is the murky depths and the hidden danger which we were blind to.

*Thassos* paused, 'I am guessing you know a little about sponges?'

'I've seen plenty of them in Harrods,' Chris replied. 'Iain used a term when we arrived at the port, "soft gold". I hadn't heard this before, but I liked the analogy.'

'Yes yes, this is true because this hunting created great riches. These sponges are of course aquatic animals, living and growing on the ocean bed or on the rocks. The surface has thousands of pores but as you know they look nothing like "Soft Gold" under the water. The process to take them from a living thing to a valuable golden sponge is our version of alchemy. For *Kalymnians* this is the oldest occupation on the island. We have been hunting them in *Rhodos*, *Kriti*, The *Peloponnese* and far into the Mediterranean towards the North African Coast.

From its very beginning it has been a dangerous and demanding occupation requiring great physical stamina and acute mental awareness. People will say the draw to these waters was the risk and the bravado associated with the hunt. But you must remember, what else was a man to do to provide for his family? You know the best sponges, these could be found in the deepest waters, maybe 30m of water. In the early days, a man would dive naked, apart from his sponge net. To help him get to the bottom and hold him down he used a flat stone, maybe marble or granite with a hole in it. This was called a "*Skandalopetra*", maybe 15 kilos and a rope would be fastened to the boat and the stone. Can you imagine the diver holding his breath this long?'

'Yes and quite a feat. You say this created great riches, for who?' Chris asked.

'The bounty was sold to merchants, shrewd businessmen who achieved enormous wealth and success. Did you know that in the early 1800's the main trade in sponges was in your country Chris?'

Chris shook his head.

'The boom time for the sponge diving was in the second half of the 19th century. At this time there were six large companies in London. The biggest and most successful merchant in *Kalymnos* was *Nikolaos Vouvalis*'

Chris interrupted 'I know this name. Iain has mentioned a little of him. We are going to see his house in *Pothia*, which I understand he left to the state, and it is now a public museum. We are also going to visit the *Kalymnian* Maritime Museum, all part of his plan apparently.' He said glancing at me.

'Ah I see, you know *Nikolaos* was a special man. He mixed in the highest circles of British society and even dined with your Queen Victoria! His father was already a wealthy businessman, based in London but *Nikolaos* decided to pursue the sponge hunting, I believe he could foresee the opportunity. His business was founded in 1882, in *Pothia*, and by the early 1900's he had an office in London followed by a number of branches and agencies in far flung places. He died in 1918 but his wife continued the business. There is more for you to know of this man, but you can find out for yourself when you visit. Everything ok so far?'

'Yes, yes but I could do with a beer, anything for you *Thassos*?'

'The same please.' Chris looked my way and I duly obliged. After settling back down *Thassos* continued.

'As I said the peak time for the hunting was 1850 onwards, by 1868 there were many boats maybe 300 in the *Kalymnian* fleet all with divers. There were other methods to catch this bounty such as harpooners and trawlers, but we will stick with the divers. They were hunting many many tonnes per year worth 2 million gold francs, I don't know what this is in today's world, maybe you find out in *Pothia* but great wealth and riches for the merchants.'

'Same old story then, some getting rich on the backs of others hard graft,' Chris opined.

'Yes maybe, but a good living for the successful captains and their divers. What you must understand is the great change that drove this upturn in bounty and fortune, a revolution in diving to match that of the motor engine "The *Skafandro*" The diving suit. You will see this in the museum.' *Thassos* topped up his glass, wiped his brow and continued.

'No more diving naked, no more diving stone, instead a rubber body suit. It was cumbersome, loose and the large bronze collar and helmet were heavy, but the helmet had a valve for the supply of compressed air, delivered by a hand operated pump on the boat. With this diving suit the divers could reach depths of 70 metres and even better sponges. Communication however was still behind the times with a fine string attached to the right wrist. Each boat would have maybe 6-15 divers, under a captain. The boat had a cook, better facilities and they worked in groups with a support ship. I guess today you would call this progress. The fleet would leave after Easter and return in the Autumn laden with a huge bounty of sponges. The divers were considered aristocrats against the old "Skin Divers". This was of course very good news for the business.'

Thassos leaned forward, to move closer to Chris. His voice even softer.

'This was undoubtedly an upturn in fortune for the divers. However, there was a foreboding spirit lurking in the deep and they would soon discover an unexpected and unknown terrible cost the sea would make them pay for its bounty.'

*Pavlos* appeared from the kitchen and made his way over to our table. 'A small *meze* my friends.' He placed a small basket of bread with three small forks, a small plate of tomatoes, olives and cucumber sprinkled with oregano, a plate of grilled octopus, the obligatory olive oil and white wine vinegar companion set and a spare glass.

'Wow, that octopus smells wonderful. I love the aroma of the grilling together with the oregano.' Chris said as he was already wearing his eating glare.

*Thassos* took the spare glass and filled it with *ouzo*. 'Iain, you know this but Chris you must try, we dip the octopus in the *ouzo*, *oraois*, (beautiful), try.' Chris grabbed a fork, selected a piece of the octopus, and dipped it in the *ouzo*.

'Very nice, I like the aniseed from the *ouzo* with this.'

'Another form of bounty from the sea,' *Thassos* exclaimed. 'Shall we continue?'

Chris nodded as he continued to pick at the *meze*.

'*Daxi*, (ok) so now my story begins, and you will also understand *Vasilas'* place in this. I believe you know we are related?'

'Yes, the wedding party, Iain explained a little.'

'So, you will imagine in these boom times there was a very upbeat atmosphere as the boats prepared to leave. This would be around Easter time and the fleet would be given an extended farewell by the people of *Pothia*. There would be the priest's blessings of the boats, street parties with dancing and singing and on the very last night a "Dinner of Love".

*Thassos* voiced wavered, he paused, swallowed hard and adjusted his stick. 'I will talk of this more shortly. I know you are to have your own dinner of love but excuse me as this is difficult for me. Simply to say, this was a party for all the captains, the crew, and the divers, to mark the farewells between friends, families, and lovers. This dinner, over the years would become more poignant as the foreboding evolved.'

He continued. 'We must now picture the boats out at sea, brave divers full of pride and optimism and full of determination to prove their skills as the hunting began. With their newfound *skafandros* the barriers to collecting the best sponges were removed. No more returning to the surface when out of breath, no more frustration at having to leave an outcrop for others to gather. Now they would be able to stay in the depths and dive for long periods, several times in a day.

We must now imagine how the pride and optimism turned to dismay the first time the foreboding cast its shadow. A diver returns to the surface, laden with sponges and full of bravado and swagger, just like the hunters in the jungle showing off their prize. As he pulls on a cigarette and regales his fellow divers and crew of his exploits, they notice a strange smell in the smoke he exhaled but ignore it. A little later something they cannot ignore. The diver starts to tremble and to cry out in torment at the pain in his limbs and chest. What was this, what devil below the water had afflicted the diver. As the hours went by, the dismay turned to utter disbelief when it becomes apparent that he cannot move one of his legs, that it is violently shaking and worse, seemingly paralysed. Imagine this scene when on one of the other boats the same affliction begins to occur, the same pain, the same symptoms, but this time the diver seems to be fading away and then without warning he dies!'

Chris was utterly immersed in the story, seemingly knowing what was coming.

'Off-course we and you now know that this devil from the sea, this incarnation of the spirit of foreboding was decompression sickness, the bends. They knew of its existence and its dangers. They knew they should rise gradually to the surface to oxygenate. The first dive of the day would be fine, but each diver would dive every two or three hours throughout the day. It was almost always after the second or third dive the affliction of this devil would surface. Nobody understood why, so they simply accepted the risk and carried on.

This continued for a very long time with the most horrific

outcome. It led to the paralysis or death of not just a few divers but a terrible majority. Can you imagine, each year over half of the men who left with the sponge fleet, full of hope and determination, of love for life, simply did not return and of those who did make it home there were many who were disabled.' *Thassos* paused for a sip of *ouzo* and seemingly to gather himself.

'In the years from 1886 – 1920 over 10,000 deaths and 20,000 cases of paralysis across the *Agean* with the majority being *Kalymnians*. The women folk of this small island lost fathers, husbands and brothers, children lost their fathers, and many young men were condemned to a lifetime of physical pain and dependence.'

Chris' shock was apparent in his face.

*Thassos* continued, 'So where do I fit in all this? I must take you back in my family line, slowly for you to follow. I was born in 1955, my father *Giorgos* was born in 1932. His father, my grandfather *Spiros* was born in 1907. He was the youngest of four brothers *Nikolas* born 1897, *Helios* born 1899, *Yainni* born 1902 and *Demetrious* born 1904. All of the men in my family were sponge divers, this was their life and ultimately their death. *Nikolas, Helios,* and *Demetrious* all died from the affliction and *Yainni* was paralysed. My Grandfather, you may think was lucky to survive but along with *Giorgos* he had two further sons and a daughter and lost the two sons to the sea and as for my father there is me.'

The emotion was clear in *Thassos's* voice. Chris leant forward. 'Let's have a little break as I need the toilet. Can I get you anything on the way back? *Thassos* gathered himself 'Some more *ouzo* and ice please.'

Chris returned to find *Thassos* deep in thought 'Everything ok?' he asked.

'Yes, yes but these memories, they carry a lot of pain, but we must continue. I mentioned *Vasilas'* place in all this. My

Grandfathers wife, *Caterina* had a sister *Theodora,* and she married a man called *Vasilas,* again a sponge diver and they had three sons. Unfortunately, the story is the same. Two die at sea and the surviving son goes on to have two sons, and one of them dies at sea. This remaining son has one boy and names him *Vasilas* in honour of his grandfather. This is the same *Vasilas* at the wedding, but he has now broken the chain. This is why he has the dance of the *Mihanikos* at the wedding, to pay his respects to his family and for his daughter's new husband to understand the history.'

'As family I thought you might have been at the wedding?' Chris asked as he dipped another piece of the octopus in the *ouzo.*

'For me this is too much. I cannot witness the dance. I understand why they must have it and what the dance is trying to say but you know the end, where the paralysed diver kicks away the stick and is once again free to dance. For me this is too painful.' *Thassos* leaned back and took a long breath. 'You understand this?'

'Yes, yes but your problems, by the time you were diving, around 1970 I'm guessing, the bends were understood, there were protocols for diving, decompression tables. What went wrong?' Chris asked, clearly perplexed.

'Greed and bravado my friend but let me finish my story and you will understand. My Mother was only blessed with one son, and you will imagine I was very precious to her. It is the way in *Kalymnos* that we follow in our father's footsteps. All the time I was at school I would tell my friends that I would follow the family tradition and I would find the best sponges. I wanted to make money and as you know working the land here is very difficult. I also had a dream, built around a girl. I met *Theodora* at school when I was fourteen. The very first time I set my eyes on her I wanted her to be mine. I find it hard to explain but the way she looked, spoke, laughed, everything she did captivated me. Every day I could not wait for school to end so we could spend time together. I lived in *Arginonda,* and she lived in *Kamari,* maybe 7 kilometres and I would walk to see her most nights. She was the most important thing to me, and we fell in love.

As we grew together, we made plans, secretly like youngsters do and she also knew of my plans to be a diver. She had an uncle who lived in *Vathi,* you know this place?'

'I think Iain mentioned this place and that maybe we would visit but that's all I know.' Chris said.

'It is on the Eastern side of the island heading South from here,' *Thassos* pointed in the direction of the mountains in the distance.

'When you drop down the other side of those mountains you enter the most fertile spot on the island. It is the largest and most productive farmland on the island, beautiful and green. Its lovely houses stand on the slopes of two hills whilst a small part of the settlement lies on a verdant valley that extends all the way to a natural gulf. There at the end you will see a picturesque port filled with some fishing boats. This uncle I mentioned, he had land in *Vathi,* and we planned to make enough money to buy a piece of this land, to build a home and to grow, oranges, lemons and figs and work the land. It would be hard work, but we were not afraid of this. Before buying the land, we would marry but we would need money to fulfil this dream. I would work the diving boats and *Thea* would work in her family shop.

Back in those days, there was a much greater understanding of the diving process and to be a diver required attendance at the *Kalymnos* diving school. You mentioned the decompression tables, the first ones adopted in Greece were produced by Jacques Cousteau, a very famous diver, you know this man?'

Chris nodded 'Yes, yes, in England for many years his expeditions were shown on television,'

'I enrolled in this school, and I remember finally telling my mother and father of my intentions. She cried and pleaded with me not to follow what she called the "family curse of diving". I expected my father to understand. It was the first time I had seen this man cry. It would not be the last time. I found out that my parents visited the diving school and pleaded with them not to enrol me. I would not be diverted from this path. At the school government representatives came to talk to us, they would bring older divers, some paralysed and they would tell their stories, which of course I already knew. I was not worried, I studied hard, driven by my dreams. I learnt all I needed to know and knew the risks but with the training I felt safe.

'I started my diving career in 1973 and for three years was making good money and we were saving hard. I was considered one of the best divers and slowly my mother and father became accustomed to my job. They also now knew of my plans and my dreams for my life with *Thea*. So, we move to 1976, I was 21 and at the celebrations for Easter *Thea* and I announced our plans to marry in late Autumn, after the year's diving season. That we would buy her uncle's piece of land and start to build our new home. I could not imagine a happier time.'

*Thassos* leaned back in his chair and called *Pavlos*.

'*Ella Thassos*, what you like?'

'Enough with the *ouzo*, a *brassino* for me, and Chris?'

'If that's a small beer then fine for me to, thankyou *Pavlos*.'

'Iain?'

'A *brassino* is good for me.'

*Thassos* continued, 'As has been the way for many years we would leave *Kalymnos* for the sponge diving just after Easter. There was of course a lot of preparation for the trip and alongside this all manner of festivities to say farewell to those leaving with the fleet. These festivities culminated in a very special celebration.' *Thassos* paused, for a moment he was lost. He regained his thoughts.

'The dinner of love, with this came all the emotion of having to say farewell to friends, family and lovers. Over the years it became symbolic of the risk that many of those leaving would not come back or would come back changed men. I have told you the high toll this island has paid in the loss or paralysis of the divers. But you must remember this would also play out dramatically in the lives of those eagerly waiting for the return of their loved ones.'

'The dinner of love I shared with *Thea* that year was very special, we had reached the point where our dreams were in sight, becoming tangible and real and we had announced our intentions to all our friends and family. We danced and there was singing, traditional songs and one called "*Thalassaki*", "My Darling Sea". It is a song about the anguish the woman feels at the absence of her man and begs the sea to treat him kindly. I remember looking into her eyes as it was being sung and she was mouthing the words to me. I felt her emotion, I felt mine. But we *Kalymnians*, we must be strong men. I could not show how I really felt. I did not know the poignancy of her words in that moment nor the foreboding nature of them. I simply felt her love.'

*Thassos's* head dropped as he struggled to compose himself. I reached out to reassuringly grab his hand.

'You ok to carry on?' I asked.

'Yes, yes, its ok, I must finish. The following morning after saying goodbye to *Thea* and being waved off, the fleet set sail and we headed down to *Kriti*. Maybe the first week the sponge hunting was not so good, and we moved to another area where the captain believed we would find better sponges. This particular day we were diving in maybe sixty metres of water and the first dive was very successful, lots of good sponges. This is where the problem began. You will know the procedures for this depth, the time to come up is one hour and the time between dives 3-4 hours but when you find good sponges you have a choice, we call it "bounce diving", returning to the surface too quickly and going back down without the proper break. After the first dive I felt the itching, but I ignored it. All I wanted to do was get back to the hunting. I think maybe after the third dive it began, I started to tremble and then my feet were paralysed. I had seen this before and I knew what was coming. I hoped maybe it would not be as bad, but it was not my day.

'*Pavlos* arrived with the beers, he noticed *Thassos's* demeanour 'Everything ok *Thassos*?'

'*Nai, Pavlos*, just memories. You know these.'

'Yes *Thassos*, painful memories, you are very brave,' *Pavlos* said as he slowly poured the beer into the glasses and headed back to the kitchen.

'I was taken to hospital in *Kriti* and then eventually back to *Kalymnos*. I must tell you that many years ago my family members were not so blessed to be able to go to hospital. When they reached the stage of trembling and unable to move the crew got to recognise that death may follow but that heat would give them some relief. They were taken to the nearest beach and their bodies were covered in the warm sand with only their heads visible. Can you imagine this? A fellow diver stayed by their side hoping they may recover but this was not the case for many of them. After their last breath their companion for death would wait until the boat returned. They were taken away and buried on a small Egyptian island, *Karavonolissi* with just a small wooden cross at their head.

In those days, the family members would only find out about such tragedies when the fleet arrived back in port. However, in my case news had travelled and once I was able to return to *Kalymnos* my family and *Thea* were waiting. My mother's screams of anguish haunt me now and I witnessed my father cry for the second time. As for *Thea*, she was inconsolable. She held my hand and told me she loved me, that she would care for me no matter what and she would help me recover. It was a dark day, and my emotions were mixed. I felt guilty putting my family and *Thea* through such pain. I was angry that the sea had chosen to treat me so bitterly.' *Thassos* could not hide his emotion as the tears welled up in his eyes.

Chris offered him one of the napkins.

'Thank you,' he said as he slowly dabbed at his eyes.

'I am sorry. These tears are not mine. They are my mother and fathers, they are *Thea*'s. I have no more tears for myself.'

Chris interrupted, 'Please no apologies required, can I ask about your mother and father, of *Thea*, how were they after the accident, how are things with *Thea* now?'

*Thassos* looked at Chris pensively 'My mother and father carried the grief of my disabilities as a great burden, they could not forgive themselves for letting this curse afflict their beautiful son. They have passed now so at least that pain is now gone.'

'As for *Thea*, I have to explain. We *Kalymnian* men are proud, strong men. Conscious of our past and what it is to be a husband and a father. To work hard and provide for the family. You will remember I told you of our dreams. I wanted all these things for *Thea* but slowly came to the conclusion that these dreams had been shattered, crushed by the depths of the sea. After maybe six months I decided I could not fulfil my promises to her and could not burden her with my affliction. I told her that my life had changed and so had my love, I lied. She pleaded with me, she reminded me of our announcement at the dinner of love, she spoke of the song. I believe I broke her heart but at the same time I broke mine. After I told her, and she left it was the last time I cried for myself.'

'What of her now, of you,' Chris asked totally engrossed in this revelation.

'She married a man from *Kos* and lives there. I believe she comes over to the island to see her family. I try not to think too much of her, of her life, it is too painful. I hope she has found a new dream. As for me this is my life now, on the pension. I worked hard on my English, to do some teaching and I also speak at the diving school. I never thought I would be like the old divers who came to the school when I was there. Some lessons are hard to learn and up until maybe five years ago I was still diving.'

'Sorry for butting in but you were still diving, how can this be after all you have been through?' Chris said somewhat bewildered by this madness.

'Well, the black money for diving is good, you know this term Chris?'

'Yes, but we call this the black market.' Chris replied.

'But also, the sea now offers me back a little piece of kindness. When I am in the water, at the right depth it relieves the pain, negates a little the effect of the nitrogen in my legs and for a short time I am fully alive. You know this world down there. It can be magical.'

Chris leaned back in his chair, somewhat aghast at *Thassos's* sorrowful tale 'Wow, that's some story,' he exclaimed.

'We all have a history my friend, so let me take you back to where we began. In all of this, the pain, the loss of my freedom to walk, to dance, the sorrow of my family, the thing that I regret most is the loss of love. I would accept all of these if I still had the love!' *Thassos* paused.

'Chris, you have told me of your pain, your affliction and I asked you a question earlier.'

Chris grimaced, he sensed what was coming.

'I asked you if you had love in your life. Your answer seemed unsure. I do not know you but maybe your friends do. Perhaps they sense something. You have your very own dinner of love on Monday?'

'Yes, I'm not sure what to expect.' Chris responded.

'Maybe it is time for you to ask the same question of your lady. What would you forsake for the love of this lady? What price would you pay? Would you be prepared like me for this to be your last dinner of love?'

Chris stared silently at *Thassos*, contemplating the questions put before him. *Thassos* put him at ease.

'Now is not the time for answers and I am not the person to hear your words. But you must think on this. I thank you for listening and now maybe Iain can tell us one of his stories, to lighten the mood.

Thassos called *Pavlos* over to refresh their glasses. Over the next hour I indulged *Thassos* and Chris in the story of when I severed my urethra when sailing in the Ionian! It certainly changed the mood! Eventually the girls made their way up to the taverna for lunch.

We headed over to join them at the set table. I introduced *Thassos* to Jen and asked if she would mind if I sat him with her. She said she would be delighted. Over the next two hours we enjoyed a tremendous lunch. Chris spent most of the time eating but also listening intently, trying to pick up Jen and *Thassos'* conversations. As *Thassos* left and said goodbye he hobbled his way over to Chris and whispered something in his ear. Chris looked at him pensively for a few seconds and then he was gone. Another part of the plan done.

# CHAPTER TEN

## THE NAUTICAL MUSEUM AND
## THE HOUSE OF VOUVALIS

It was Friday morning, and we were all gathered round our normal breakfast table. Thursday night had been quiet on the basis that we were heading off to *Pothia* this morning and nobody fancied that with a hangover. Milos was in his usual early morning shaking phase and as any trip to *Pothia* was strictly off limits he was on countdown for the bus.

I had discussed the trip to *Pothia* with *Pavlos* last night and he agreed he would take us down there and whilst we were visiting the Nautical Museum and house of *Vouvalis* he would do some "shopping".

Also, last night when we arrived for pinkles, a little late, due to Jane asking me to 'rub some after sun on her back!', I was surprised to see Chris sat at the table on his own. I asked where Jen was and Chris told us that she had gone down to the mini market, about an hour ago. Apparently, she thought it would be a good idea if we had a few nibbles with the pinkles. He added that she had taken her book and he wouldn't be surprised if is she had stopped off for a little quiet reading time. When she eventually returned the few nibbles were a very nice addition....

'*Pavlos* appeared at the table with breakfast. He was shaking his head. 'Ahh Iain, I don't believe. Big problem at Alberto's house with the swimming pool. I will have to look. I can't take you to *Pothia* this morning, maybe the bus.'

'Ah, the *Pavlos* system and just a tad too late chaps.' Milos said as he got up from the table. 'It's leaving!' he added as he made his way to the bar.

'Iain, no problem. I call Mike, you know for the bikes,' *Pavlos* offered.

'Surely it's too far to ride to *Pothia*.' Jen exclaimed.

'Not pushbikes Jen, motorbikes, well scooters more like.' I said.

'Did you say motorbikes? Now you're talking.' Chris said.

In the past, prior to his accident Chris had an in between job as a motorcycle courier and I could sense the excitement in his voice.

'Well yes, me and Jane always have a couple of days out on the scooter, but *Pothia,* even I'm not sure that's a good idea.'

'I hope you're insured,' Milos said as he returned with his beer.

'I speak to Mike, no problem, maybe just for today, two bikes only 20 euros,' *Pavlos* said.

'Blimey that's cheap, what cc are they,' Chris asked.

'We usually get the 100cc version, plenty good enough for here, even with a pillion passenger.'

'I'm up for it,' Jane confirmed.

'Jen?'

'Well, if Chris' happy to take me then fine.' I didn't wait for his response.

'Okay *Pavlos*, it's a deal. What's the plan?'

'I take you to *Myrties* before I go to Alberto's. You sort the bikes and bye bye. Then ring me later when finished and I pick you up, after my sleep, maybe 5.30pm,'

'Done, what time do we leave?' I asked.

'Maybe half an hour.' *Pavlos* said as he made his way back to the kitchen.

'In that case I suggest we get breakfast down our necks and get sorted asap.'

'What do we need?' Jen asked.

'Well, I suggest we go via *Vathi*, you'll like it there and….'

Chris interrupted 'Yes *Thassos* mentioned this place yesterday, sounds lovely.'

'Ok so then it's over the top of the mountain to drop down into *Pothia*. After *Pothia* and the Museum and house of *Vouvalis* if we have time maybe visit *Vlichadia*.'

'Oh, *Vlichadia* is lovely,' Mary said excitedly.

'Don't even ask,' Milos interrupted sternly.

'Sorry Jen, before I was rudely interrupted. Just to finish you'll need some swimming gear and that's about it,' I advised.

'Should we wear jeans, you know for protection,' Chris asked.

'Jesus Chris, it'll be 34 degrees and who the fuck brings jeans to *Kalymnos?*' Milos exclaimed. Chris' look said it all.

'It'll be shorts and flip flops for us. This isn't the TT races on the Isle of Man! It's *Kalymnos*. Besides, I have a simple protection strategy, don't fall off!'

'That's what they all say. You bloody amateurs are all the same.' Chris said shaking his head.

'Well, that's your call Chris. Jane and I have all we need so if you need anything, I suggest you get sorted and be back here in 20 minutes.'

Jen stood up 'How exciting, it'll be just like the old days.'

'Yeh, but I'll have you on the back.' Was Chris' final acerbic comment as they made their way back to their room.

'Fuck me Youth, are you sure this is a good idea?' Milos asked.

'It wasn't part of the plan, but this is the system. In the scheme of things, it might help Chris see that there is still fun to be had past 70,' I replied.

'I'm not sure it's going to be fun for Jen on the back after hearing Chris' comment,' Mary wisely noted.

'You wait until he gets on the bike, that'll liven him up,' I suggested.

'Especially going vertical up the side of the mountain, on a bloody scooter!' Milos added laughing.

Chris and Jen returned, readied for our little escapade. Chris must have been listening as he was still adorned in shorts. However, he did have on a pair of sensible pumps. *Pavlos* gave us the shout and before we knew it we were on our way to *Myrties*. The girls joined *Pavlos* in the cab of the truck and Chris and I assumed our usual position in the back. The short journey to *Myrties* passed quickly with everyone simply taking in the wonderful scenery. We did have the odd moment dealing with the goat's, clearly on a suicide mission as they crossed the road.

*Pavlos* dropped us off at Mike's motorbike hire shop and we sorted the scooters. Chris was pleasantly surprised when I asked Mike for helmets for us and the girls. As much as l liked the freedom of riding round the island as lightly dressed as possible, the sensible side of me kicked in when it came to protecting my bonce, especially with kamikaze goats roaming the hills.

Before we set off, I told Chris that I would keep him in sight in my mirrors and that generally I pootled around at about 25mph max. He dismissed this nonchalantly and his look was very much a "been there, done it" one.

'Ok you two, we'll head to *Vathi* first. The journey there will take us right up to the top of the mountains and the views are breath-taking. I suggest a little stop, to take a few pictures and then a gentle ride down the mountain to take in the wonderful green nature of the lush valley. It's one straight road all the way down so you can't get lost, and the tiny port has a lovely little inlet, ideal for a swim. We can have a drink at one of the *tavernas* and then we can head to Pothia for the Museum and the House of *Vouvalis*. Any questions?'

'Sounds lovely honey in *Pothia* can we get some of the sandals Jane mentioned?'

'Christ, can't we go somewhere without shopping,' Chris said somewhat vexatiously.

'Now, now Chris, you're sounding like Milos.' I responded.

'Don't bag me up with him, sitting back at the *taverna* with his "art of doing nothing" nonsense.'

Jen gave me one of her little looks.

'Chris, I'm sure the girls won't want to see the Nautical Museum so whilst we are there, Jane can take Jen to the little sandals shop. We'll sort it out when we get there. Saddle up and let's get these horses underway.'

Chris muttered something under his breath as Jen climbed on the back of the scooter. As soon as Jane was ready off we went.

The journey to the top of the mountain was as expected. Initially a wonderful meander along the coastal road, slowly enough to take in the wonderful scenery and to be able to pick up the intense aromas of the oregano and thyme (plus the odd billy goat!). Then once at the bottom of the small village *Argoninda*, we took the left turn to commence the climb to the top of the mountain that divides the North of the island from the East. The first part of the climb is not too steep and the main sensation you feel is one of the intense heat from the tarmac road. As we progressed upwards the incline increased as did the wind gusting through the mountain pass, providing a little bit of solace from the heat. I kept a close eye on Chris and ever the "biker" he had his lights on. Very useful I thought, but only if you see any traffic!

'How are Chris and Jen doing?' Jane shouted in my ear.

'I can still see them in my mirror so all good.'

We continued our climb, ever steeper with the 100cc engine

screaming and whining with the effort of traversing its way to the top. After about ten minutes and several twists and turns we reached the top. I spotted a place to pull over and brought the bike to a stop. Chris sidled up alongside.

'Why are you stopping? I was just beginning to enjoy myself.' Chris exclaimed.

'Put the scooter on the stand, jump off and I'll show you.' I shouted over the engine noise.

'We turned off the engines. As Chris and Jen got off and removed their helmets, I tapped them on the shoulder and pointed behind them.

They both turned round. 'Wow, that is absolutely stunning,' Jen remarked as she took in the wonderful vista of the mountain pass we had traversed.

'Well, I've seen some fantastic views in my time, but this is right up there,' Chris added.

'If you look carefully,' I pointed down the valley 'to the right in the distance, that's *Emporios.*'

'Gosh it looks so tiny,' Jen remarked.

'That's because it is! Let's take a little snap of you two and Jane with the view in the background.'

They duly lined up for the snap, I was going to suggest Chris and Jen got a little closer but decided against it and took the shot. After a few minutes I suggested we commence the run down to *Vathi.*

'Chris, come over here. I pointed in the opposite direction. See down there, we are going to sweep down the side of the mountain and then at the bottom the road turns sharp to the left and then it's a straight road all the way to the little port. It's fairly steep on the way down so I'll be steady as we go.' Chris nodded and before we knew it we were back on the bikes and underway.

After a very short while I noticed Chris' scooter light right up behind me in the rear-view mirror. With his shades on I could sense he was now taking this seriously. I continued to dab my brakes as without the need for power we were already swooping down the pass at over 30mph. Suddenly he passed me and was heading off at increasing speed.

'Blimey, what's he doing,' Jane shouted.

'About 40+ and re-living his past! I've told him it's a straight road all the way down so good luck to them.'

The distance between us continued to lengthen but I wasn't going to rush. Both Jane and I loved the little ride down the valley, taking in the oasis of greenery with hundreds of trees and bushes, laden with oranges, lemons, pomegranates, and figs. The contrast with the remainder of the island was as stark as ever. Once at the bottom of the pass we made our left turn to take the final piece of road through the middle of the valley down to the port. By now Chris was out of sight.

As we neared the village the road changed, taking on a different nature. Winding its way through the small streets of the village, small houses on each side that force you to slow down and give you a real sense of a traditional *Kalymnian* fishing village. Before we knew it we were at the port, and I could see Chris positioned at the start of the inlet. I pulled alongside and signalled for him to follow me. We slowly made our way along the side of the port, passing a couple of shops and tavernas, eventually reaching the end of the road. Jane and I jumped off, I put the scooter on the stand and turned to Chris and Jen.

'What took you so long?' Chris exclaimed smirking.

'The sights!' I countered.

'That was fantastic, I really enjoyed the ride. I should have got a bigger bike though.'

'Well honey, it's not the size of the bike, it's the way you ride it!' Jen said rather salaciously.

'Anyway, that was fast enough for me, I was hanging on for dear life.' She added.

'Where's your sense of adventure?' Chris asked a tad frustrated.

'Well, I might ask you the same question. One bike ride does not an adventure make.'

I sensed the conversation was moving in the wrong direction. The inlet leading to the picturesque port was one of my favourite places to swim. The passage out to the sea is bounded by vertical rock faces and the water is crystal clear.

'Right, who fancies joining me in a little swim?' I knew Jane's answer already.

'Not for me darling,' Jane confirmed.

'That sounds lovely, the water looks very inviting, and I could do with a cool off,' Jen responded.

'I don't want to wear wet trunks whilst riding the bike, so I'll give it a miss,' was Chris' strange response. Very adventurous I thought!

'Ok, why don't you two have a little wander and maybe have a little drink in *Poppy's taverna*? It's the one on the corner back by the entrance to the port and then when we are done we'll come over and join you.'

'What about the bikes?' Chris asked.

'Leave them here, they will be fine. Shall we see you in around half an hour?' I asked.

Jane came up to give me a little peck on the cheek 'Don't be too long,' she whispered in my ear. As Jane and Chris headed up to the *taverna* Jen and I readied ourselves for our little swim.

Jen had stripped down to her bikini.

'Bloody hell Jen, you're really in great shape for a 70-year-old,'

'Well thanks Iain, you really know how to make a woman feel good,' she said somewhat sarcastically.

'Sorry, but you know what I mean.'

'Indeed, and frankly I'll take what I can get, compliments are in short supply these days!'

With that we made our way to the little set of steps to access the water and off we went. The water was as expected, and we slowly made our way up the channel in unison. It was lovely, peaceful, and somewhat idyllic.

'How's things, we haven't had a proper chance to catch up following Chris' meeting and the lunch with *Thassos*,'

'Yes, I know, I was sort of hoping that maybe we would head down to the *Artistico* that evening, but it didn't quite work out and on reflection it wasn't a bad thing.'

'Well, if you had let me know earlier in the day you were going to head down to the village to buy some nibbles I could have popped down with you, anyway what do you mean not a bad thing?'

'Oh, the nibbles were just a spur of the moment thing, more about reading my book in peace. Anyway, in the light of what happened later, after we went to bed it was a good job we didn't go to the *Artistico*.

'I thought you were going off for an early night?' I cheekily suggested.

'Not that sort of early night. It just meant we had some time to talk. There's some things I need to share with you.' She said a little sheepishly.

'And?'

'Well let's swim back, I think you've bought us half an hour or so and we can talk.'

We made our way back, dried ourselves off and found a nice little spot under the shade of a ubiquitous tamarind tree.

'I'm all ears Jen.'

She leaned back, for once seeming to be a little unsure of herself.

'I told you that we have been talking a lot more since we've been out here.' I nodded.

'And that it still always seems to be on Chris' terms. Well, we got into a little discussion about why we were out here, you know your plans and all that.' I nodded again.

'Chris asked me what I thought the purpose of your plans

were.' She stalled a little.

'And?

'I asked him if he remembered the time at your house, earlier in the year, when you and I stayed up and talked after dinner, you remember?'

'How could I forget.' I was intrigued.

'I told him that you and I had a very open discussion about where our relationship was. I told him how I was feeling about things and that as he wasn't listening and that I needed someone who would listen. Anyway, I was about to tell him that I thought the purpose of your plans was to try and give us some time away from our current environment, to talk.'

'And then what happened?'

'I hope you are ready.' She paused. 'He stopped me in my tracks and said I was very late to bed that night, and somewhat surprisingly asked me if there was something going on,' she added raising her eyebrows and wearing a rather coy look.

'Do you mean what I think you mean, between us?' I said a little incredulously.

'Well yes, and he thinks this plan thing is all a bit of a ruse, that you are spending more time with me and....' She paused again.

'He cited the night at the *Artistico*, he asked if anything happened after he had gone, that I was rather late back?'

'Like what, is he mad?'

'Oh, come on Iain, I don't need to spell it out to you! Remember I've heard all about the ten years of debauchery at Pollards, with the constant stream of young ladies wanting to party with you,' She paused for thought.

'Anyway, is it really that incredulous?' her look had changed, it felt like she was testing me.

'Well, firstly before I answer that this is so typical of Chris, trying to create a diversion away from the heart of the problem, continuing to hide behind his shield,' I paused. 'Frankly with his past record that's a bit rich coming from him! And secondly, and more importantly to answer your question, no it's not that incredulous and, fuck me Jen in some ways I wish it was true, but you and I know that isn't the answer to this problem. How did you respond?'

'I told him I had a wonderful evening, listening to *Ireni* sing and wasn't going to be drawn into a ridiculous perception brought about by his imagination.'

'So, you didn't tell him about the beach?' For a second she shied away from my gaze.

'I didn't see the need, I also told him that if there was a problem it wasn't my making. The conversation ended with me telling him one of your favourite little lines, one you told me that evening, that if he wanted to know where the problem lies, go take a look in the mirror.'

We both stared intently at each other for what seemed an age.

'Jesus Jen, this puts a whole new spin on Monday's dinner of love, I suppose he thinks that's a dinner for you and me! Christ I thought the plans were going well, the joy of this place, sharing it with you, the wedding, the dance of the *Mihanikos*, *Thassos'* story, the sheer fun and madness of *Emporios*. Is he blind?'

'Well perhaps not as much as we think,' Jen knowingly replied

'Ok but fuck me it's so frustrating. This has made my mind up.'

'And' she asked.

'I've spent a little time thinking about how I would play the dinner of love, but this has now re-enforced my thinking.'

'And' she asked a tad more imploringly this time.

'Look I'm sorry Jen but if I tell you now, it will lose its impact on the night. However, two things before we go and join them. One, this conversation stays between you and me, please' I implored.

'Ok, that's a deal.'

'And two, and I don't want you to answer this question. Would playing around with me give you what you're looking for?'

Jen leant back, I could see the intensity of thought in her eyes. I sensed she wanted to respond.

I leant forward and for a short moment placed my finger on her lips.

'As I said, don't answer the question just think about it and its relevance in all this. Shall we go?'

I could sense Jen composing herself as we readied ourselves for the short walk to the *taverna*.

'I'm glad I got that off my chest, it's been playing on my mind. I am trying not to let it colour my judgement, but it now feels like Chris' eyes are on me.'

'Look, I'm going to have a little time with him when we get to *Pothia*. I will put a little thought in his mind.'

I grabbed her face, looked intensely into her eyes. 'You deserve better than this, and that includes me! It shows perhaps that he's woken up, you remember the big question.'

'Yes' she replied.

'It feels to me you are getting closer to the answer.' I kissed her gently on the lips.

'Maybe,' she whispered.

'One last thing, as I said his accusation of a little dalliance between us is a bit rich knowing his history. I've never really thought about this too much and we've certainly never discussed it, but you've always seemed to deal with his womanising in a calm and steady manner. How so?'

'Remember Iain, Chris and I are both of the same 60's cloth and my attitude has always been "What's good for the goose!" ' she replied in a surreptitious manner.

'Blimey you never fail to surprise me. You are a very special lady, let's hope he realises that before it's too late. Perhaps he's wooing Jane as we speak!' We both laughed.

'That's better, shall we go?'

We gathered up our belongings and made our way to the *taverna*.

Jane and Chris were deep in conversation when we arrived. I
announced our arrival. 'You two having fun?'

'Just talking, did you have a nice swim?' Jane asked.

'Yes indeed, very good for the soul,' I smiled at Jen.

'Are you having a drink?' Jane enquired.

'No, I think we should head down to *Pothia*. I believe the
museum and house close around 2.30pm. It's midday now and it
will take around twenty minutes to get there.'

'Is the ride over similar territory?' Chris asked.

'For maybe fifteen minutes, but the last five minutes down into
the town will be interesting.'

'How so?' Jen asked.

'The traffic system is a tad chaotic to say the least. Cars, trucks,
motorbikes, carts, pedestrians, all crammed into the town centre
with their own view as to how the road system works. Throw a few
tourists on scooters into the mix and that should give you a sense of
what is to come.'

'Sounds like my idea of fun,' Chris said.

'Well remember I'll be hanging on behind you,' Jen cautioned.
Chris' look said it all.

After settling the bill, we headed back to the scooters, donned
our helmets, saddled up and off we went. The first fifteen minutes
were as expected. Climbing uphill out of the village the views
across to Turkey on the East and Kos straight ahead were
magnificent. I kept the speed right down so we could enjoy the
scenery. I sensed Chris' desire to speed off again but maybe my
warning and Jen's request did the trick.

The last five minutes of the journey involved dropping down
into *Pothia*. Like all islands the hustle and bustle of life away from
tourism is generally hidden but to get to the town you must
navigate your way past various municipal operations and
buildings, not least the islands waste and power stations with their
not so pleasant aroma. The trucks and cars were coming thick and

fast, we were steering our way through the sharp twists and turns, never knowing what was round the corner. I was concentrating totally on myself and decided Chris should do the same. As the town came into view the final part of the journey was down a road designed, in my view for nothing more than a donkey and a cart. Jane was laughing in my ear as well as hollering at various cars, people, and trucks as we tried to dodge round them. The pressure and concentration seemed to intensify the heat. Milos' prophetic words were ringing in my head.

We finally dropped onto the main harbour road skirting the town. It was as busy as expected. I checked in the mirror and Chris' was right behind me. The lights weren't a bad idea after all. I knew the museum was right by the main square and *Pavlos'* advice on parking was if you see a space grab it. As we made our way towards the square I spotted a gap big enough for two scooters and after traversing the junction, without really knowing who had the right of way I wedged the scooter into the space, immediately followed by Chris.

'Wow, that was great, what a gas,' Chris exclaimed excitedly. 'You alright honey?'

'I think so, I had my eyes closed for that last bit!' Jen said, clearly relieved to be off the scooter in one piece.

'Don't worry the journey back isn't as fraught. I suggest we head over to a little *taverna* I know on the main drag. *Pavlos* has taken me there on the odd "shopping" trip. It's very nice and has a terrace across from the main road next to the harbour. Very close to where *Pavlos* and the family kept their *kaiki (boat)*. We can make it our base for the next couple of hours. I think a beer is in order after that little ride!'

We made our way over to the *taverna*, grabbed a table and were relieved to sit down and relax. It was called the *Ibiscus* and even though it was in a lovely spot it still couldn't hide the hustle and bustle of the town. I suggested that after a drink Chris and I head off to the museum and house whilst Jane and Jen went shopping for sandals. Thinking an hour would be long enough for the museum and the house we agreed to meet back at the *Ibiscus* for a late lunch around 2pm. I had a word with the waiter and told him we would be back for lunch. He kindly let us leave our helmets inside the *taverna*.

After pointing Jane in the right direction and reminding her to ask for directions to the *Ibiscus* if they got lost, navigation wasn't her greatest skill, Chris and I headed to the museum. It was only a short walk and in five minutes we arrived. It is situated next to the town hall, another building bequeathed to the island by the great sponge merchant and was originally the "*Vouvalis* Technical School". On the walk over I told Chris that I simply wanted him to get a sense of the archaic nature of the early sponge divers and to reflect on *Thassos'* story. Outside the building was a beautiful bronze statue of *Nikolaos*, looking suitably austere and dignified. We were greeted warmly as we entered by the lady on the desk, who introduced herself as *Nomiki* and told us she was the museum curator. I explained that Chris had met my friend *Thassos* and I gave her a little insight into the afternoon discussion we had with him. She was clearly thrilled by this, so much so that she offered to escort us round. I said that was very kind and if Chris wanted to take up the offer that would be great. He agreed and off we went.

For the next half hour *Nomiki* guided us round the museum which was made up of four rooms. The history of the diving techniques was on display from the 19th century to today. I could see Chris was captivated. The "*skandalopetres*" stones, used by the early divers to facilitate the drop to the ocean floor, a stark reminder of the precarious nature of the early hunters. The diving suits and air pumps had Chris shaking his head in disbelief and the rich collection of photos and artwork from the beginning of the 20th century captivated him. I was delighted when *Nomiki* pointed to one in particular, a photo of a painting called "Departure of The Fleet", by a local artist *Antonis Karafillakis*. I had seen this before and felt the artist had brilliantly captured the sense of foreboding on the faces of those saying farewell to the divers. I decided I didn't need to say anything as *Nomiki's* commentary provided all the backdrop that was needed. She explained how inextricably connected *Kalymnian* social life was with the sponge hunting.

Everywhere we looked there was an array of sponges. I asked *Nomiki* if she had any photos of *Nikolaos Vouvalis*. She nodded and guided us over to an area in one of the rooms. She explained that this part of the display was dedicated to the *Vouvalis* family and there in front of us in the centre of the display was a picture of this *Kalymnian* legend, with his wife *Katerina* dutifully sat beside him. He bore all the hallmarks of a *kalymnian* and the setting for the picture bore all the accoutrements of his status and wealth. She was delighted again when I told her of my knowledge of this man, but not so when I told her we were going to visit the house. Unfortunately, it was having some extensive work carried out and was shut until next year. Shit I thought, all the times I had passed through *Pothia* and when finally sorting out a visit it was closed. Next year maybe?

Before we moved on to the last room I asked *Nomiki* if I could ask her a question. 'But of course' she said obligingly.

I began, 'The story of the sponge diving is one of those fascinating tales that mixes great wealth with human tragedy. As with all these tales there are those that gain and those that lose. In my history, on my mothers' side of the family, the men folk, they were all coal miners in Wales. I presume you know about this?'

'Maybe not this place Wales but yes, yes, I understand. We have a history around mining, going right back to ancient times,' she confirmed.

I continued, 'As with the sponge diving there were great

merchants, selling the coal and creating huge wealth for themselves whilst the miners, like my family were working in terrible conditions often suffering from tragedy and long-term illness. I see parallels but I have this question in my mind, about the status of the *Vouvalis* family. I know *Nikolaos* was recognised as a great benefactor for provision of the school, the hospital, and many other things. How is this reconciled with the terrible loss and disabilities inflicted on the divers?'

*Nomiki* paused in thought 'This is not a subject I have given much thought to. We *Kalymnians* accept the way things are, this is our life, our history. Maybe these things he bestowed on our people were some sort of redemption, I don't know. There is a book, written by an English Lady, Faith Warn it's called Bitter Sea. She lived on the island for a while. It is the real story of Greek sponge diving. I know she spent a lot of time researching the history. Maybe in that book you will find the answer.'

As we passed through the final room I asked Chris if he wanted to see anything else. He said he had seen enough but would like a little memory of the visit and asked *Nomiki* if he could purchase something. *She* disappeared and returned with what she said was a special gift, to remind Chris of his visit and of *Thassos*, a small copy of the painting we had seen earlier depicting the "Departure of the Fleet". I could see Chris was genuinely touched. I was even jealous myself as it was a lovely gift and a truly captivating depiction of my vision of this special moment. After thanking *Nomiki* we left and made our way back to the *Ibiscus*. As we hadn't visited the *Vouvalis* house I knew we would have a little time to ourselves before the ladies made it back to the *taverna*. I ordered a couple of beers which duly arrived.

'Well Chris, what did you think of the Museum?'

Chris paused for thought 'It was a fascinating. I learnt so much more about the history of the sponge diving and as for those stones and suits. I can't say I would have enjoyed that way of diving.'

'Yes, it brings a little perspective to modern diving methods. I hope it gave you a little insight into the world *Thassos'* family lived in. Very harsh way to make a living and even with all that progress, the improved methods, *Thassos* still ended up with his afflictions.'

'I guess diving has a way of reminding us of who is in charge down there. Even with all the modern methods adopted in our time divers still end up with issues to deal with.' Chris declared.

I saw an opening in his response 'Everyone has issues Chris, to me it's all about how you deal with them.' I waited for Chris' response and all I got was a stare.

'I thought that was a lovely gesture from *Nomiki,* to let you have that picture. With our dinner of love round the corner you'd almost think it was part of the plans.'

Chris took a sip of his beer 'Yes it was and as for the plans, I have been giving them some thought.'

Jens earlier confession came into sharp focus in my mind 'And?' I asked.

'I've been trying to wrestle with what it's all about. I've had a lot of time to think and had some very frank discussions with Jen,' I could sense him poking for a response.

'And?' again was all I offered.

'Look, that doesn't really help. You invited us out here and from what's gone on so far you clearly had some idea in your mind that you wanted to achieve. Was it for your benefit or mine?' His tone a little aggressive.

I held his glare 'You can take whatever you want from this holiday, this place, what has happened and what is still to happen. My aim was to open your eyes, to let you get a sense of the history, the hardship of life past and present, the people and their dogged determination to live their lives to the full. Most of all that in amongst all the madness there is one thing that bonds these people... Love! Their love of life, of friends, of family and their immense love and respect of the *Kalymnian* way. That is why everything ends with the dinner of love. You must take whatever benefit you want from this. As for me I would suggest my benefit is clear for you to see!'

Chris leant back in his chair. I knew I had more than nudged him. I wondered whether this would push him to take the next step.

'Hi guys.' I looked round and there was Jane and Jen, smiling with bags in hand approaching the *taverna,* great timing I thought. I leant across the table.

'Chris, the answer to all of this is before your very eyes.'

'Do you ladies want a drink?'

'Yes please, you know Milos is right about this place. It's too bloody hot!' Jane exclaimed.

'Hi honey, I've got some sandals, how was the museum and the house?' Jen asked as she wearily plonked herself down next to Chris.

'The museum was great, really fascinating. We didn't make the house, it was closed! I'll tell you about it later. I got my own little present from the lady at the museum whilst you were shopping.' Chris passed Jen the picture.

'It's a depiction of the departing of the fleet, you know when it leaves for the sponge hunting. The artist seems to have really captured the emotion of the farewell in the people's faces. The lady said it was closely linked to the dinner of love.'

'Wow, that's really nice. I am rather looking forward to our dinner of love.' Jen said eagerly.

'Indeed, aren't we all,' said Chris a little sarcastically, glancing my way.

We decided on a small *meze* for lunch which was duly dispatched. We all agreed with Jane's view that *Pothia* was 'Too bloody hot!' so we paid our bill, made our way to the scooters and I took the corporate decision that *Vlychadia* was not a good idea, maybe another time and we should head back to *Emporios.*

Having fought our way precariously out of *Pothia* and through the main residential areas of the town it wasn't long before we were back at Mike's Bikes at *Myrties*. Having dropped them off we made our way across the road to a bar, I phoned *Pavlos* and after a couple of beers he arrived.

'Ok Iain, how was *Pothia*?'

Before I could answer 'Too bloody hot!' Jane exclaimed.

I decided Chris should sit in the front with Jen as I fancied spending the last part of the journey in the back of the truck with Jane. She asked me if everything had gone to plan. I simply told her the plot had thickened.

The evening followed its usual routine, pinkles, with Jen doing her village and nibbles routine, dinner, copious drinks, and plenty of talking rubbish. After our earlier skirmish at the *Ibiscus* I decided it was a night to leave Chris, Jen and the plans alone and instead focussed on enjoying the evening with Jane. I was duly awarded with a very nice lovemaking session when we returned to our room.

# CHAPTER ELEVEN

## KALYMNIAN VIGNETTE NO. 3:
## "HUNTING KALYMNIAN STYLE"

The weekend arrived, not that Saturday or Sunday were any different from the weekdays for us, but in *Emporios* in general it meant most of "the boys" were not working and just like us at home this was "me" time for them. This usually involved some sort of madness, mixed in with drinking, smoking and if the situation arose, womanising! However, today was a little different as it was a significant day for them, the beginning of the *Kalymnian* hunting season! But this season had nothing to do with hunting of sponges, this was landlubbers' territory and all about *kynigi paichnidiou, (game hunting)*.

For "the boys" this was a very special day, a sort of lad's day out, but for the life of me I could not think of a worse place to go hunting. Firstly, it was extremely hot up in the mountains, secondly the terrain made it very difficult to sneak up on anything, and thirdly, and in my view most importantly, there was not a lot to shoot! The tradition of hunting, just like the fishing had its roots in the need to find food and sustenance. However, now the hunting season was simply a good excuse to get their guns out and for a short moment blast away at anything that moved on the mountains. I suspect it was also a way to celebrate the many occasions the *Kalymnians* had battled with the various marauders occupying their land.

I had discussed this with Milos earlier in the week when we were up at the *taverna* on our own and we'd decided to say nothing to Chris and Jen about this impending shoot-out. You can therefore imagine their surprise when turning up for breakfast this particular morning they were greeted by "the boys" hovering around a table full of weaponry.

'Jesus, have the Turks invaded,' was Chris' rather witty comment.

'My what a lot of guns!' was Jen's somewhat obvious and prosaic response followed with something a little more imaginative and typically mischievous. 'Well, they do say men treat their guns like their penis, they like to get it out and shoot it off as regularly as possible.'

'Fuck me Jen, where do you pull that sort of shit from?' Milos remarked.

'Years of practice Miles! Any particular reason why we have a full-scale armoury in the *taverna*?' Jen asked, 'It's a little disconcerting,' Jen added.

'It's the hunting season,' Milos replied, as he lit another customary *Assos*.

'Hunting for what?' Chris asked. 'It seems pretty barren here.'

'Partridge and rabbit.'

'Oh, I love a bit of Rabbit *stifado*,' Mary interrupted and exclaimed rather excitedly.

'I think Miles wished you loved another sort of stiffy,' I said chuckling to myself.

'Very funny Youth now let me finish. In the past hunting for wild partridge and rabbit was all about food. Unfortunately, over the years with the number of guns on the island they wiped out the wild partridges, but you know what rabbits are like. Anyway, to get round the problem with the partridges they arrange for shed loads to be brought to the island just before the season starts and they let them loose in the mountains. Then off go "the boys", along with all the other cowboys on the island and the shoot-out at the "Ok *Kalymnos*" commences. My advice is to avoid the mountains for the next two days.'

'Is *Pavlos* going shooting?' Chris asked.

'No, he reckons "the boys" should have been on the mountains hours ago and will now be lucky to find anything left that moves.'

*Pavlos* arrived with the usual morning accoutrements for breakfast and dished them out accordingly. He pulled up a seat and took his usual position in between Milos and me, leant back in his chair, pulled out an *Assos* and surveyed the scene as some sort of commotion erupted around "the boys" table with the usual shouting and gesticulating.

'*Pavlos*, what's that all about, I heard the word *oplo*, *(*gun*)* is there a problem?' I asked.

'Ah pa pa, big problem here with the shooting. I believe *Nikolas* forget the ammunition for some of the guns. Maybe a little drunk last night,' he explained as he chuckled to himself.

'Well, I wouldn't be the one to tell *Nikolas* he's fucked up,' Milos wisely noted.

*Pavlos* shouted something across to "the boys" and they all laughed.

'What was that *Pavlos*?' Milos asked.

'I said maybe no ammunition needed, especially for *Skevros*,' with a comment in Greek that would be best aligned in English with "He couldn't hit a cow's arse with a banjo".

*Skevros* was one of *Pavlos* oldest and closest friends. Like *Pavlos*, he was born and raised in *Emporios*, one of the few non-*Michas* and we had got to know him well. He was a little unlike a *Kalymnian* in that he was very slight in build, without the mop of black hair or a *moustaki*. His English was very good, and he was also softly spoken. He was also devoted to his family, was married to *Polymnia*, a beautiful lady, not just in looks but in nature. They had two children, both girls who had inherited their mothers looks and *Skevros* doted on them. They also had a pet *skillos*, (dog) a funny white curly haired mongrel called Arkoudaki, (teddy bear) which the girls and *Polymnia* constantly fussed over. This was out of kilter with most *Kalymnian* family's approach to having a dog. Generally, dogs didn't hold the same place in *Kalymnian* life as they do in British life. Their purpose was either as a guard dog, a goat herding dog, and come the hunting season, a hound to support the hunt. Most family's dogs were kept in the yard and in my view seemed a little unloved.

*Skevros* was also a little different to most *Kalymnian* men when it came to his family. He took his role of being a husband and a father very seriously. On many occasions when "the boys" were up to something or *Pavlos* had some "shopping" to do he would decline the offer to join in, giving some excuse as to why he could not participate. The usual mickey taking would follow along the lines of who wore the trousers in his house. His mother still lived in the village and with his father now passed he visited her most days. In the summer he spent a large portion of his time sat on the beach wall taking the money for the rented sunbeds and sunshades for the family's particular part of the beach. A few years back he decided to build a beautiful house on a piece of land owned by his father, just up the hill that leads into the village. It was a fantastic spot, with wonderful views of *Emporios*, the bay and the distant mountains. His original plan was to move the family in but by the time it was finished his other job as a general builder was not producing enough cash for family life. He decided that the best option was to rent the place out as a holiday let. I believe it is the only time he went against *Polymnia,* and the girls' wishes.

Irrespective of all the above, the one event he never missed was "the boys" day out on the shoot and this year was no different. Now when it came to guns, *Pavlos* had told me that most men on the island had one or two weapons. There was a legal requirement that all guns should be registered but part of the problem here was that lots of guns had been passed down through the family and these tended to be unregistered. Mainly because they were either pre-war or German guns from the war and were considered a little dangerous, just like the dynamite. These older guns also presented a problem regarding ammunition and apparently whilst big *Nikolas* accepted he was guilty as charged being drunk the previous evening, when it came to the ammunition he simply couldn't get his hands on any that was suited for *Skevros'* favourite gun. This rifle had been handed down to him by his father, who had it handed down to him from his father who had carried it with courage and pride during the German occupation. However, it seemed this time he would have to opt for his registered rifle as there was ammunition a plenty for this gun.

*Skevros* shouted something across to *Pavlos* and the only part I caught was my name. *Pavlos* laughed.

'What was that *Pavlos*, I heard my name?'

'Ah "the boys", they want to know if you will join them on the hunt. They have a special rifle for you, no ammunition!' he responded chuckling to himself.

I looked at Jane and her look told me all I needed to know. 'Go on Youth, give it a go. You've been a cowboy builder all your life, now you can do the real thing,' Milos said glibly, adding more importantly that the bus was leaving.

I got up to make my way to the bar, 'Not strictly true you twat. As you well know Milos I was, and still am technically a quantity surveyor, just like your good self and you will therefore know that the job requires an adroit hand, however using them to blast off a gun at some unsuspecting defenceless little creature is not one of the actions I like to turn my hand to!'

Jane needn't have bothered with the look. There was no way I was going to head up into the mountains in this heat.

......

I had learned my lesson maybe fifteen or sixteen years ago on what was I think our second or third trip here. It was the year Mary's daughter and her then beau Dave came along for the trip. Dave was around twenty-seven and clearly fancied himself a little as an action man and apart from his day job as a plumber was taking lessons in acting. The quietness of the surroundings and the "art of doing nothing" was not sitting comfortably with his persona. One lunchtime, sat in the *taverna* Dave was chatting with *Pavlos* about the mountain terrain and one part in particular, a large cave entrance in the distance that was visible from the terrace. *Pavlos* told him a few stories (lies) about what was in the cave and that it was a relatively easy climb (another lie) to reach the entrance.

Dave decided that trying to reach this cave and explore its contents would be a great adventure and far more fun than sitting in the *taverna* doing nothing. He suddenly announced that after lunch he was going make his foray into the wilds beyond the village and climb the escarpment in the distance. His acting lessons had clearly given him a presumption for over-the-top language. The response to this announcement was firstly Mary went scuttling of to the toilet, for once not down to me, and secondly Jodie declared he could only go if I went with him. Dave's imploring looks at me, together with the luncheon's *retsina* gave me no option but to regrettably agree to join him on this adventure.

By the time we finished lunch it was around 3pm, the hottest part of the day! We readied ourselves for the trip, i.e., not wearing flip flops, and with us both adorned in baseball caps we asked *Pavlos* for a few pointers. His first response, which was typical

*Pavlos* was, 'Maybe cancel the trip,' which we foolishly ignored. This was followed by some very rough directions and a warning to watch out for the local dogs as we made our way round the back of the village and lastly, to keep away from the beehives as we made our way up the mountain. As we set off Milos said he would arrange the funerals, which made *Pavlos* and Jane laugh, and sent Mary scuttling away again. Jane told me to be careful and to take some water so on our way out of the *taverna* I grabbed a couple of large bottles of *nero* (water).

As we made our way down the hill towards the village, I immediately realised we had made a mistake as it was fuckin hot and hard work just walking! However, the resounding cheers and clapping from the *taverna* as we left made it impossible to bottle out. As we made our way through the village I decided we should avoid the back route (and hence most of the dogs) and as we passed along the beach road I could feel the temptation to blag it and simply go for a swim. However, *Pavlos* had a rather good set of binoculars and had announced that he was going to track our progress. As we turned up the main route out of the village, we were both already dipping into the water supply. *Pavlos* had told us to head up the main hill out of the village and at the top, by *Michali's* place, which was the last house turn left and then simply follow our noses. By the time we reached the top of the hill Dave had removed his top and was moaning about the heat. Not quite the adventurous type after all I thought. There was a small track visible up the side of *Michali's* house which we gamely followed. Just as we reached the end of his garden wall, we both shat ourselves when we were startled by his gnashing and snarling dog who clearly relished his guard dog duties. Fortunately, he was on the end of a chain, and we delicately edged past the reach of his tether. As we started the incline up the mountain, we could see the cave entrance. It already looked a lot higher up than it did when we viewed it from the *taverna,* and the terrain looked a little tricky.

After circumnavigating the various beehives and somehow manging not to trip up on the rocky terrain we reached the start of the proper climb to the cave entrance. My water supply was already gone, and Dave wasn't far from finishing his. We decided a quick five-minute rest was a good call before we attempted the final escarpment. I used this last five minutes to try and persuade Dave to bottle it and take the flack. Unfortunately, he did not bite and thought as we'd come this far, we should give it a go. The initial climb to the part directly below the cave entrance was relatively easy other than the searing heat. However, grabbing the sharp rocky crags was already affecting my pen-pusher's hands. When we reached the last part of the climb, directly below the cave entrance the reality of *Pavlos'* lie became apparent. The entrance was around six metres above us and whilst I could see plenty of places for foot and hand holds it was somewhat precipitous. At this point my bottle went. I declared this was only fit for goat herding types like *Pavlos.* Having reached what I termed close enough to the summit of our escapade, there was too much of the holiday left to risk injury and I would be happy to fail. Dave didn't share this view and said that he thought he could make it. Apparently *Pavlos* had told him that there was a rope inside the cave which had been there for years, originally used to hide stuff away from the Germans during the occupation and that once up he could lower it down to me. My response was to ask him if he knew the word gullible wasn't actually in the dictionary. He gave me a funny stare!

Taking his last slug of water, he commenced his climb, very quickly reaching about halfway up. Then the problems started. He shouted down that he could not reach the next hand hold and was not sure where to head next. After about a minute, which seemed an eternity he told me that the thought of falling had entered his head and he was now panicking and frozen to the rocks. Not the action of some future James Bond I thought, and my next response was to give him the advice my good mate Wacks would give when anything like this happened, which was, "Not to panic like an amateur". Generally good advice but in this instance, we were amateurs! Whilst three metres did not seem that high, when the ground below is solid igneous rock the thought of falling becomes a little more intensified. For a moment all I could think about was *Pavlos* staring at us through the binoculars and reporting back what he was seeing. I knew where Mary would be. My brain then kicked in and I decided to take the "what goes up must come down" approach and that whatever way he did it there was only one option. After five minutes of persuasion, he was ready to give it a go. I positioned myself below him and watched as he gingerly made his first moves. All went well for the first metre until taking a short rest, he balanced on what appeared to be a safe foothold when it suddenly gave way and down he came, wailing like a banshee with me clumsily breaking his fall. Other than Dave having a bit of a gash to his cheek, miraculously we both escaped with a few scrapes and bruises, with the only thing broken being his pride. I surveyed the gash and told him his acting career was over when it came to looks and he would be resigned to playing baddies. His response was a little melodramatic saying he was simply glad to be alive. I then turned in the direction of the *taverna* and held a thumbs up position hoping *Pavlos* was watching.

When we finally made it back, having stopped off at the *Artistico* for a bit of a clean-up and a stiff drink we headed up the stairs to the *taverna*. We were greeted with cheers and shouts of *Bravo, Bravo.* Very strange I thought, until I saw *Pavlos* grinning. It seemed his ability to lie knew no boundaries and he had clearly painted a very different picture to the reality of our final descent! Whilst Dave attempted to blag his way out of why he had a gashed cheek and regaled the others with his momentous climb I went over to *Pavlos* and told him surreptitiously I owed him one. "No problem" was his simple response...

......

Having furnished Milos with his morning *Mythos* beer I went over to "the boys" and politely declined their offer to join the hunt. I told them *Pavlos,* and I had a wager, with him insisting that they would bag nothing. I told them that my money was on them and furthermore that Mary was expecting a large haul of *kunelli,* (rabbit) for a nice *stifado.* I asked *Skevros* about his gun and the problem with the ammunition and he told me that he would have to use a different gun, not as good as his favoured weapon but with his shooting skills no problem. The shooting party numbered five. They gathered up their armoury, cigarettes, and a few bottles of retsina. They made their way out of the *taverna,* jumped into Big *Nikolas'* pick up and headed off into the horizon. As I sat back down, I asked *Pavlos* where they were going. He pointed towards the mountain stretch to the west of the island that led to *Palionisis.* I asked how long they would be, and he laughed.

'Ah... maybe 2-3 hours, maybe less if there is nothing to shoot. Maybe Mary has nothing to eat tonight!' he said as he poured himself a little drop of *raki.*

Jane suddenly announced she was heading to the beach and asked if I was joining her for the morning session. I said yes, particularly as I planned to spend all of Sunday in the *taverna.* I hoped Chris would stay up in the *taverna* as I really wanted to spend some more time with Jen, but when Jen asked him he decided to join us on the beach leaving Milos and *Pavlos* to have some "quality time" together.

We positioned ourselves on the sunbeds, under the shade of the trees in the usual manner, with Mary setting out somewhat in hope, a sunbed next to her for Milos. No chance, as Milos had given me one of his looks when responding to Mary's question as to whether he was coming down to the beach with a, 'Maybe.' As we settled down for a quiet Saturday morning beach session the first gang of locals appeared. The weekends were the only time we ever had to share our little piece of *Emporios*. I could not blame them for wanting to share this little piece of heaven and frankly this was more their home than ours. On some occasions entire families would turn up, kitted out with everything they needed for an overnight stay. This was another reason why Milos did not venture down to the beach on a Saturday or Sunday.

It was another beautiful day, very warm with a little smidgen of wind gently caressing the trees. The shade was doing its job of softening the heat and the intermittent crackling and popping of the cicadas up in the tree was the only noise breaking the silence. I laid back on the sunbed and spent the next couple of hours dozing with the odd swim thrown in. We had a little bit of fun when a very nice 60' yacht arrived at one of *Pavlos'* buoys and displayed the seamanship skills of a complete amateur, taking five attempts to catch the buoy. At each attempt, the skipper was roundly abused by Chris saying that he clearly didn't have a clue and he asked me if I could tell where they were from. Using Jane's binoculars, I scanned the stern of the yacht. Having looked a little closer, he was a little perturbed when I told him it was displaying a Royal Navy white ensign! And therefore, must be from blighty! Chris shook his head in disbelief.

I kept a little eye on Chris and Jen and was pleased to notice them having a few little chats in between cooling off in the sea. After Jen's revelations to me on the Friday I was conscious that at some stage Chris may collar me, but I soon realised I was ok for now when Mary announced it was time for lunch and we all readied ourselves for the short walk up the hill to the *taverna*. This little three-minute walk, at this hour of day was best treated as a meander and whilst very hot with the tarmac road intensifying the heat it was still made pleasant by the wonderful view of the bay and the odd goat stumbling across our path. I liked to see them nibbling away at the wild oregano, knowing how this heavenly herb would be helping to create the unique aroma and flavour of the *katsidi* stew.

When we reached the terrace, our table was waiting whilst Milos and *Pavlos* were sat in exactly the same positions.

'How was the sea today Youth?' Milos enquired.

'Nice temperature and very refreshing, did you see the yacht attempting to catch the swing mooring?'

Chris interrupted me, 'What a moron, I thought you were only allowed to fly a white ensign if you were associated with the Navy? He can't be with seamanship skills like that.'

'Well we can soon find out' Milos responded. 'Youth, *Pavlos* wants you to swim out later and remind him about the conditions of using the mooring, tell him that he should visit the *taverna* tonight. You can then ask him about the flag.'

'Actually Milos, I may not be going back down so sounds like a job for you!' I remarked as we all settled ourselves round the table. *Pavlos* disappeared into the kitchen and Milos ambled his way over and leant across the table.

'*Affroula* has made some nice *gigantes,* (beans) for lunch, very smoky and there is also some *horta* (greens) if you fancy it'

'That sounds lovely,' said Jen 'Can we have a Greek salad as well and a *tsatsiki*?'

'No problem, I'll sort it when *Pavlos* appears.' Said Milos as he filled his and my glass with *restsina*.

Jane coughed melodramatically in Milos' direction, eyeing up the *retsina's*. 'Yes, ok Pipe Up, what do you want?'

'Blimey Miles, are you alright?' exclaimed Mary.

'Yes and no need for you to join in Perks,' Milos said as he waited for the others to select their poison.

'Any news from the shooting party?' I enquired.

'Literally not a dicky bird, *Pavlos* reckons that's because they've probably drawn a blank.'

'Just like Skevros' ammunition then.' I added.

'Shall we go on the red?' Jane enquired of the ladies.

'Well why not, it is the weekend.' Jen responded giving Milos a little knowing glance.

'And for you Chris?' Milos asked.

'A beer will do thanks.' Chris replied.

As Milos disappeared to the bar *Pavlos* made his way out of the kitchen across to our table. 'What you like Iain?'

'Milos says you have *gigantes, nai?*'

'Yes, yes, fresh today.' *Pavlos* confirmed.

'Ok, *gigantes* it is, some *horta, apo exi,* (greens for six) *horiatiki salata,* (Greek salad) *apo desiris,* (for four) and some *tsatsiki,*' ordered in my best Greek.

'*Bravo* Iain.'

'*Pavlos,* Milos says no news from "the boys" '.

'*Nai, nai,* maybe big problem for Maria.' *Pavlos* said with a chuckle

'What was that?' Mary said obviously hearing her name.

'No news on the hunt for the *kunelli* (rabbit), maybe no *stifado!*' I said laughing.

*Pavlos* headed back to the kitchen just as Milos made his way to the table with the drinks. Once distributed we chatted amongst ourselves as we waited for lunch to arrive.

I heard *Pavlos'* mobile phone ringing from the bar. *Pavlos* appeared from the kitchen and answered the phone. What followed was a typical *Pavlos* conversation, delivered at full volume and at breakneck speed. Suddenly he stopped, listening with a look of incredulity. Milos asked if I was getting any of it and I said it was too fast apart from the fact that it was definitely big *Nikolas* so probably to do with the shooting. Suddenly *Pavlos* broke out into uncontrollable laughing followed intermittently with more shouting. We waited impatiently for the call to end and eventually he hung up.

*Pavlos* stood staring at the phone with the same incredulous look.

'Ahh pa pa, pa pa, this I don't believe, I don't believe,' spurted from his lips.

*Pavlos* made his way over to his normal table, grabbed his cigarettes, glass of *retsina* and a chair and came over to join us, adopting his normal position between Milos and me.

'Ah Milos, this I don't believe, crazy system.' *Pavlos* said shaking his head as he lit an *Assos*.

I couldn't hold back 'What's happened *Pavlos*, I gathered it was big *Nikolas*, something about the shooting?'

'Yes, yes Iain. They have been on the far mountains all this time, nothing to shoot. They were doing their last… I don't know this word in English but in Greek *anagnorisi*,'

'Like patrol?' I asked.

'Maybe?' Pavlos shrugged his shoulders.

'Reconnaissance?'

'Ah yes, this the last look for the hunt. *Skevros* was with big *Nikolas* positioned for the shot as the others pushed up from below, you know this? to scare them out. *Skevros* says to *Nikolas* be very still, he has spotted something moving and has his sights on the target, he waits and then suddenly shoots his gun and shouts to *Nikolas* that he hit it and shouted down to the others to come up. As he and *Nikolas* made their way over *Nikolas* says what was it, partridge, or rabbit? *Skevros* says rabbit he believes. As they got nearer the others joined them and *Skevros* says it's just behind this rock. They follow him and suddenly *Skevros* lets out a big shout.'

'What, in celebration?' I asked.

'*Oki, oki,* (no, no,)' I noticed *Pavlos* was struggling to contain himself.

'When the others joined him there it was. He had shot his dog!' *Pavlos* erupted into laughter.

Jane screamed, along with Mary 'No!!!'

Milos and I joined *Pavlos* howling with laughter.

'Oh my god, should you be laughing?' Exclaimed Jen while Chris sat wide mouthed and totally perplexed.

'What he shot *Arkoudaki?*' I managed to spurt out still howling.

'*Nai, nai*' Pavlos confirmed as he struggled to contain himself.

'Fuck me, I don't know about the dog but he's dead. *Polymnia* and the girls will kill him... Is it dead?' I asked.

'*Oki, (no)* luckily just hurt in the leg. *Nikolas* rang me to tell me that they have taken it to the hospital, you know... for the animals, but not sure what the problem with the leg will be.' *Pavlos* responded as he continued shaking his head.

'What about *Skevros?*' I asked.

'Ah big problem for *Skevros*. He is heading home to tell *Polymnia* and the girls. Maybe tonight he sleeps at *Pandalis* with you!' *Pavlos* said once again breaking out into a chuckle.

'Well, that puts a whole new meaning to being in the doghouse!' was Milos' witty retort.

'*Pavlos*, will "the boys" still be up at the *taverna* tonight?' I asked. 'They usually come up and have a few beers after the days shooting.'

'Ah yes Iain, definitely but *Skevros* I don't know. Maybe at the hospital.'

'What with the dog?'

'Maybe with a sore head!'

*Affroulla* appeared with the lunch, and we tucked in. I decided a little joke about now having to cook *skillos stifado,* (dog stew) instead of the *kunelli,* (rabbit) was perhaps a tad inappropriate and furthermore it would be lost on *Affroulla*. It was at this moment I had a little idea. The conversation continued along the same lines over lunch with much mickey taking and the girls finding it very difficult to understand why we found the incident so funny. "Boys Humour", which clearly travels was my take together with the thought of the tongue lashing *Skevros* would undoubtedly get from *Polymnia*. I could also imagine the ribbing he would get from *Pavlos* and "the boys"!

When it was time for another *retsina* I offered to get the round in, made my way into the bar and called *Pavlos*. I asked him if he would do me a little favour in return for me swimming out to the yacht for him later. Just a little 20-minute round trip to *Myrties* after lunch and on the way back drop me at the beach. He agreed and the usual subterfuge would apply.

Having returned to the table with the drinks and settled back into our very nice lunch *Pavlos* appeared at the table and announced he had a little "shopping" to do. He told me I was needed, and he would give me a shout when required. The plan worked as no one batted an eyelid. After finishing lunch, which was washed down with a decent load of *retsina Pavlos* called me from inside the bar saying we were leaving in five minutes.

I told Jane I would get *Pavlos* to drop me off down the beach and would see her in around half an hour. I made my way to the truck, and we headed off to *Myrties*. On the way I told him what sort of shop I wanted to visit and he duly obliged. Having got what I wanted we headed back to what I thought would be *Emporios*. However, *Pavlos*, who is never one to miss an opportunity announced there would be a little detour. I soon recognised the route we were taking which was to a very nice little bar, which he had taken me and Milos to before which was mostly frequented by the locals but most importantly was run by a very feisty blonde *Kalymnian* temptress. We had a few beers and I looked on as *Pavlos* engaged in his version of flirting, with loads of shouting and gesticulating together with plenty back from the temptress. I decided not to ask any questions and doubted anyway that *Pavlos* would have answered them. She was a very tasty treat for the eyes!

As we arrived back at *Emporios* I asked *Pavlos* to store the little package I had bought and that he would see what it was tonight. He dropped me off and I made my way across to our little spot on the beach and was surprised to see that even Milos had made his way down for the afternoon.

'How was the shopping trip? Jane asked, 'Took a little longer than the half hour,' she added.

'Usual madness, I'll fill you in later. I need to swim out and give the guys on the boat the message from *Pavlos*.'

Milos was laid out on his sunbed, smoking an *Assos*. 'I didn't expect to see you down here Milos. It's the weekend.'

'I thought I might swim out and help you give the twats on the boat the message.' he responded.

'Bloody hell Miles, are you ill?' Mary exclaimed.

'No Maria, I need to unload the ballast tanks and I thought the Youth might need some assistance.'

'Having a drunken idiot swimming out to those buoys is hardly assistance, more a liability but if you insist get your arse off the sunbed and we'll crack on,' I said.

'And by the way Mary, the nearest toilet is a trot back up the hill' I added playfully.

Once Milos had finished his *Assos* we made our way over to the entrance channel, I waded in followed by Milos' usual introduction to the water which was to throw himself in headfirst and then surface spluttering and making the sort of noises associated with a walrus. I decided to swim a little upstream as I had no doubt what Milos' next actions would be, and the ahs and oohs were a sure sign he was unloading! As we made our way out, Chris shouted from the beach that based on the white ensign the captain was likely to be ex-Navy, and we should address him accordingly. Having witnessed his attempt at mooring up to the buoy, I knew exactly how he would be addressed by Milos!

The water was lovely, and the swim out was very pleasant. Whilst a little slow, due to having Milos tagging along, we eventually made it out to the stern of the boat. All was very quiet, but the tender was tied up alongside and I guessed maybe the crew were inside sheltering from the heat.

I called out a couple of times with no response. Milos decided it was time for him to step in.

'Whatever twat in there who goes by the name of the captain, get yourself out here!' I heard movement and then the cabin door opened.

A young rapscallion appeared, tall with a big fop of blond hair and a garish pair of surf type shorts.

'I say, did someone call' he enquired in an accent that could only be described as proper posh.

'Yes, it was me and if you're the captain of this boat, god help the crew. My wife could park this boat better than you and she's a crap driver!' Milos exclaimed.

'Oh gosh, you saw that. A tad amateurish I know but it was a bit windy, and my crew had a little too much to drink on the sail over from Kos.'

'Did you mean motor over? I didn't see any sheets on the masts as you came into the bay. Also, how the fuck did you get a white ensign?' Milos asked.

'Ahhhh, I see, well that's my papa's. I stole it from him. He's a Rear Admiral in the Navy. A bit naughty I know, but bloody hell looks good when you come into port' he explained.

Suddenly a couple of bits of bikini clad totty appeared from the cabin. 'I say Bertie, what's going on?' one of them enquired, equally as posh.

'Nothing much Lottie, just a couple of chaps from the beach, sorry what is it you wanted?'

'Are they locals?' the other piece of totty enquired.

'No I'm fuckin not' was Milos' erudite response.

'Sorry guys let me explain. You see the *taverna* up on the hill,' I gestured towards *Pavlos* place.

'This is his buoy and in essence, if you use it you need to visit the *taverna*. It's a local thing.'

'Oh gosh, we'd really love too but we've booked to eat in the village tonight. We were told to visit *Harry's Paradise*, apparently, it's a wonderful setting and the food is supposed to be great.'

'Well, you're not wrong there, but how long are you staying?' Milos asked.

'We are planning to visit *Leros* on Monday and..'

Milos interrupted 'Right you twat, I can't spend any longer treading water out here. Get yourself up to *Pavlos* taverna Sunday night and we'll get the owner to do something special for you. Some proper local grub,' and off he swam towards the beach.

'Oh Bertie, that sounds like fun, can we go, please, please,' implored one of the bits of totty as she draped herself around the captain.

The captain wisely made the right call 'Righty ho then, tell him we'll be up around 8pm. Will you be there?'

'Yes, we'll be there, and I look forward to meeting you all. One last thing I hope you all like goat stew!' I shouted as I started my swim back.

'Did he say boat?' asked the other bit of totty.

'No Goat, crikey I wonder if it's curried?' was the last thing I heard. By the time I reached the beach Milos was draped across his sunbed and toking on an *Assos*.

'Was the captain anything to do with the Navy?' Chris asked.

'Sort of, anyway you'll find out as they are coming up to *Pavlos* for dinner on Sunday,' I responded

'Isn't that *Katsidi* day?' Jane asked.

'Indeed, and I have a little plan!' I exclaimed.

We spent the rest of the afternoon lounging by the sea and watching the madness of the local's slapping octopus on the rocks, to tenderise them before throwing them on the BBQ. After a quickie and a shower Jane and I headed down for pinkles. Milos and Mary were knee deep in gin and tonics. Shortly after we arrived Chris wandered over. Apparently Jen had decided the nibbles last night were so good that she would get some more. She eventually returned armed with pistachios and pringles and around

9pm we headed to the *taverna*. The usual system followed with drinks and food, and we had the pleasure of "The boys" excluding *Skevros*, sitting across from us indulging in their version of Greek banter which I quickly deduced was directed at *Skevros* and the incident with "*Arkoudaki*".

We were delighted when around 10pm the noise of a motorbike could be heard approaching the *taverna* and *Pavlos* announced it was *Skevros*. As a somewhat sheepish *Skevros* made his way through the gate the shouting, hollering, laughing, and chanting began. As best I could make out, they were championing *Skevros* as the great and skilled "*Skillos kynigos*" (Dog Hunter) of *Kalymnos* and generally taking the piss out of his sharp shooting skills. *Skevros* tried his best to convince them it was all down to not being able to use his favourite gun stating, 'There was a problem with the sight.' You can imagine the response to this! A proper ribbing along with plenty of stick about the tongue lashing he got from *Polymnia* and the girls. Once things had settled a little, I asked *Pavlos* where he had stored my little package, from the "shopping" earlier today. He told me where it was and I made my way into the *taverna*, grabbed the bag, and headed back out.

I made my way to "the boys" table.

'*Signomee* (Excuse me). Everybody, can I have your attention.' A hush fell over the *taverna*.

'We understand today is a special day. The beginning of the *Kalymnian* hunting season, an opportunity for the great hunters of *Kalymnos* to demonstrate their prowess on land rather than at sea. I am reminded of the God of Hunting Orion, a companion of the deity Artemis, who when out hunting with Artemis boasted that he could hunt and kill any living thing on Earth!'. I noticed *Pavlos* translating for some of "the boys" and a few giggles followed.

I continued 'I understand that today we have our very own Orion amongst us, a man who has demonstrated his ability to hunt any living thing on earth!' some further giggles with *Skevros* sat still looking a little sheepish.

'Fortunately, this great hunter's shooting skills didn't match up to the boast and all he did was wing his prey.' The giggles turned to laughter.

'To honour this great achievement, we have a trophy which I would like to present to *Skevros,* to remind him of this great day.'

'I opened the bag and pulled out a large toy dog, on which I had tied a bloodied bandage to the leg and held it up for all to see.'

The boys burst into joyous laughter and the whole *taverna* erupted into applause, followed by *Skevros* gamely accepting the trophy.

I waited a moment for things to settle.

'My friends, my friends, let me just close things off and take you back to *Orion's* boast to *Artemis.* You may not know that following this, the Goddess *Gaia,* ancestral mother of all life objected to such a boast and sent a giant scorpion to kill him.' I paused 'Let us hope that the Goddess *Polymnia* doesn't put a scorpion in *Skevros* bed tonight!' Great merriment followed.

As for the trophy, *Skevros* decided it was best kept at the *taverna!*

# CHAPTER TWELVE

## KATSIDI DAY AND "THE SPECIALS"

Waking up on the Sunday morning listening to the soft and warming sounds of the goat bells, tinkling as the they traversed the hill behind our room searching out the oregano plants, was one of my favourite simple pleasures that *Emporios* continually heaped upon us. It was also very apposite as Sunday was *Katsidi day,* (Goat Stew Day). This generally meant a mad day in the *taverna,* with family, friends and any other unsuspecting tourists witnessing the *Emporios* version of a Sunday roast.

After our ablutions we made our way across to the *taverna* for breakfast. Having arrived slightly after 9.30am we were surprised to see that Milos and Mary were not in position. Whilst we waited for them to arrive *Pavlos* sorted our breakfast. I popped into the bar area where he was making our coffee to confirm that I had spoken to the so-called captain of the yacht moored on his buoy and that they would be coming up that evening for dinner. There were eight on board and I had informed them that it was goat stew day and that he would ensure there was plenty for them. I also asked *Pavlos* if we could arrange for some of the "Goat Specials" we had several years ago, to celebrate Milos' 60th birthday.

'No problem,' he responded, wearing a big grin.

'Oh, and one last thing *Pavlos*. This lot are proper posh, so I suggest we pull all the stops out and get Milos to do the silver service.'

'Explain Iain?' Pavlos asked.

'You know this *Pavlos*, like the Queen. The way she speaks, all plummy,' I said as I mimicked the Queen.

'And all the service she gets, Milos will be like one of her butlers,' I explained.

'Ah yes, this I know. You think Miles is good for this?'

'Absolutely,' I replied, grinning as I made my way back to the table.

Just as I did so Milos and Mary were making their way to the *taverna*.

'Morning Lofty, you're late. Most unusual, what happened?'

'Had a problem this morning with the chalfonts,' he said grimacing.

'Oh Miles, they don't want to know about that thank you,' Mary exclaimed.

'Sorry, but he did ask, anyway the Youth knows the crack. How is *Pavlos* this morning?'

'All good, I just confirmed to him that the posh brigade from the yacht are coming up for dinner tonight. I've asked him to do a few "specials".'

'Like what?' Jane enquired.

'Wait and see Jane By the way, as they are proper posh *Pavlos* and I think they should get the special service. Which basically means Milos will be on waiter duties, like their own personal butler!' I said laughing.

'Do you want me to knock up a dickie bow?' Jane asked mischievously.

'Very funny Pipe Up. If you're not careful I'll do it in my special smugglers!' Milos responded.

'I take it from that you're up for the crack then?' I asked.

'Why not, it's a Sunday, what can go wrong?'

Jen and Chris arrived at the taverna. 'Morning Miles, did I hear you say something has gone wrong?'

'No, but the day is still young. The Youth has stitched me up and I'm on waitering duties tonight for the toffs on the yacht.'

'Do we get the same service?' Chris politely enquired.

'In a word no!' Milos abruptly replied.

'Any reason why?' Jen asked.

'Since when have you two been toffs?' Milos responded. A fair point I thought.

Breakfast followed its usual routine with the delightful addition of *Poppi*, who turned up to see us and to collect the money for the use of her sunbeds. This was always a good crack with Milos trying to remember how many times he'd been to the beach and attempting to work out how much he owed. This always seemed a little unnecessary as at three euros a day for two beds they were nothing short of peanuts. I suspect Milos enjoyed winding her up and would use this as nothing more than a ruse to enable him to accuse *Poppi* of treating him like a Turk. A general discussion would follow with *Poppi* sharing her simple view that they were murderous bastards!

The other good thing about *Poppi* turning up was that she would bring us all a leaving gift, large bags of the local dried *threbe* (oregano) and a tin of the local *mela* (honey), which I deemed to be the elixir of life and simply the best on the planet. Jen was particularly delighted as she said they would be able to make their own version of the yoghurt, fruit, and honey at home. That's if you get to it before Chris I thought.

At around the usual time Jane announced she was going down to the beach for the morning session and asked if the girls were

coming. She didn't bother asking me, after all it was Sunday!
Chris announced to Jen and all that he was staying up as he
fancied witnessing the pre-cursor to the Sunday Lunch. I was
pleased at this announcement as I wanted a last little session with
Chris ahead of the dinner of love on Monday.

Once the girls had set off for the beach, we settled ourselves
down for whatever the rest of the morning would throw at us.

'Milos, time for a *retsina* and you're in the chair. Chris, what
are you going to have?'

'As it's a Sunday I'll join you in a *retsina*.'

Milos made his way into the *taverna*. Just as he did so I noticed
*Thoris'* truck pull into the car park. He made his way through the
gate and across the *taverna* towards the kitchen. There were two
other things I noticed. Firstly, he was carrying a rather large bin
bag and was shouting something to *Pavlos* about the *Katsidis,* and
secondly, following behind him was a guy I recognised
immediately as *Lavros*, also carrying a large bin bag. As Milos came
back with the *retsina* and sat down I informed him of *Thoris*
arrival and that he had *Lavros* in tow. I already knew how Milos
would respond.

'Catastrophe, the lunchtime could get very interesting.'

'What was that?' Chris enquired.

'I said catastrophe, *Thoris* is here, with his best mate *Lavros*. Tell
him Youth.'

I explained to Chris that on Sundays it was not unusual for
*Thoris* to turn up for a very long lunch session with a few of his
family and mates, which generally included *Lavros*. They would sit
at the table at the end of the terrace, directly overlooking the bay
and would shout up all manner of food and drink, whilst doing a
very good Greek version of talking rubbish. I went on to further
explain that *Lavros* was a little "different" and that the Greek
system for dealing with mental illness was somewhat laissez faire,
especially when it came to diagnosis and that the support

mechanism, just like the pensions was a tad generous.

Early in his formative years *Lavros* had worked out that playing this system, when it came to mental illness could be a very nice way to avoid having to earn a living and adopted a persona that could only be described as bonkers. Initially this plan worked well, with his seemingly innate ability to act as if he'd lost the plot. Before long he was living fully at the behest of a very lucrative mental health order. The only problem with this was that the longer it went on the more accustomed he came to acting strangely and before long had lost the ability to separate the play acting from the reality of life. The line between normality and madness was now completely blurred, but fortunately his close friends, including *Thoris,* had worked out a way to keep a semblance of control. Finally, I told him to expect some madness!

Following a bout of shouting and hollering from the kitchen *Pavlos* appeared and made his way over to join us. He was shaking his head and chuckling away to himself. He lit an *Assos*, took a sip on his *raki* and turned to Milos.

'Ah Miles, big problem today for lunch.'

'Indeed, the Youth told me *Thoris* was here, with *Lavros*. I heard all the shouting. What's happening?'

*Pavlos* took another sip 'Thoris* told *Lavros* that he had to bring some supplies to the *taverna* today, for me to cook for the special starters, for the English boat people.'

'Yes, the Youth told me about this, is there a problem?' Milos asked.

'It's ok, this is no problem, *Thoris* brings now to *Affroula*, but *Lavros*, when he heard this he decides he should bring something special as well. That was what all the shouting was about. You will see.' *Pavlos* explained with a chuckle.

Shortly thereafter *Thoris* appeared from the kitchen, followed by *Lavros*. They made their way over to our table, greeted us accordingly and then parked themselves at their Sunday table. Before doing so *Lavros* decided that he should help himself to our *retsina* and duly took the bottle with him. *Pavlos* simply shook his head.

They settled at their table and commenced the "talking rubbish". After around ten minutes another truck pulled up and three guys got out. All instantly recognisable. There was *Thoris* son-in-law, *Thassos*, *Giorgios*, a builder from *Arginonda* and *Nikolas*, a teacher who lived over in *Pallionisos*. They made their way over to *Thoris* table and settled themselves down for the afternoon. It would be no understatement to say the talking rubbish ratcheted up a notch or two. Over the next hour several *meze* dishes turned up at their table with the same turning up at ours. Suddenly *Lavros* got up and announced he was heading to the *korzina, (*kitchen*)* and upon arrival there followed an inordinate amount of shouting, shrieking and laughter. After around ten minutes *Lavros* re-appeared shouting the Greek equivalent of "dinner is served" and sat on this very nice silver salver was an extremely large, cooked pigs head, presented wearing sunglasses. The presentation got the reaction it deserved with looks of complete amazement all round, lots of shouting and laughter and all manner of Greek swearing which I decided I wouldn't translate.

*Lavros* proudly placed the tray at *Thoris'* table and announced he would carve. This was when the fun began. As much as he tried he could not get the carving knife to penetrate the pig. The more he tried, the more frustrated he became and the more everyone laughed. *Pavlos* shouted across to *Lavros* to ask him how long he had cooked it for and apparently he had it on the boil for three hours this morning. When arriving at the taverna *Affroula* had bunged it in the oven for another couple.

*Affroula* appeared with some side dishes and roundly chastised *Lavros,* telling him and all present that she had already told him that it should have been cooked low and slow for a very long time and that simply it wasn't cooked! A row followed with

*Affroula* suggesting he should put it back in the oven, but *Lavros* refused point blank and there it sat, on display for the next couple of hours with all manner of appendages being added to the poor creature's head. It was undoubtedly the strangest dinner companion ever to grace either the *taverna* or *Thoris'* Sunday lunch table.

You can imagine the reaction when Jane, Mary and Jen arrived for lunch. *Lavros*, ever the charmer decided that the best thing he could do was offer the pigs head as a photo opportunity. The ladies declined. The remainder of the lunchtime session was just as mad with *Lavros* visiting every table with his pig's head in tow, offering all manner of uses whilst *Thoris* and his mates continued to work their way through everything on the menu. The one thing that didn't happen was the eating of the said pig! In amongst all this madness, I suddenly remembered that I'd wanted to have a final chat with Chris about the impending dinner of love, but that would have to wait. The remainder of the day followed the standard routine.

We arrived as usual that evening for pinkles. Milos was ensconced in a rather large Dark and Stormy and Mary was gently sipping a gin and tonic. Jen, minus Chris was busy adorning the table with more nibbles.

'Blimey Jen, been on another shopping expedition have we. You must have cleaned the shop out of pistachios.' I asked.

'To be honest, it's more about a little book reading time, but they do seem to add a little "je ne sais quoi" to the evenings pinkles,' Jen replied, elegantly as ever and with a perfect French timbre.

'Well, whatever that means, fine and yes they are very moorish,' Jane commented.

'Where's Chris?' I asked.

'He was giving his leg a little more rest. It was playing up and he really didn't want to use his stick tonight. Hopefully it will have settled by the time he gets here.'

'Ok, Maria, your turn for the music tonight, what's your selection?'

'Oh, I don't know, let me think… how about a bit of Santana?'

'Supernatural or Shaman?' I asked.

'Miles?' Mary said as she looked imploringly to Milos for help.

'Is my name Maria?'

'No, but your good lady wife is asking for some assistance,' Jane remarked.

'Thankyou Pipe Up. I don't need your assistance. Supernatural it is.'

'Good call Milos, and whilst you're at it, you can assist on the drinks front, usual for me and Jane. It will be good practice for your waitering duties tonight.'

Milos stood up 'Ahh, I'd forgotten about that, catastrophe awaits.'

As Milos made his way inside to sort the drinks I hit the button and the sounds of Carlos drifted across the terrace. Whilst he was inside Chris turned up, minus the stick. I shouted out to Milos to sort him a little Dark and Stormy and we were soon all sat enjoying the vibe. On the basis that Chris was looking at one with himself I thought that this might be a good time to mention the bill.

I turned to Chris and Jen 'Just so you two know, tomorrow morning over breakfast I will be sorting the bill.'

'What does that mean?' Jen asked.

'Well. Like all things here there is a system. As you already know sorting *Pandalis* for the room is straightforward. Just go and see him tomorrow when suits and square him away. However, with *Pavlos* it's a little different. As much as we have tried over the past, Milos and I can't fathom how he works things out.'

'Can't you simply ask him' Chris softly enquired.

Milos responded 'In a word no. I work on the basis that as he is good enough to let us run a tab for two weeks and virtually have free run of the *taverna* I'm not going to quibble over his billing system. Besides, it will be dirt cheap.'

'Well maybe to you but what if we don't agree,' Chris replied.

'You want to argue with a *Michas*?' Milos rasped back.

I sensed this wasn't going the way I wanted.

'No, but you spend a lot of time up there when we are down the beach, am I paying for all your drinks? Chris asked accusingly.

Milos gave Chris his own version of a Chris stare. 'The *retsina* is three euros a bottle, hardly breaking the bank and the red wine, which your good lady has been sinking at a rate is twelve euros a bottle. I think it might be the other way round! And as for you paying for all my drinks shall I mention the investment?'

This definitely wasn't going the way I wanted.

I intervened, 'Let me explain before you two start World War three.' Milos' look said it all.

'*Pavlos* will give me a bit of paper with a number on it. I will do my usual and overreact and so the negotiations will begin, a little bit like when the Germans were negotiating with the Greeks over their austerity measures during the European debt crisis,'

'What?' asked Jane.

'Fuck me Youth, that's not quite the analogy I'd use,' Milos added.

'Yes ok, a little OTT but you know how it goes, like the time I adopted the Marlon Brando Godfather routine, with the paper serviettes stuffed in my mouth.'

'Oh yes that was really funny, until you realised Alberto was at the next table,' Mary said laughing.

'Indeed, I thought I was done for. Anyway, the point is it's all in the negotiations but ultimately it never comes out much different each year. My guess is 850 euros per couple for the two weeks which equates to 30 euros a day per person.'

'Oh gosh, that's very cheap.' Jen commented.

'Exactly,' Milos responded.

'Does that exclude all Milos' fags,' Chris sarcastically asked.

'Very funny and you can go fuck yourself!' Milos said followed by him announcing that he was heading up for dinner. I looked at

Jen and she raised her eyebrows and grimaced. Maybe tonight wouldn't be a good time for my final chat with Chris.

We made our way up to the *taverna* and to our usual table. It was great to see the terrace tables close to full, usual Sunday evening carnage I thought and following a quick scout of the tables I soon spotted the toffs.

*Pavlos* appeared. 'Ok tonight very busy. Miles and Iain, you look after the English boat people and maybe the two Swiss Italian boys, *Daxi*?'

'I wouldn't mind looking after them,' Jen said somewhat lasciviously.

'Sorry Jen, nothing personal but I reckon the Youths got more chance than you, if you know what I mean. Anyway, he still has to sort the bet out!'

'Ok Milos, you do the Toffs and I'll do "the boys", metaphorically speaking of course. Oh, and by the way when you sort their order tell them that I have arranged a special starter for them, a very traditional little *meze*. The rest of the meal they can pick for themselves.' Milos nodded.

'Ladies, as we are going to be busy tonight it's your job to sort our grub and Chris you're on drinks duty,'

'What was that?' Chris enquired.

I sensed he was currently in his own little space. 'I said what do you want to drink?'

I took the rest of the orders and made my way into the bar as Milos made his way over to the toffs' table. This would be fun.

'*Kalispera* captain, my name is Miles, remember me?' Milos announced himself, immediately grabbing the attention of the whole table, which was made up of four fellas and four fillies.

'Yes, indeed I do, you swam out to see us the other day with another chap to invite us for dinner here at the *taverna*. It was very nice of you. Do you remember Camilla?'

'Sorry, I didn't recognise you with your clothes on.'

The whole table giggled. 'Can I introduce my crew?' The captain asked.

'If you must, but don't expect me to remember the names. Very shortly I will be pissed!'

'Ah, ok then, so I'm Bertie by the way, I've already introduced Camilla, she's my girlfriend, then going round the table we have Ryan, his father is a banker in Singapore, his girlfriend Laila, then it's Fin, short for Finlay, does social media type stuff together with his girlfriend Hattie and finally Laurence, bit of an entrepreneur and his girlfriend Lottie, short for Charlotte. Us boys were all together at Eton.'

'Eton eh, would never have guessed. Right, you'll have noticed the *taverna's* busy so bad luck, you've got me for the service. Just so you know, any tip is paid in *retsina*. My mate over there Iain, he told me that when we swam out to see you he mentioned he would sort some "special" local starters and that Sunday is *katsidi* day, which, for those of you that don't speak Greek, and I'm guessing that's all of you, this means goat day. I highly recommend the goat stew, but just in case you want something else the other main dishes tonight is *moussaka, keftedes,* a sort of meatball dish, chicken or pork *souvlaki* and some fresh fish, which you have to go into the kitchen to pick, a tad expensive but very nice. I'll take your drinks orders and sort them and then I'll be having a fag before I take your mains. All *daxi*?'

'Fine sir, and we are all looking forward to the specials. Very important to do as the Romans do as they say when abroad,' Bertie replied.

Milos gave him a look of nonchalance and after sorting their drinks he returned to the table, grabbed an *Assos*, fiddled around in his top pocket, pulled out his lighter and sparked up.

'Fuck me they are proper posh. All the guys were at Eton together and the ladies are their girlfriends and very nice too I might add. You sorted "the boys" out Youth?'

2off2

'Yes, and I have persuaded them to have the special starters as well, they'll be right up their street. Oh, and by the way we are having them too. I presume you ladies have sorted the mains for us?'

'I'm very much looking forward to the special starters and we all thought that as it was our last Sunday we should feast on the goat, so it's stew all round,' Jen announced.

'Lovely,' I replied. Wait until they see the starters I thought.

'Miles, which one is the captain?' Chris asked. 'We should have a word about the ensign.'

Milos pointed to Bertie 'The geezer sat there, called Bertie. Turns out he stole the white ensign of his old man, a rear admiral in the Navy. Not quite Eton behaviour, but l like his style.'

'Not on in my books,' Chris declared.

I could sense Chris and Milos were more than a little agitated with each other. Fortunately, the shout went up from the Kitchen.

'*Ella* Iain, *Ella* Milos.' The unmistakeable shout from *Pavlos* for me and Milos to head to the kitchen.

We entered the kitchen to be met with three trays. Milos' reaction told me all I needed to know.

'Fuck me, this should be fun,' Milos declared.

'Ok Iain, this tray for you to take to the Italia boys. Miles this tray for you to take to the English people and I take this tray for the company.' *Pavlos* was grinning ear to ear.

We made our way out to the tables, holding the trays in the air. As we reached the tables I declared to all that the special starters were served, and we placed the trays on the table.

The first scream, from one of the English ladies in full plumb was 'Oh my fucking god!' with the second one, just as plummy 'I think I'm going to be sick!'

The Italia boys were next who just looked at the trays, then each other incredulously and then finally our table, which on the basis that both Jane and Mary had tried this delicacy before were simply laughing.

There sat on each tray was an array of roasted goat heads, fully laden with the brains, tongues, cheeks, and the eyes staring eerily at their waiting guests. I then announced that the little delicacies surrounding the heads and looking remarkably like chicken nuggets were in fact goat testicles!

This time the scream was from one of the English boys, also in full plumb 'No fucking way am I chewing on goats nuts.'

'Well Ryan, you expect us to chew on yours,' was the very witty comment from Laila.

The rest of the tables in the *taverna*, which were mainly occupied by Greeks found it all hilarious and *Pavlos* was already delivering them little trays of the specials.

The Italia boys were clearly made of sterner stuff and were tucking in whilst the toffs were still staring nervously. I made my way over to our table and asked Jane to follow me.

'Right you lot, this is my lovely wife Jane and she'll show you how it's done. *Pavlos*, the owner of the *taverna* would tell you that she eats like a Greek, with her mouth and not with her eyes. Show them Jane,'

They all watched as Jane fearlessly leant forward, pulled at one of the eyes and popped it into her mouth. I grabbed one of the testicles and in it went. All was going well until Milos decided to join in, pulled at one of the eyes, popped it in his mouth and on commencement of chewing, gagged and ran to the little sloped garden area alongside the terrace and gobbed it out. The lady who thought she was going to be sick ran for the toilet.

Slowly things began to settle and with some more coercion and perhaps not wanting to upset their hosts the English table finally got stuck in, soon realising that in fact these delicacies were quite tasty. As for our table and knowing Chris and Jens penchant for food it was no surprise to me that everyone was tucking in.

*Pavlos* appeared and reminded me and Milos that we were on waitering duties and that he needed the orders for the main

courses for our tables. Before we got up I told Milos to ask his
table if they fancied a little bit of fun after dinner, a little bit of the
left, right, centre game of chance and if so I would show them the
ropes. He thought this would be a great idea and I would see if
the Italia boys fancied joining in. Off we went and fulfilled our
duties. On returning Milos advised that after a very simple
explanation of the game the English table said they were up for
that and said to pass on their thanks for "the specials".

'Do the Italia boys fancy joining in?' Milos asked, 'Oh and by
the way, any the wiser on the bet?'

'No, they just want to watch, I think you put them off after
you played Jenga with *Sascha*. And on the bet front I didn't ask,'
which was true, 'and I'm still no wiser,' which was a lie!

After Miles and I delivered our respective tables' main courses
we re-joined Chris and the ladies to ready ourselves for the main
event, the goat stew. I had decided that after missing the
opportunity to talk to Chris at lunchtime that I would park
myself next to him for dinner tonight and duly settled myself
down. I was still mindful of the chat
with Jen in *Vathi* and thought I would simply focus on Chris'
reflections on the holiday.

The goat stew arrived, and everybody tucked in. It was superb.
I thought I would bide my time and let them enjoy the food
before entering the fray. After around ten minutes I decided I was
good to go.

'Chris, only one more day, in the evening the dinner of love
and then the holiday will be over. Has it lived up to your
expectations?' I asked.

Chris looked at me, it was a look of disdain. 'Let me have a
little think on that and I'll come back to you.' I soon realised that
this had nothing to do with my question but simply that I was
disturbing his final demolition of the goat.

'Ok, so same question to you Jen,' I knew Chris would be all ears.

'When you first invited us out here and having heard Miles constantly talk about his "art of doing nothing", I expected a very quiet holiday. Nothing could have been further from the truth. I certainly didn't expect all your so called "plans", but frankly it has exceeded all my expectations. I've had a truly wonderful time and now I'm just looking forward to your so-called dinner of love.'

'Ok, but any particular highlights?' I asked.

'I'd have to think more about that before answering. What I would say is that the whole experience has been quite intoxicating.'

'Chris, you ready to proffer up your thoughts now?' He leant back, clearly happy that he had now given the goat a good going over. He looked at Jen and then me. I wondered where he would go.

'I've been massively taken aback, and this place is truly mesmerising. I have to say that when you invited us out here I was a little unsure about coming. Jen knows this.'

I noticed Jen raise her eyebrows 'Well honey, I would say it was a little stronger than unsure.'

Chris gave her one of his stares 'Well the thought of sitting all day watching Miles drink and smoke until he falls over was not high on my bucket list of things to do or my idea of a holiday. But like Jen, the way things have unfolded, right from the start when we arrived at the port, and you mentioned the "soft gold". I had no expectations of these things and blimey, some of the experiences have really got me thinking.' He took a sip of *retsina* and continued.

'Your plans, now they have really played on my mind.' I held his stare, wondering if this would be the moment. Jen looked a little uncomfortable.

'You've given me a few hints here and there but have never really set out what the plans were leading to.'

I jumped in quickly, 'Not strictly true Chris, I made it very clear from the start when I told you about the "soft gold" that there was a story here I wanted you to witness. Early in the holiday, when I outlined most of the plans I said they were all leading towards the dinner of love.'

Chris interrupted 'Yes, yes I get that, but what's the purpose of all this, who are the plans really for, what outcome do you expect?' He was now giving me one of his stares. I leant back whilst still engaging his stare. I was determined not to go where he wanted, not yet anyway.

'Look Chris, I expect the dinner of love to define this holiday and my plans. As it is tomorrow I believe you will get your answer then. Let me just remind you of some key moments for you to muse on. This is for you Jen as well?'

'I am all ears.'

'This island, you've now seen that behind the splendour and beauty lies a tragic past. It reminds me that sometimes in life all is not what it seems. The people of this island, you've witnessed how this tragedy has played out in their lives. How it has shaped the way they are today. Yet despite all of this at the heart of everything they do is love, for each other, for family, for friends and for the *Kalymnian* way of life. You have witnessed the dance of the *Mihanikos*, a painful reminder of that tragedy but what that dance really speaks of is hope, of never giving up and accepting that life is not about being wrapped up in cotton wool.' I stopped, filled my glass. I hadn't noticed but Miles, Mary and Jane were also listening intently.

'And Thassos, what can I say. When I first met him, and he told me his story I'm not embarrassed to say I cried. You Chris will know from your time with him that he doesn't cry for himself, he is selfless. And what of his frailties? Does he wallow in the mire of them or seek pity? No, he doesn't because this is not his way, this is not how *Kalymnian's* live. However, if there is one thing from his story that strikes at the heart, it's the sacrifice he made for love!' I focused on Chris 'The poignancy of his dinner of love with

Theodora should be etched in your mind.' I took another drink.

I looked at everyone round the table staring at me expectantly 'That is enough for tonight and I'll explain a little more at pinkles tomorrow, suffice to say I have a question for all of you. Not for you to answer now but to muse on ready for tomorrow night.' I took my time to engage eye to eye with each of them.

'What does to love mean to you?'

The table was silent. 'Right before any of you get carried away let's leave it there and get on with tonight's business, getting the Toffs pissed. If any of you lot want to join in come on over.'

'Well, I might like to watch' Jen declared. That will go down well I thought.

'Anyone else?' I asked.

'Youth, I'll give that a swerve. I've finished the service and am going to stick at what I do best. Besides, I've seen the sort of carnage that evolves playing that game!' Milos wisely said.

'Not for me,' Chris added

'Jane?'

'I might come over in a while, but for now I'll keep Mary and Chris company.'

'What about me Vera?' Milos remonstrated.

'You'll be off with *Pavlos* and "the boys",' Jane knowingly responded.

'Fair cop Vera.'

I made my way over to the Toffs table with Jen in tow, introduced her and announced that it was time for a little bit of fun. I noticed that a few of them already looked a few sheets to the wind and that they would be ideal candidates for the game. I explained that I needed around five to six people as any more made it a tad difficult to manage and those five to six needed to be sat in close proximity. After a little discussion we had five willing volunteers. I then announced that whenever we played this game *Pavlos'* son *Nikolas* liked to play and on the basis of us having just five volunteers we would rope him in.

'*Ella Nikolas, Ella,*' I shouted

*Nikolas* came to the table 'We are playing Left, Right, Centre.

You joining us?'

'Ah yes, this you know I like,' *Nikolas* replied.

'Great.'

I then asked everyone to shuffle around and announced that I would sit at the head of the table to monitor proceedings. Once everyone was settled I explained the rules.

'Right, I am giving you all three coins and in the middle of the table is a pot. I have three large dice and on these dice are various letters, not in Greek I may add. The letters are L for left, R for right, C for centre and K for keep. The game is very simple, you throw the dice and whatever comes up on the three dice you follow by distributing your coins. So, let me give you a quick example.'

I threw the dice. 'Ok so I have L, L and K. On this basis I would give two of my coins to the person on the left and keep the third coin. I'll do one more roll.'

I threw the dice again 'R, L and C. On this basis I give one of my coins to the person on the left, one to the person on my right and the C one goes in the pot. All nice and simple yes?'

'I think we can all manage that,' Camilla announced, 'But how do you win?'

'You don't, there is only a loser and that's the last person with a coin,' I explained.

Ryan interrupted 'All seems a bit pointless to me.'

'Well Ryan if you let me finish. The loser then has to take the "Punishment" drink.'

'What's one of those?' Hattie asked in her best plum.

'It's whatever I decide to put in the middle of the table,' I confirmed. I could see *Nikolas* grinning.

'*Nikolas*, sort everyone with the coins and I'll be back.'

I headed into the bar. We had played this game many times, with various guests over the years and using the stash of spirits and liqueurs in *Pavlos* bar. I had perfected any number of punishment drinks that were either highly potent or frankly nothing short of disgusting.

I made my way back to the table and placed the punishment drink by the coin collection pot

'What is that?' Laila exclaimed, clearly disturbed at the content of the glass.

'Let's hope you don't find out,' I stated.

As ever the game started very quietly with the players dutifully rolling the dice and placing their coins in line with the corresponding letters. Within a short time, *Nikolas* being a veritable expert started the shouting. If someone next to him was shuffling the dice either to his left or right he would shout "no left" or "no right". If he was shuffling the dice he would shout "Centre, Centre" or "No Keep". His involvement did the trick and before long all the players were following suit, which with their plummy accents was very funny. The shouting got louder as the coins moved left, right, were kept, or disappeared into the pot. As the coins diminished the realisation of what was waiting for the loser intensified until the first round culminated with Camilla being our first loser.

The cheers were followed with a very colloquial 'Oh my fucking God' from Camilla.

I reminded her that the punishment drink had to be downed in one, with the empty glass being held upside down above her head as she exclaimed "*Yammas* you bastards". She duly obliged and whilst *Nikolas* dished out the coins for the next round I went to the bar to replenish the glass.

This went on for the next two hours with each round getting more raucous and each punishment drink a little more repugnant.

The Italia boys, along with a few others had joined Jen to witness the carnage and join the cheering. As ever when we played this game some people seemed to have good luck and some bad luck. Tonight, the bad luck fell on Camilla and Hattie and whilst most players got a taste of a punishment drink they got a very hefty share of the prize!

By the time Bertie the Captain had decided enough was enough most of the players were pissed. He voiced his concern as to how he was going to get some of his crew back on the boat and frankly I could see his predicament. Camilla, because of her bad luck was in the toilet making a very unedifying noise and Hattie was draped across *Nikolas* declaring her undying love! The remaining boys announced their desire to continue partying and were asking *Nikolas* where the nearest club was. *Pavlos*, ever the wise host decided this would not be a good idea and declared he was closing shortly. But before doing so he would help Bertie with the obvious predicament of getting his crew safely back on board their yacht. As they noisily made their way down to their tender we all decided it was time for bed. We never encountered the Toffs again!

# CHAPTER THIRTEEN

## THE DINNER OF LOVE

It was Monday morning, our last day in *Emporios* and despite last night's shenanigans I awoke feeling unblemished. As I looked over towards Jane she was still asleep with just a cotton sheet draped across her lower half. Her body was now carrying a beautiful bronze hue and she looked ravishing. As it was our last morning I thought we ought to share a final intimate moment. I gently woke her up and we had a wonderful, slow lovemaking session and afterwards just lay in each other's arms, enjoying the peace and serenity of this beautiful place. At around 8.30am we decided it was time for a shower and jumped in together. Another great pleasure I enjoyed when spending time with Jane in *Emporios*.

After towelling ourselves Jane sat in front of the mirror, it was make-up time.

'Can I ask you a question?' Jane asked as she peered closely at her reflection.

'Of-course, what's on your mind?'

'You know the question you asked last night, about love. Why did you ask all of us? I thought all these plans of yours were aimed at Chris and Jen?'

'Yes, that's true and originally I planned for the dinner of love to be just for Chris and Jen. But over the last two weeks there have been a number of incidents that have led me to believe that leaving Jen on her own won't draw out the answer she needs.'

Jane turned to look at me 'And what answer is that?'

'You remember how this all started when they came down for the weekend.'

'Yes.'

'And on the Friday night you and Chris went to bed and left me and Jen downstairs.'

'Yes, to finish off the Port!, get on with it,' Jane said impatiently.

'Indeed, and very nice it was too. In amongst all the talk and the tears, I asked Jen what I called the big question.'

'No, I don't remember you telling me that bit. And it was?' She asked inquisitively.

'Well, I said I would keep it between me and her, but in essence I asked if it was all over for her.'

Jane looked a little shocked. 'I didn't realise you got that deep.'

'I didn't intend to, it just kind of happened. However, her answer was not a simple yes or no. She said if she could get back the Chris of old, the person she fell in love with, then she could see a way through.'

'Okay so what happened next?'

'We left things at that but when I came to bed I had one of my thinking moments. I've known Chris a long time and it's struck me that he carries the burden of some of his decisions that have shaped his life uneasily. That's when *Thassos* came to mind. I thought about his story, the decisions he had made, how they had changed and shaped his life. I thought about the similarities between them, but also the main difference.' I paused. I wanted to get the right words for this.

'And?'

'That *Thassos* lost the one thing that he cherished above all things. I thought that Chris should hear his story, should understand the decisions he made and the terrible impact it had made on his life. The sacrifice he made for love and that this was his decision. I want Chris to have an epiphany, to realise that his sometimes malevolence towards Jen, the one thing that at his stage in life that he should treasure above all is going to be lost if he carries on, but unlike *Thassos* it's not going to be his decision.'

'Blimey, I really wonder sometimes how your mind works. A couple of questions though, why do you think this is something you should get involved in? Don't you think Chris will resent that?'

'On your first question, I've known Chris and Jen a long time, must be getting near forty years. They are good friends and if I get this right not only will they have had a great experience but can look forward to an assured future. On your second question I didn't think so originally but probably now it's a yes.' I paused again.

'Let me re-phrase that, never mind think, or probably, definitely yes.'

Jane interrupted 'That sounds very definitive, and on what basis?' She asked as she picked up her hairbrush and set to sorting her hair.

'Things Jen has said. We've had a few chats. I wanted to see how things were progressing with Chris. I knew Chris wouldn't open up to me, so I've been using her to gauge where he's at.'

Jane interrupted again 'So what did she say to make you so sure that Chris will resent your involvement?'

'Ok, so usual rules apply, just you and me on this' I insisted as I sat down on the bed next to the dresser where Jane was perched.

She turned to face me, 'Yes.' She said inquisitively.

'You know when we were down at *Vathi*, on the bikes. Me and Jen went for a swim and you and Chris had a coffee.'

'Yes.'

'We didn't swim for very long. She said she had something to tell me. In one of their chats Chris asked her who she thought my plans were really for.'

'Well, I don't see how you get resentment from that.' She said as she softly brushed her damp hair.

'Wait a minute, wait a minute. He then said it looked like the plans were for me and her, to spend time together and wait for it, he asked her whether we were we having an affair!'

'Bloody hell, that's ridiculous, how did he get that?' Jane exclaimed.

She looked at me and frowned 'You're not are you?'

'Bloody hell, now who's being ridiculous. Apart from the facts that we live 120 miles apart and I see her once in a blue moon I am very happily married thank you. '

'Yes I know, but I had to ask,' Jane said as she reassuringly placed her hand on my knee.

'What did you say to Jen?'

'I told her that was typical of Chris at the moment, trying to deflect the issue away from him. Furthermore, based on his past exploits I thought it was a bit rich. In some ways it's helped as I've got a clearer picture of where he's at and as I said earlier it's helped me shape the way the dinner of love should be.'

'And what was Jen's reaction to this revelation?'

'Pretty typical, she said in her inimitable way that whilst the thought was nice some things are best left as fantasy.' Jane and I laughed.

'Do you think he'll say something tonight?' Jane asked looking a little worried.

'Who knows? But if things go the way I plan, I suggest not. That's why I am getting everyone to answer the question.' I grabbed Jane's hand. 'I'll be leaving him in no doubt about my views on love.'

'Ahhh, now I see and how nice,' Jane said as she squeezed my hand.

'You haven't heard my answer yet,' I said mockingly and gave her a big hug.

'Let's get ourselves sorted. I want a nice quiet day ready for tonight.'

I had already decided that I would have a day on the beach with Jane. We had a very nice leisurely breakfast at the *taverna* with the company and I told them that other than lunch Jane and I were going to spend the day lazing on the beach and as normal, they were welcome to join us. Surprisingly, Milos agreed that this was a great idea and Chris and Jen followed suit. I also told them that I didn't want to discuss anything more regarding the dinner of love until I kicked off proceedings with a special pinkles at 8pm. We spent the day sunbathing, reading, swimming, unloading the ballast tanks and generally talking rubbish. As it was a Monday we had the beach to ourselves with only the odd yacht mooring up to *Pavlos'* buoy to disturb the peace. Lunch followed its usual routine followed by our return to the beach. At one stage in the afternoon a solitary seagull landed on a nearby rock which Mary christened "Nobby no mates". Milos spent half an hour gently sneaking his way towards him to see how close he could get only for me to launch a huge boulder near to the rock causing Nobby to take flight and Milos to declare I was a twat! So much for the "art of doing nothing".

As the shade hit the beach and the sun started on its inexorable way towards sunset we decided it was time to call it a day. On the slow walk up to the hotel I suggested that as we were not eating at *Pavlos'* tonight we would have pinkles at his, which also meant we could settle the bill. I also reminded Jen that she should sort *Pandalis* for the room. As we made our way up to our room I told Jane that when she had a little doze I would get myself sorted early and pop down and pay *Pandalis*. I told her I also needed to drop down into the village to see *Evdokia* at *Harrys*, and *Giorgos* and *Ireni* at the *Artistico,* to sort some final arrangements for tonight's dinner of love.

I had a quick shower, put on one of my favourite flowery shirts, twinned with my blue Ted Baker trilby, gave Jane a quick kiss as she lay dozing on the bed and headed down to see *Pandalis*. As ever the transaction with *Pandalis* was quick and simple. He grabbed his old-fashioned calculator, did a quick sum on it, and showed me the result. Same as ever I said, handed over the ready prepared sum of cash and he handed me two tins of *mela, (honey)* which I said I would pick up on the way back. I set off for the village. The temperature had cooled, and I took in the simple joy of the slow walk from the *Asteri* to the village square. I didn't bother reminiscing over this final walk of the holiday. It wasn't needed, I knew I would be coming back. I popped in to the *Artistico* first. *Giorgos* and *Ireni* were busying themselves ready for the night's service. I persuaded them to have a ten-minute break and join me for a drink. They confirmed everything was ok for tonight and they would see me later as planned. I then made my way across the square and took the back route to *Harrys*. The *taverna* was quiet, but I knew where *Evdokia* would be. I made my way through the *taverna* and to the entrance of the kitchen and sure enough there she was, slaving away with *Maria, Thoris'* daughter, preparing the evening's fayre. They didn't spot me at first and I decided to watch. They were great friends, having grown up together in the village, and whenever I saw them working in the kitchen they would be laughing, gossiping, and generally enjoying both each other's company and the tasks ahead of them.

'Ella Evdokia, Ella Maria, Yassas,' I called out. They both turned and I was greeted with their beaming smiles followed by the usual shrieks. They downed tools and made their way over.

'Iain *mou*, Iain *mou*, how are you?' *Evdokia* asked as she grabbed my hand.

'I am well, like the hair colour.' She had a penchant for dying her hair all manner of colours and the current vogue was a kind of deep purple.

'Ah Iain, always commenting on my hair. You never comment on *Maria's*'.

'That's because she doesn't do anything daft with it!' *Maria* laughed.

'Everything ok for tonight?' *Evdokia* asked.

'Yes, yes, I just thought I'd pop in to make sure everything was ok with you and to let you know the arrangements.'

'Everything is fine, the menu just as you asked. It's so exciting and special to be holding a dinner of love. *Maria* and I were talking about it this morning.' She looked at *Maria* 'We thought maybe we should get *Dimitris* and *Thassos* to follow your lead,' *Evdokia* said jokingly.

'I'm not sure your husbands are the romantic types.' They both laughed as *Maria* made her way back to the kitchen.

'Ok so we'll be looking to get here for 9pm, maybe a little cocktail and then the special *meze* to begin at 9.15. I have arranged a little surprise for around 10.15.pm, Is that ok?'

'Yes, yes that should give us plenty of time,' She confirmed.

'Will your mum be about?' I enquired.

'Yes, I have told her you are coming and about the dinner of love. She was so pleased that you know about these things and the *Kalymnian* ways. She is very fond of you all.'

'That's nice, she is a lovely special lady. We will raise a glass to her tonight and of course to *Harry*.'

'She will like that.' *Evdokia* responded smiling.

I grabbed her other hand, leant forward, and gave her a little kiss on the cheek. 'Thank you *Evdokia*, I am so looking forward to tonight, see you later,'

'*Daxi* Iain, see you later.'

As she made her way back to the kitchen I decided to leave by the main entrance, which meant I could walk across the terrace and through the garden. *Harrys* Paradise was a very apt name for the *taverna*. *Evdokia's* parents *Haralambos* (Harry for short) and *Aleka*, spent many years turning the *taverna*, the terrace and the garden into a veritable oasis, that whenever I visited gave me a complete sense of serenity. I couldn't think of a better setting for the dinner of love.

*Aleka* had carefully positioned and planted olive and tamarisk trees, creating a natural green canopy across the whole area. In between and intertwined with the trees were many *Bougainvillea* and *Olianda* plants that when in bloom provided a wonderful backdrop of colour and fragrance. The little pathways through the garden were marked by pristine whitewashed stones and all manner of bric a brac and pastel painted plant pots added to the shabby but chic nature of the restaurant. Once darkness descended upon the garden the loops of soft golden lights hidden amongst the trees and the small lamps and jasmine candles provided a wonderful ambience that truly matched anywhere else I had ever been. As quick as a click of the fingers the rasping noise of the *cicadas* would fill the evening air and then just as quickly dissipate. The only thing missing these days was *Harry*, who had sadly died some fifteen years ago. I would give Chris and Jen a taste of his rumbunctious character later.

The other great decision *Harry* and *Aleka* made was to send *Evdokia,* when she was eighteen, off to work around Europe to learn to cook. This had given her the skills and ability to take the very traditional and basic recipes of the island and use her experience of the Mediterranean to transform them into wonderful, elegant, and truly scrumptious dishes. Her version of a Greek *meze* was really something to behold.

Just as I made my way under the entrance arch and onto the road I nearly walked straight into *Thassos'* unmistakable Mazda as it went by. It was unusual to see him more than once whenever we were here, but I didn't have time to catch his gaze which was a shame, maybe next year. I made my way back along the beach road and up to the hotel. Climbing the steps towards our room I noticed Chris was sitting out on his balcony.

'What time did you say pinkles was?' he asked.

'8pm and don't forget they are up at the *taverna* tonight. I've just been down the village to finalise the plans for tonight. You and Jen will love *Harrys*.'

'Yes, I'm looking forward to it. Did you see Jen down there?' Chris enquired.

'Didn't spot her matey, but maybe she's on the beach. I only popped into the *Artistico* and *Harrys*. I imagine she'll be back soon if she's going to get ready for tonight. See you in a while. I'm going to be up there a little earlier, I have my negotiations with *Pavlos* for the bill!.'

As I made my way up the final flight of stairs I could just imagine what Chris was thinking. Jen down the village, me going down there as well. Would fit in perfectly with the little picture he had created of our so-called trysts. Not my problem I thought and anyway tonight would take care of that. I made my way into the room and Jane was close to ready.

'How do I look,' she asked as she did a little sashay.

'As beautiful as *Harry's* Garden, a real picture.'

'Aaaaww, how romantic.' She grabbed me and we embraced.

'All sorted for tonight?'

'Yes, all the plans are in place.'

'I'm really looking forward to tonight, apart from one thing,' She had her worried look.

'And?'

She grimaced 'You and your bloody questions. I'm not very good at articulating or sharing my emotions.'

'You'll be fine, say it as it is, nice and simple,' I said reassuringly.

'Ok, but what about Chris, how will he respond following your little revelation.'

'Only one person knows the answer to that question. Should be interesting though,' I replied.

'For whom?'

'A very wise question and I'm sure all will be revealed. You ready?'

'As I'll ever be,' Jane said with a slightly nervous tone.

We made our way up to the *taverna*. We passed Chris and Jen's balcony and whilst the doors were open there was no sign of them.

As we made our way past Milos and Mary's terrace I peered inside their open door to see Mary doubled over, in just her knickers attempting to pull up her dress.

'Very nice Mary, I didn't realise there was a full moon tonight!'
Mary shrieked which prompted Milos to appear from the shower.
'What's happening?' he enquired.
'It's Iain, he passed by just as I was bent over and pulling up my dress,' Mary explained.
'Milos, you should warn her about that.' I suggested.
'About what?' he enquired.
'Trying to smuggle that amount of crack into the country!'
'Iain, that's terrible,' Jane declared.
'And also very funny,' Milos added laughing. 'You're a tad early' he noted.
'We're heading up to the *taverna*, to sort the bill. See you up there. Love you Mary,' I shouted as we moved on.
'Yes, thanks Iain, love you too,' she replied sarcastically.
We made our way to our table. The *taverna* was empty although we could hear action in the kitchen. I made my way into the bar and sorted drinks for me and Jane. I stuck my head in the kitchen.
'*Kalispera Pavlos, Kalispera Affroulla*, you two ok?'
'Yes, everything ok. I thought you said 8pm for the drinks,' *Pavlos* said
'I did, but I thought I would have an early one and you and I can sort the bill.'
'Ah yes, I will come and join you.'
I made my way back out to the terrace, gave Jane her drink, sat down and contemplated the wonderful vista in front of me and the night ahead.
'*Yammas* Vera'
'*Yammas* darling'
'Here's to us and a great evening,' I said as I leant over and gave Jane a little kiss. *Pavlos* appeared and joined us at the table. Pulled out

an Assos, lit up and took a deep sigh.

'A big night for you yes, the dinner of love. Maybe a dinner of catastrophe?' he said laughing.

'We shall see and talking of catastrophes what's the bill?'

*Pavlos* reached inside his pocket and pulled out a piece of paper. This was his standard approach.

'Ok Iain, I have worked everything out and the bill for six people is here,' he said, ashen faced as ever when it came to the bill time.

'Does this include the cigarettes for Milos?' I cheekily enquired.

'No, separate bill for Miles,' He responded still straight faced.

I opened the piece of folded paper and gasped. I stared in silence at *Pavlos*.

'*Pavlos*, are you serious? I asked.

'Yes, yes this is the system.'

'Then I think you've made a mistake,' I said looking as stern as possible.

'No, no this is for everything.' He confirmed.

I turned to Jane, 'What is it Iain?' she asked looking a little concerned.

'It's bloody cheap, that's what it is.' I exclaimed.

*Pavlos* look had changed 'Ah maybe I added it up wrong, I look.'

'No, no *Pavlos*, as you said this is the system,' I said staring at him until I could hold on no longer and burst out laughing.

'Ah *malaka, (*wanker) this is what you call a… a wind up?' he said as he started to laugh.

'Yes *Pavlos*, this is my system. The bill is fine but maybe you wind up Milos with the cigarettes, yes?'

'Good idea,' *Pavlos* said. After we hatched a plan he got up and made for the kitchen.

'How much then?' Jane asked.

'About usual, works out roughly 890 euros per couple for the two weeks,'

'Blimey it' so cheap,' Jane said.

'Let's hope Chris thinks so, as it won't be a great start to the night otherwise'.

We looked over as we heard Miles, Mary, Chris, and Jen making their way up the stairs and across to the terrace.

I stood up. 'Ladies, you look stunning,' and they did. 'And you boys haven't made a bad effort either. Take a seat.'

'A drink would be in order Youth.'

'Patience old fellow.'

*Pavlos* appeared, for once perfectly on time brandishing a silver salver loaded with a bottle of champagne and six fluted glasses.

'Oh, how wonderful,' Jen declared.

'Yes, and so is the bill I hope,' Milos responded.

'As it happens folks, this is on me and Jane. A little last night gift.'

'That's very kind,' Mary commented.

'Our pleasure.' I replied as *Pavlos* passed out the glasses. He then opened the bottle and charged the glasses.

I stood up and raised my glass 'I'd firstly like to say a big thank you to *Pavlos* and the family for being, as ever, wonderful hosts. To *Pavlos* and the Family "*Yammas*"!'

'*Yammas Pavlos* and the family' we collectively shouted.

'By the way for those of you holding the purse strings, I have negotiated the bill and you all need to give *Pavlos* the princely sum of 890 euros, and before you ask that is per couple.'

'Blimey, that's cheap' Jen declared.

'Correct and by the way there isn't a bill and it's cash only!' I added and *Pavlos* laughed.

'I can also confirm that it doesn't include Milos' fags.' I gave *Pavlos* the nod.

'Ah yes, Miles for the cigarettes for the two weeks 400 euros.'

'Oh my god Miles, how many cigarettes have you been smoking?' Mary said clearly concerned.

'Sounds like enough to keep the whole islands tobacco supplier in clover,' I commented.

Milos turned to *Pavlos*. 'Have I really smoked that much?' Clearly just as concerned.

'Nai, yes,' *Pavlos* replied biting his tongue before eventually bursting into laughter.

'*Malaka* Youth, this is your doing isn't it,' Milos barked.

'I may have mentioned something, anyway back to the toasts. So secondly, on behalf of Milos, Chris, and myself I would like to raise a glass to our wonderful ladies, in my view we are lucky to have you.'

'Chance would be a nice thing,' Milos lamented.

'Oh Miles, stop it,' Mary chided as Milos chuckled to himself.

'Now now you two, let me continue before the old fella ruins the moment. As I said, in my view we are lucky to have you and if ever this island tells you one thing, it's that family and love is at the heart of everything so *Yammas* Ladies,'

'*Yammas*' Milos and Chris responded. At least Chris was joining in.

'So lastly, I turn to the dinner of love. I have a few little things to say. I asked you all a question the other night, and I told you I would ask for your answer at tonight's dinner of love. I hope you feel you've had plenty of time to reflect on your answer and are ready to reveal your thoughts.

Just to remind you it was "what does love mean to you?" and just so you are clear, this about love for each other, not for family, not for friends and not for the love of life itself. I know these other forms of love are important but what is life without the special bond of a love shared between two people?'

'Christ youth, what have you been drinking. I didn't have you down as a romantic,' Milos interrupted somewhat sardonically.

'Well, I think that's rather lovely,' Jen responded.

'And I can assure you he's got a romantic streak.' Jane added.

'I knew you would Pipe Up!'

'Right Milos, that's enough for now, we'll have plenty of time later for your romanticisms on this so let's raise our glasses for the last time, the dinner of love.'

'The dinner of love,' resounded across the terrace.

Having quickly finished the bottle of champagne, we ordered another round of drinks and tucked into a little *meze* courtesy of *Pavlos*. On arrival of the *meze* Mary asked Jen where her nibbles were as she had spotted her heading down the village earlier. She gave a very quick dismissive response along the lines that there wasn't anything left in the shop worth having. At around 8.40pm I announced that we needed to leave in five minutes and that those paying the bill had a simple choice, do it now or very early tomorrow before we leave. Everyone decided now was a good time and having collected everyone's share I gave *Pavlos* his bounty. I could just imagine the good use this fat bag of cash would be put to, a few "shopping" trips no doubt. Although we would probably see *Pavlos* in the morning we said our fond farewells to the family.

We set off for the village and *Harrys*. We were accompanied by the usual warm breeze, the cackle of the cicada and Milos moaning about the walk, which was all of five minutes. I reminded him that the walk back, which included a few uphill moments was what he should be moaning about, but his simple response was that he would be pissed and wouldn't remember it. As Jane and I wandered down hand in hand I noticed that Chris and Jen were not following suit. I mentioned this to Jane, and she dismissed it as not relevant. I told her I was a little surprised, particularly as we were heading down for the dinner of love and perhaps Chris could show this as a little expression of their closeness.

As we made our way to the square Milos announced he was taking the back route. I told him we would be entering via the front entrance as I wanted Chris and Jen to experience the simple pleasure of the walk through the garden. Within a couple of minutes, we reached the entrance to *Harrys*. The vividly coloured welcome board adorned with flowers simply stated, "Welcome to

*Harry's* Paradise".

I asked Chris and Jen to wait a minute whilst we made our way to the *taverna* as I wanted them to experience the garden on their own. Jane and I made our way along the main path and onto the restaurants terrace. Milos and Mary were already seated and engaging in conversation with *Evdokia*.

'*Yassas Evdokia,*' I said to announce our arrival.

She turned towards us. '*Yassas* Iain, *yassas* Jane. Lovely to see you. I thought there was going to be six of you for dinner?'

'Yes, yes, Chris and Jen. They're just taking a little moment in the garden'.

'*Daxi,* now is the time for cocktails?' She politely asked.

'Yes indeed, you know the order, *epharisto',* (thanks)

'*Parakalo,* (you're welcome)' she said as she made her way into the *taverna.*

'Youth, what's the crack with the cocktails,' Milos asked as Jane, and I sat down.

'Don't worry Milos, I sorted the order earlier. You gotta love this place though, absolutely wonderful and paradise personified.'

'And look how she's set the table, with the lovely delicate tablecloths, the little heart mementos and the posy of flowers. It's so romantic,' Jane said.

'Well, it is the dinner of love,' I exclaimed.

'You ok Mary?'

'Yes, I love this place. We should have come here earlier in the holiday though,' Mary responded.

'I know but with all the plans and the dinner of love I thought the magic of the night wouldn't have been the same if we'd already been.' I explained.

'Fair shout Youth, but in terms of magic I hope you've got this right with Chris and Jen. Could be an interesting night!' Milos wisely stated.

'Best laid plans and all that, it's up to them. I intend to

thoroughly enjoy myself. I have to say I have no clue what sort of response we'll get from them on the question,'

'I'm more interested in Mary's response,' Jane cheekily added grinning at Milos.

'Don't you start Pipe Up. Anyway, my wife loves me.' Milos boldly declared.

Mary just smiled and then stuck her tongue out.

'Oh Iain, this place is simply wonderful,' Jen announced as she and Chris suddenly appeared from the garden.

'I can't take it all in. We've been up all the little paths and there are lots of little places to hideaway. Why didn't you bring us here before? I could have read to my heart's content sat in one of the little alcoves.'

'Yes, I know Jen, we were just talking about that. It's my fault, but the plans and the dinner of love. I needed this to be a special surprise.'

'You've definitely passed on that one, hasn't he Chris?'

'*Harry's Paradise* eh, they got that right when they named it,' Chris responded stoically as ever.

'Grab a pew,' I said.

Just as they were seating themselves *Evdokia* arrived with a tray laden with drinks.

I stood up '*Evdokia*, this is Chris, Miles' old school friend and his other half Jen.'

'Very nice to meet you both. 'I have the drinks' *Evdokia* announced.

'Cocktails, how wonderful, but we haven't ordered,' Jen stated.

'Don't worry, it's all sorted along with the grub.' I replied.

'I have two Dark and sSormys.'

'That Me and Milos.'

'Two Cosmopolitans.'

'Mary and Jen.' Jen gave me a knowing smile.

'A Harvey Wallbanger.'

'For Jane.'

'And lastly a Mojito'

'Chris.'

'Very nice,' said Chris.

'Ok, the *meze* will start shortly and then I will bring the red wine and *retsina*,' *Evdokia* said as she left for the kitchen.

'And make sure it's the cheap shit,' Milos shouted in her direction.

'Oh Miles, not tonight,' Mary scolded.

'What?'

'Right you lot, here's to a great evening, *Yammas*,'

'*Yammas,*' they responded.

As I sat down I turned to Chris and Jen 'We of course have had the pleasure of eating at this place many times. We were also fortunate enough for that to be when *Harry* was still alive. With his wife *Aleka* they created the vision for this place and I'm sure you'll agree that they've certainly delivered on that. *Harry* was quite a rambunctious character but in his later years spent most of his time sat at the table just in front of the *taverna*. Alongside the table he kept a barrel of *retsina* which he used to continually top up his glass. You can see why him, and Milos got on so well!' I took a long sip on my rather nice Dark and Stormy.

'So, before the food arrives I want Milos to give you a little taste of the character of *Harry* but please don't let it spoil your meal!' I said tantalisingly. 'Over to you Milos.'

'Ah' Milos exclaimed as he gave me a knowing glance. He pulled out an *Assos*, lit it and took a long draw.

'This little anecdote was not amusing to everyone who witnessed it, namely Maria and Jane.'

I could see on their faces, instantly, they knew what was coming.

'We were sat on that table just over there on the left,' he said pointing accordingly. 'Fortunately, the *taverna* wasn't particularly busy.'

Another long draw on the *Assos*. 'I think we were getting stuck into a little starter when *Harry* shouted across to us to keep still. We looked in his direction and he put his finger up to his lips. We also noticed he was reaching down the side of his chair and suddenly he pulled up a rifle. He lifted it, slowly took aim, which frankly looked to me that it was straight at us and pulled the trigger.'

We all ducked and heard 'Take that you bastard' and as we regained our composure *Harry* was belly laughing and pointing at a dead rat, that had the temerity to try and steal some food off the adjoining bird table!'

'Bloody Hell!' Chris exclaimed.

'Yes, there was a tad of blood around. *Harry* simply congratulated himself on a wonderful shot, put his rifle down and went about his normal business, re-filling his *retsina* glass. With this *Aleka* came running out of the kitchen and what followed was the classic Kalymnian shouting match followed by *Aleka* removing the said rat, apologising profusely and *Harry* acting as if nothing had happened.'

'Well, I suppose as he's no longer with us we won't be experiencing anything like that tonight,' Jen remarked somewhat hopefully.

'I can assure you that we are in for a very different treat tonight,' I replied.

And indeed, we were. We spent the next hour being treated to an absolute triumph of a meal. As the *meze* dishes arrived the joy on everyone's faces was only surpassed by their expressions as they tucked into each of the delightful treats laid before them. Chris was in complete overdrive gazing impatiently for each dish to be passed his way. Milos had clearly noticed this and was revelling in taking as much time as possible to serve out his portion and pass the plate on, always to the ladies first. The *retsina*, red wine and conversation was flowing, the soft music and the wonderful ambience of this little piece of paradise was already providing the perfect backdrop I had anticipated for our dinner of love.

Having delivered around eight wonderful dishes of food *Evdokia* announced that the next and final course would be a sweet dish and that she needed my assistance in the kitchen.

'What little surprise have you got in-store for us next?' Jane excitedly asked.

'You'll find out very shortly,' I said as I got up to follow *Evdokia* into the taverna. We had already agreed this would be her sign to tell me my next part of the plan for the evening was ready.

Inside the *taverna* were *Giorgos,* guitar in hand and *Ireni* as planned. I greeted them and asked if they were ready and if so we would head out to the table. They said they were, and I called out to *Evdokia* to ask if she was ready and she shouted 'yes, but one minute'.

She came out of the kitchen with a big smile. I asked her where the special pastries were, and she gestured behind her and *Aleka* appeared carrying an even bigger smile and a tray of pastries.

'*Aleka*, I was wondering where you were, what a lovely surprise and bearing gifts I see.'

'*Yassas* Iain *mou*, I am your waitress for this moment. Just like the old times eh,' she said in her beautiful, soft lilt. *Aleka* had adopted the island tradition of wearing black since the passing of Harry. However, it was no surprise that she followed her own interpretation of this. Always black, but always stylish and elegant and with her willowy frame she seemed to glide rather than walk.

'Shall we go and see our waiting friends?' Even I was getting excited.

'*Nai, nai*' they all responded.

We made our way out of the *taverna* and over to the table. Mary was the first to spot us and gave out a shriek of excitement, especially when she saw *Aleka*.

Mary got up and headed straight for *Aleka*, followed by Milos and Jane.

'Hang on a minute,' I shouted. 'Let her put the tray down.'

Once the tray was down *Aleka* and Mary warmly embraced with

Milos and Jane following suit. Jane's tears were already falling before she got to her, and I could see the commotion was not lost on the other guests.

I asked everyone to sit down and grabbed two chairs that *Evdokia* had placed for me near our table. *Evdokia* whispered in my ear that *Aleka* was aware of what was about to happen and wanted to sit and listen.

I looked around and saw a spare chair, grabbed it, and placed it next to Mary's.

'*Aleka*, as you have been so kind to deliver us such wonderful pastries, you must join us as we celebrate their arrival. Please take a seat with Mary.'

'I would love to, but only if that is ok with your other guests. These people I do not know,' she said gesturing towards Chris and Jen.

'Then so you shall and I'm so sorry *Aleka*, in all the commotion I forget my duties. This is Chris, Milos' old school friend and his partner Jen.'

*Giorgios* and *Ireni* were already sat waiting for my sign. Whilst all this was going on *Maria* and *Dimitri* were delivering pastries to all the other tables. It was time for me to do my thing.

I picked up a glass and a spoon, held it up and started tapping loudly to gather everyone's attention. It worked.

'*Signome, Signome*, and for those who don't speak Greek excuse me. I am sorry if I am breaking the peace and tranquillity of this wonderful night. My name is Iain, and I am here with my friends tonight to have a very special dinner. I simply want to invite you to witness a very special moment within this dinner and you will see you have been given a tray of delicate pastries. These have been made by our lovely hosts, *Evdokia* and *Maria* and are a gift from us, for allowing us to momentarily disturb your evening but to also allow you to be part of this special moment. I am sure you all know something of the *Kalymnian* sponge diving history and tonight we are re-enacting what was known as the dinner of love. This was a special ritual for families, friends, betrothed lovers, held around Easter just before the sponge fleet left *Kalymnos* to ply its trade. Over the years it became a dinner tinged with sadness and foreboding as the sea took its toll on the brave sponge hunters of *Kalymnos*.' The *taverna* was silent.

'These two wonderful people sat beside me, some of you may know are *Giorgos* and *Ireni*, from the *Artistico*. I wanted my friends and you all to witness a special song, associated with the dinner of love and they have kindly offered to sing it for us. Music and dance remain the traditional heartbeat of life in *Kalymnos* and many of the traditions around these songs bear witness to the tragedy of the hunt for what I call "Soft Gold". This particular song touched me when I first heard it, even more so when I understood the words. The delicate sweet gifts we have placed before you have great resonance in this song so please enjoy them. To all of you here tonight, to our wonderful hosts, to my dear friends sat here and last, but not least to all those touched in some way by the pain of loss, there is always love.' I paused.

*Kiries and Kirio,* (Ladies and Gentlemen) I give you "A Taste of Heaven".

Just as before when they sang for Jen in the *Artistico* the same ritual began. *Giorgos* announced that as this dinner was for us, tonight *Ireni* would sing this song in English. The *taverna* remained silent as *Giorgos* began playing, softly and intently, once again as if this music was the heart of his soul. The acoustic hum drifted beautifully across this paradise setting. *Ireni* had closed her eyes and was gently swaying in her chair, letting the emotion of the moment build. I let my gaze wander around the table and could see the intensity in Jen's face. Jane's hands were resting on the table. I made a very deliberate gesture of resting my hand on hers. I wanted Chris to see this moment. I glanced at *Aleka*, I could already see this was touching her. *Ireni* began:

Pastries drowned in milk and honey
I prepare for the bridal feasts
Milk is like the galaxy
That you sail above, alone
When they found you in the sea
Were your final thoughts of me
In your arms I tasted heaven
But you left me for the deep
Syrup oozes from the pastry
As seawater from a sponge
They found you bound in ropes and weeds
In your arms a diving stone

For a moment silence. *Giorgos'* gaze transfixed on *Ireni*. They didn't need words. Suddenly the silence was broken with rapturous applause and shouts of *bravo,* whistling and whooping. I had kept my eyes on Jane throughout the song, again deliberately. Her tears started way before *Ireni* finished, but that was Jane. As I looked around she was not alone. Jen, just as in the *Artistico* was clearly emotionally shaken by this beautiful lament and *Aleka* and Mary were hugging. Even the old fella had a tear in his eyes. I glanced at Chris, and he just seemed lost as to how to deal with the moment.

*Giorgos* stood up 'Iain, thank you for letting us be part of this. I hope you enjoyed.' I made my way round to him.

'No, thank you *Giorgos* and thank you *Ireni*, that was magical.'

I hadn't noticed, *Aleka* had left her seat and was suddenly beside me.

She gently grasped my hand 'Iain *mou*, that was wonderful. This dinner of love, so many memories filled my mind. This history is special to us, and I thank you for keeping it alive. Ah if *Harry* were here... he would have loved that.'

'I know, and this wonderful place, all of your making has made it a very special evening.' We embraced and she kissed me gently before heading back to the kitchen with *Giorgios* and *Ireni*.

I sat back down and as I looked around the *taverna* the other guests were eagerly tucking into their little pastries. As I caught their eyes a few of them nodded in appreciation with the odd one mouthing *yammas*.

'Well Youth. That's one of your plans that definitely hit the spot. I wasn't expecting that, made me quite emotional.' Milos said breaking the silence.

'Yes, it was lovely to hear *Ireni* sing, I was really disappointed when we missed her singing at the *Artistico*' Mary added.

'How did you know about that song? It was perfect for tonight, and the words were so fitting. All I could think about was *Thassos* and it instantly made me cry,' Jane said.

'Somewhere in the memory banks I guess.'

'Well, I'm still teary now' Jen added 'And I'm a little lost for words.'

Chris was sitting quietly, looking on somewhat pensively as this wave of emotion was washing over the table. Now was the time I thought.

'So, you lot, in amongst all the madness of this island, the sometimes crazy but truly wonderful nature of the people, my plans and all that has unfolded, here we are, and everything comes down to this, the dinner of love. Over the last two weeks we have laughed, cried, and indulged ourselves in food and wine. We have met old friends, made some new ones and there are some we will never see again. But in the end this is the life we have made, and this is the life we choose to share. You may recall one evening I remarked "what is a life without love?" I paused but the table remained silent. I took a sip of *retsina*.

'I followed this up with a question, and now is the time for you all to answer this question. What does love mean to you?'

I looked around the table 'Milos, following your outburst earlier why don't you fill us with your wisdom first?'

Milos leant forward, paused for what seemed and age, 'That's easy

Youth, love, want, need.' He stared at Mary. 'You know this Mary!'

'Yes,' she replied rather coyly. 'How could I forget. You always put it in my birthday and Christmas cards,'

'Correct and for me it's very simple, love means I want you and I need you. I couldn't live without you babe, that's it.' As he leant back looking very self-satisfied Mary blew him a kiss.

'How nice Miles, I'm going to cry,' Jane added unsurprisingly.

I turned to Mary 'Your turn.' She was already wearing her furrowed brow.

'I've been thinking about this ever since you first mentioned it. You know me I get all confused and worried about what to say.'

'Just say it as it is,' I said reassuringly.

'Well, I know he's an old git and can be a bit cantankerous.'

I interrupted 'A bit!... sorry Mary, but I'm loving this.'

She looked at me and then Milos 'What love means to me is caring for someone, accepting the way they are but that's why I am always worrying about him. It's my nature I know, but it's also how I express my love. Is that alright?'

'Of-course it's alright, if that's what it means to you?'

'Jane?'

'Can't you go before me?'

'No' I replied with a cheeky grin.

'Ok, I can't express things like this easily, but to me love is everything,' she kept my gaze. 'I know it's a bit soppy, but you are my everything, that's it.' Her bottom lip gave away her emotions. She leant towards me and gave me a little kiss.

'I can happily live with that!'

'Jen, do you want to go next?'

'I think you should respond to Jane before I put my head above the parapet.' Jen said raising her eyebrows. Perfect I thought, this was my opportunity to make things clear to Chris.

I looked at Jane 'Ok, Love to me is all about emotions and the way those emotions manifest themselves in everything I do with you. They strengthen the way I feel about you and I couldn't imagine sharing these emotions with anyone else.'

'That's nice' Jane mouthed.

I looked around the table 'I have a joke I often share with Jane: I tell her I'd never leave her… I couldn't bear to be happy again.' They all laughed.

I let things settle 'But the thing is, this couldn't be further from the truth. Being in love with Jane makes me emotionally content in so many ways. That's it for me,'

'She's off again,' Milos declared as Jane's eyes welled up.

Chris, Jen, who wants to go first. They looked at each other. I sensed a bit of trepidation in them both.

'C'mon you two, it's not that difficult,'

'Not for you maybe,' Jen said somewhat ominously. 'I'll give it a go.' She added.

'In my view we women love in a very different way to men, a good example of this is the way we communicate about love. When it comes to love, and all that love means, women want to talk about it, to find some common ground for that love. However, most of the men in my life just simply stop talking when it comes to discussing love. I have no doubt they want to love, but very much on their terms.'

I knew where this was aimed, and it didn't miss. Chris interrupted.

'Are you saying we don't talk?'

'Honey, we talk all the time, but not about love and certainly not in the way I want to talk about it. It's one of the most important things to me so let me finish.' Chris was clearly agitated.

'To answer the question, what does love mean to me? It's about companionship, honesty, and respect. These are the things that have touched me the most in reflecting on the question. When I hear you lot talk about the one, it doesn't resonate with me, in my view there's no such thing'.

Chris interrupted again, somewhat aggressively 'Ok so what about intimacy? Where does that sit in your little world, eh?'

'Well, that would be nice,' Jen responded sarcastically. I wondered whether I should jump in.

'I guess what I'm saying is that for me I accept that what love means changes over time. If those changes push you in different directions it's a difficult conundrum to solve,' Jen said with an air of frustration.

This time I did 'So Chris, are you saying that your answer to the question is intimacy?'

Chris stared at me for what seemed an age. I could sense the change in the mood of the table. An air of uneasiness was evident as we waited expectantly for his answer.

'Before I answer that just clarify what these plans have all been for. I recollect that I asked you this before, but you said it would become evident.' He leaned back, glanced at Jen and back to me.

'Because at the moment they aren't apparent to me.' Chris was now very clearly agitated.

I took another sip of *retsina* just to give a little air to the table.

'Listen Chris. As you know Milos, Mary, Jane, and I have been to this island many times. We keep coming back because of the joy it brings just being here. I wanted to give you and Jen the chance to share in this. I wanted to indulge you in the fun and madness to be had, even as we enter our later years. This island and the sponge diving history, I thought it would resonate with you. I'm sorry but I'm not blind, I believe I see what you either don't see or are choosing not to see. I guess I wanted some sort of epiphany, for you to see that the one thing that you have, especially at this stage of your life, that should be precious above all other things, is love. Something I remind you that *Thassos* lost never to regain,' I paused but the tension had the table in a vice like grip.

'Whatever you think of my plans, let me make it clear. They weren't for me.' I turned to Jane 'I have everything I want.'

I looked around the table and was greeted with faces in complete shock. I turned back to Chris, and he was gone!

'What happened?'

Jen looked forlorn 'He just stared at me and then suddenly he was gone' The arrival of her tears was imminent.

'This is driving me crazy, I just don't know what to do next. I've had such a wonderful time, and this dinner, the people, the singing I am so grateful to you all for sharing this place. I just don't know where he is at,' she said in a tone imploring help.

'Jen, he's been my friend for over 50 years, and I haven't got a clue where his mind is at. Good luck with that one,' Milos said as he lit another *Assos*.

'Do you think you should go and talk to him?' Jane asked.

'Probably, but our talking never seems to go anywhere. I think I should go.' And with that she hurriedly collected herself and was gone.

*Evdokia* appeared, her timing was great 'Is everything ok, your friends enjoyed their evening?'

'Everything is fine, and we've had a wonderful evening. One more bottle of *retsina*, the bill and then it will be time for my bed,' Milos declared.

'*Daxi* Miles. I will sort' and off she went.

'Youth, I can honestly say that tonight, along with all the other lunacy has been magnificent. As for your plans, only you will know what outcomes you expected. In terms of what happens next you know the score.'

'Yes I know Milos, not your problem!'

'Precisely, so let's do the *retsina* and then head for the sack. It's an early start' Milos declared.

We did precisely that, along with a few anecdotes and simply enjoying our last evening in *Emporios*. Having settled the bill, we bade our farewells to *Evdokia, Dimitri, Aleka* and *Maria* and set off for the *Asteri*. Milos was his usual self, walking or should I say stumbling back, ably supported by Mary and continually declaring his love for her. We left them at their door and as we passed Chris and Jens room all was dark and quiet.

'Have you set the alarm?' Jane asked. 'We've got to be up at 5.30am.'

'I'll leave that to you this time.' I didn't remember falling asleep.

Before I knew it the alarm was ringing in my ears. Jane switched it off, asked if I was awake and then made her way to the shower. I laid in bed for 10 minutes contemplating last night's dinner of love and what would have been said when Jen caught up with Chris. I guessed I would find out shortly and what would be would be.

The taxi was booked for 6.30am. Once I was ready I told Jane I would take the bags down to the front of the hotel and pop up and see *Pavlos* to say goodbye. I just wanted to say a final goodbye but also see if there was any sign of Chris and Jen. I made my way down the sets of steps, under the arch and out onto the terrace. I dropped the bags and took a short moment to take in the peace and tranquillity of the bay at this early hour. I turned to see Jen making her way across the terrace.

'Do you want a hand down with anything?' I asked.

'No, we're fine thanks. Chris will be down shortly with the remainder of the luggage.'

'How's things?'

'As if nothing happened, when I got back he was asleep, and this morning he just doesn't want to hear anything more on the subject. What can I do?'

'Answer the question?' Her expression told me she knew what I meant.

'Indeed, let's just see if we can have a pleasant journey home' Jen said mournfully.

I left Jen and headed up to see *Pavlos*. As I did Milos appeared from his room followed by Mary, clearly ready to go. As I reached the *taverna Pavlos* was sat outside having a cigarette.

'*Kalimera* Iain, look the taxis.'

'Ah yes maybe a couple of minutes. Thank you *Pavlos* for everything. Pass mine and Jane's love to *Affroulla* and the family. See you next year.'

'Yes Iain, how was the dinner of love last night?'

'Didn't quite go to plan,' I exclaimed.

'This is the system eh!' We laughed, embraced and I made my way back down where everyone was waiting, including *Pandalis*.

I had already agreed with Jane I would jump in the taxi with Chris and Jen, as she didn't quite fancy it, but this time I would sit in the front. We loaded everything into the car and left. I decided that I would sit quietly and enjoy the magnificent scenery for the last time. We pulled into the port and there waiting was the Kalymnos Star. No problem I thought as on the journey back I didn't care too much on the choice of travel. After settling with the taxis Milos reminded me that I was on ticket duty.

I made my way over and joined the short queue. I ordered six tickets, in my best Greek and the man in the kiosk acknowledged my skill and duly processed six tickets. I made my way back to the edge of the quay where they were all waiting.

'Here are your tickets, eight euros each. Chris and Jen, you owe me sixteen euros and Milos you owe me sixty-six euros.'

'How the fuck did you work that out?' Milos asked.

'Well, it's sixteen euros for the tickets and fifty euros for the bet!' I announced.

'Hang on, how do you know who the giver or taker was?' Milos questioned.

'I'm confused' Mary stated.

'You know Mary, the bet about the two Italia Boys, Sacha and Jeremiah' I replied.

'Yes, we all remember that but how do you know?' Jane added.

'Well, you remember that night we made love on the balcony,

and you made me stop because you thought you heard some noise,'

'Yes, but I'm not sure I want this broadcast,' Jane announced.

'And you made me look over the balcony to see if I could see anything,'

'Yes' again.

'And I said I couldn't see or hear anyone, which I have to admit was a lie. That's literally when I got to the bottom of the noise and the bet,' I said now smirking.

'And?' This time from Milos.

'Well let's just say that Sacha wasn't bending over and touching his toes for exercise!'

'Oh my god Iain, I am so embarrassed,' Jane announced.

'I'm not, fifty quid is fifty quid and Milos, it's cash only,'

'You twat.'

......

## THE END

# THE EPILOGUE

As I have said many times to the members of the company
that have made the trip with us to *Kalymnos*, there are those
that visit the island, fall in love with the place and the
people, get what it's all about and return again and again.
Then there are those that simply don't get it and never
return. I was firmly of the opinion that whilst Jen got it,
Chris didn't and was therefore of the view that they would
never return.

What happened next shocked even me. Within a couple of
weeks of returning to blighty I received a call from Jen. After
the usual pleasantries and asking how they had settled back to
normality her response completely flummoxed me. She told me
that normality, as it was before the trip to *Kalymnos* was gone
for ever. She said that the whole adventure had been captivating
and whilst all the plans were aimed at Chris having an

epiphany, it was in fact her who had been enlightened. She went on to tell me that she could now answer the big question and shocked me even more when she announced that she had left Chris!

What we all thought were her little trips down to the shop to stock up on nibbles for the evening pinkles and a moment of peace away from Chris to read was nothing of the sort. Her visits, whilst resulting in a fresh supply of pistachios and crisps were nothing more than a ruse to meet *Thassos*!

It transpired that my unwittingly seating *Thassos* next to her, when he joined us for lunch at the *taverna* had resulted in him being completely enchanted by her company. Furthermore, Jen felt something herself and whilst not sure what it was she was feeling, she wanted to explore it. *Thassos* had asked her to meet him down in the village the next day and told her that he would be there at 5.30pm. If she didn't make it he would accept the rebuttal.

On the basis that Jen continued this ruse for the remaining days of the holiday it was clear that rather than receive her rebuttal he received, for their short meetings, her full and undivided attention. She told me that *Thassos* told her that in a special moment during the lunch, for the first time since giving up his love for *Thea* he felt a desire to love again. He couldn't explain why this had happened but could not let the moment pass without expressing how he felt.

She also told me that during their meetings they talked, really talked openly and incessantly about companionship, honesty, trust, and love. Her response to the question at the dinner of love was resonating in my mind. She then told me the nub of these dalliances was *Thassos* asking her to spend the rest of her life with him and telling her that he had so much love to give he hoped she would not drown in it. He gave her the words to his favourite song:

Thalassaki "My Darling Sea"
Sea, sea
The sailors, my darling sea
Don't beat them with your waves.
I'm out at sea
I stay awake all night thinking of you.
Turn into rosewater
My darling sea
To sprinkle on their hair
My darling sea
Bring my bird back to me.
Swallows and birds,
My darling sea
You who fly close to the ground,
My darling sea
Bring my bird back to me.
If you see, if you see
My love, my darling sea
Give her my greetings
My darling sea
Bring my bird back to me.
Chorus:
Sea and salt water,
I cannot forget you.
I cannot forget you,
Sea and salt water.

I knew in her formative years she had an impulsive nature
when it came to her relationships, but she had remained loyal to
Chris for many years. However, with the background of all that
had passed in the last six months I wasn't surprised when she told
me she was taking up his offer. One last thing, I reminded her that
when *Thassos* left the table after the lunch at the taverna he

whispered something in Chris' ear and that I had forgotten during the holiday to pick this up with Chris. She told me he had simply told him how lucky he was to have such a wonderful lady! She told me she was leaving for *Kalymnos* next week and that she looked forward to seeing us when we made her next trip out there.

When I told Jane, she was just as flabbergasted. She asked me how I felt, did I feel responsible, had my plans gone terribly wrong, and what about Chris. I felt fine and I didn't feel responsible. I had told Jane many years ago, when we first met, that I didn't do guilt and that in my view it is a wasted emotion. If you're going to do something, do it with your full commitment and without regret.

As for the plans and how they turned out? In the main they were everything I wanted them to be and in some cases more. As for the result, I simply used *Pavlos*' well-worn response "This is the system."

As for Chris I could not deny an element of sympathy. He had been a friend for a long time. But friendships, especially when linked to a wife or partner always result in someone losing when that relationship falls apart. We never spoke again. Did he blame me? Who knows.

Finally, I was minded towards the dinner of love. For years it had been a dinner of foreboding and once again, although in a very different way it had delivered on its promise.

- Anagrorisi: Reconnaissance
- Apo Desiris: For four
- Apo Exi: For Six
- Arkoudaki: Teddy bear
- Assos: Greek Cigarettes
- Avro: Egg
- Brassino: Slang for a small beer/ Green
- Ciga Ciga: Slowly
- Daxi: ok
- Dinamatives: Dynamite
- Dolmades: Greek stuffed vine leaves
- Ella: Colloquial term for hi, come here, oi
- Epharisto: Thankyou
- Eperochi Epliki: Lovely surprise
- Esi: And you
- Gigantes: Greek bean dish
- Horiatiki Salata: Greek salad
- Horos: Dance
- Horta: Greek greens
- Ime Kala: I am good
- Kaiki: Traditional Greek fishing boat

- Kalismera: Good morning
- Kalispera: Good afternoon
- Kalanichta: Good night
- Kala: Good
- Kala Kardia: Good heart
- Kalamari: Squid
- Katsidi: Goat
- Keftedes: Greek meatballs
- Kotopolo: Chicken
- Koimamai: Sleep
- Kunelli: Rabbit
- Kyma: Wave
- Kynigi Paichnidou: Game hunting
- Lauto: Greek instrument
- Magirevo: Cook
- Malaka: Greek derogatory term!
- Mbarba: Grandfather
- Metrios: Greek coffee
- Meze: A group of Greek dishes
- Mihanikos: Engineer
- Moustaki: Moustache
- Mou: My
- Moussaka: Greek lamb dish

- Nai: Yes

- Nero: Water

- Nes: Nescafe

- Oki: No

- Oplo: Gun

- Orais: Beautiful

- Ouzo: Greek aniseed spirit

- Parakalo: You're welcome

- Poli Kala: Very good

- Pou Eina: Where is

- Proino: Breakfast

- Raki: Greek hooch

- Restsina: Greek white wine

- Saganaki: Fried dish

- Sagapo: Love you

- Sapsari: Fish

- Skafandro: Diving suit

- Skandolopetres: Diving stone

- Skillos: Dog

- Simera: Today

- Signome: Excuse me or Sorry

- Silos: Tall

- Souvlaki: Skewered and barbecued meat

- Spiti: House

- Stifado: Stew

- Taverna: Greek restaurant

- Threbe: Greek oregano

- Ti ora fuevyee to polio yia tin Kalymnos: What time does the boat leave for Kalymnos

- Touristes: Tourists

- Tsambouna: Greek instrument

- Tsatsiki: Greek yoghurt dip

- Vlepo kai Gelo: I watch and laugh

- Yammas: Cheers

- Yassas / Yassou: Hello

Jane – For your patience and support, and most importantly your love.

Milos and Maria – For giving us Emporios and letting my imagination run riot.

Tricia –Your wise counsel, time, and encouraging support.

Steve Greenfield – This book simply would not have been finished without you.

Pavlos and Family – Friendship and love beyond words.

The people of Emporios and Kalymnos –You are the reason we keep coming back!

Faith Warn –Your wonderful book 'Bitter Sea' made writing this book so much easier.

Jodie Perkins: Bob Marketing – For making things happen!

Simon Davies – 'A picture paints a thousand words'

Antonis Karafillakis – For your wonderful painting "Departure of the Fleet". Many thanks to your Niece for her kind permission.

The Sponge Divers of Kalymnos –You are the inspiration behind this book. May your story never be forgotten.